VORTEX

Other Soviet Science Fiction available

PATH INTO THE UNKNOWN

VORTEX

NEW SOVIET SCIENCE FICTION

Edited by
C. G. BEARNE

UNABRIDGED

PAN BOOKS LTD : LONDON

First published 1970 by MacGibbon and Kee Ltd.
This edition published 1971 by Pan Books Ltd,
33 Tothill Street, London, S.W.1

ISBN 0 330 02705 0

Printed and bound in England by
Hazell Watson & Viney Ltd,
Aylesbury, Bucks

CONTENTS

EDITOR'S PREFACE

THIS collection of seven stories is representative of the writings of a group of young SF enthusiasts in the USSR. Stories by nearly all of them now appear regularly in Russian literary journals of a serious nature, an indication of the status already achieved by these young men, none of whom is primarily a literary man by training or profession. The collection is unusual in that it includes the work of no less than two sets of brothers who work in collaboration. It must be left to the reader to decide whether this factor is in any way apparent in the writing.

There seem to be two basic problems which these writers are exploring: man in society, and man and the passing of time. Time and its interpretation indeed form the basis of stories by the brothers Abramov, Boris Smagin, and Andrei Gorbovskii. Mirer, of whose works two excerpts from a cycle of stories entitled *Artificial Jam* are included here, is much more concerned with the position of man, weak and irrational, in a machine-ridden world. The brothers Strugatskii are concerned essentially with people in a society which has us under some kind of mysterious threat. They explore the actions of their characters against a background which is fictional yet has tantalizingly pervasive echoes of a kind of reality.

The collection is prefaced by an excellent analysis of the position of contemporary SF. The writer, Ariadne Gromova, is adept at presenting Soviet attitudes in a precise and readable manner. Her sociological analysis of SF in East and West is unique and highly provocative.

Ariadne Gromova

Introduction

At the Frontier of the Present Age

WHEN reading the articles and literary critical works on science fiction which have appeared with increasing regularity (although still not often enough) in recent years in England, America, France and other countries one usually reaches the somewhat bitter conclusion that the writers either make no mention of Soviet science fiction, as though they were blissfully unaware of its existence, or that, at most, they level quite justified criticism at those bad, untalented products which, in one way, represent the present-day level of our science fiction, but which are, for some unknown reason, more readily and avidly seized upon by the foreign publishing houses than those vivid and original books which really deserve to be translated. Soviet readers, in the last ten years at least, have been provided with a much broader view of the science fiction of other countries, although, naturally, even here our own house needs putting in order.

It is not a matter of Soviet science-fiction writers taking offence at not being mentioned – no, the question goes much deeper, and is one of principle.

In order to explain, however, why an acquaintance with contemporary Soviet science fiction might be of basic interest to readers in other countries, we must first discuss what present-day science fiction is, and what position it occupies in contemporary human culture.

Science fiction (Russ. *nauchnaya fantastika*) – a term we use for want of a better one – is at the moment a worldwide phenomenon. In literature it is a whole field on its own. Its scope is very broad, encompassing the most varied genres and stylistic devices, and authors who write from differing ideological standpoints. It is a concept, however, which is limited by the existence of certain general laws specific to it, laws and rules of the manner of experiencing and depicting reality.

The theory of science fiction is only just in the process of formation; there is still much which is unexplored and unclear. One is also hampered by the lack of decently presented information on a worldwide scale. There is also the fact that science fiction is in the midst of a process of rapid development, and that its outlines are constantly blurring together and changing. Finally, there is also the glaring lack of qualified theoreticians and critics (these functions are partly fulfilled, with varying degrees of success, by the science-fiction writers themselves).

At the present time science fiction enjoys a very great degree of popularity in the USSR. Books which appear in editions of 2–300,000 copies are sold out almost at once. Science fiction, moreover, is read by people of all ages, from schoolchildren to old-age pensioners. Yet the overwhelming percentage of our readership is composed of scientifically and technically minded intellectuals and students.

There is here another definite and regularly recurring factor. The majority of present-day science-fiction writers come to literature from science (or continue parallel work in both fields). At present there are amongst them scientists with world reputations – Fred Hoyle, Arthur Clarke, Isaac Azimov, Leo Szillard, to name just a few. The majority of Soviet science-fiction writers are also scientists: Ivan Yefremov is a palaeontologist, Boris Strugatskii is an astronomer, Arkadii Strugatskii, a specialist in Japanese affairs, M. Yemtsev and E. Parnov are chemists, A. Dneprov, a physicist.

All this goes to show that some kind of relationship exists at the present time between science and science fiction. What then is this relationship?

In his basic work, *Science in the History of Society* (1954), G. Bernal, studying the mutual interaction between science and society from an historical point of view, comes to the conclusion that our epoch represents a new stage in the history of mankind, precisely as a result of the radically altered role of science in the life of contemporary society. Scientific progress has become one of the active forces in economic and political life. A present-day state can only exist on condition that it thoroughly develops and uses science, therefore our contemporary political forms are also to a certain extent the material and technical consequences of the development of science. The fact that science is now a basic factor to social progress, G. Bernal evaluates as a decisive and irrevocable step in human history. He considers it to be an event of as much importance as the evolution of man himself, or of his early civilizations.

Mankind has already recognized the commanding role of science in our age. The 'average' earthman's impression of the scientist has altered radically: the study-bound, grey-haired hermit, amusingly absent-minded and impractical, has been superseded by the awesome omniscient and omnipotent magus, holding the fate of the human race in his hands. Of course, such general impressions, arising in the consciousness of the 'normal' person, are inescapably bound to be hyperbolic and schematic, and, in fact, in our day scientists correspond as little with the impressions of them as was the case in the nineteenth century. Yet, if we put these 'general' impressions side by side, we will see that, in the broad view, they do reflect a certain objective reality: in other words, that basic change in the role of science and the degree of its influence on society about which Bernal is talking. True, people are aware that spacecraft and atomic plants, television and computers, originate in the scientist's laboratory. Yet everyone is also aware that the unprecedented threat of destruction on a world scale originated there – the work of famous scientists, the best sons of their age. Without even knowing the details, the majority of our contemporaries have reacted emotionally to this fact: it could be said that this information is an integral part of Man's consciousness in our age, and plays an active role in moulding mass psychology. In fact, it was precisely after Hiroshima that the concept of the awesome scientist-magus first arose in the public mind: any further knowledge has only tended to confirm this picture.

If we compare this mass concept of the scientist with the true state of things we will be convinced of how inaccurate and unjust are the views of the majority of our contemporaries on the role of science. Furthermore, this inaccuracy is quite natural and unavoidable, especially in our epoch.

The fact is that it is really only rarely that scientific and technical achievements impinge on the consciousness of the majority of people. Even if information about these achievements were well ordered, and its imparting were well planned and well thought out (and there is as yet no basis for such an optimistic view of affairs in this field), then it would still be seriously impeded by the inert opposition of the human mentality. For the vast majority of people information about scientific and technical achievements does not form an integral part of their perception of the world: in relation to the deeper strata of consciousness it remains neutral.

In principle this has always been so. At the present time it has merely become more obvious than ever. Propositions such as: 'The Earth is round', 'It is not the Sun which revolves around the Earth, but the Earth around the Sun', 'Man is descended from the apes', are accepted or, conversely, rejected, on emotional grounds. One can here be excited or annoyed without knowing anything about the finer points of the scientific argument. Yet what emotions are aroused in the 'average' man nowadays by something like, say, the quantum theory? In fact, in the whole sphere of present-day science there is only one problem which arouses strong emotions, of the positive and negative variety, and that is the question of 'thought machines'. Speculation about the possibilities of cybernetics (albeit in a most primitive and sensational form) does have a real effect on the emotions of our contemporaries, if only because it attacks the myth of the unique nature of the human consciousness. In principle, though, what actually 'reaches' the majority of people is not the scientific discoveries themselves, however significant they might be in scope, but their practical, so to speak, everyday results: it is these which mould the mass psychology. The discovery of atomic energy (and even the existence of atomic power-stations) would in itself have no significant effect on the consciousness of the majority: though the destruction of Hiroshima was a step forward in contemporary man's view of the world. Of course, such a turning point in perceptions is not always evident. A large proportion of changes in consciousness take place slowly, imperceptibly and subconsciously, then we suddenly realize that we already accept as an integral part of our 'personal' world not only refrigerators and synthetic materials, but even space-flights and cybernetic apparata (in the form in which they exist at the moment), and that no one is surprised by the fabulous speeds of jet planes, which seem to have brought the ends of the earth closer together, nor by the television screen which brings what is happening on the other side of the world, or even in space, into our sitting-room.

At the same time the interactions of these various scientific and technical achievements have gradually provided one unforeseen result: mankind in our epoch is willy-nilly bound by a common fate. The links between countries, even between those far distant from each other, have become stronger and more numerous. The process of history has now become a single one, in all its immense complexity. In the final analysis the fate of the whole of mankind now depends on the fate of one country, whether it is the USSR or the USA, China or Vietnam. This fate shared in common by the whole world is a factor gaining an increasing recognition amongst our contemporaries, and is having an ever more significant influence on the formation of psychology. The threat of atomic war and the pollution of the atmosphere, water and soil by radioactive fallout – these are problems which, by their very nature, cannot confront merely one country or group of countries – they concern the whole of mankind. Neither can future space flights, nor future advances in cybernetics, biochemistry, genetics, fail to concern humanity as a whole.

Thus our average contemporary man is brought willy-nilly to consider the majority of problems on a global scale, and to take into account at least the more obvious results of scientific discoveries. Even if such an 'average' earthman has an extremely conservative attitude towards science and technology, and is only capable of appreciating the negative results of scientific and technological progress – then even these negative results have a far too significant importance for the whole of mankind (including our 'average' earthman himself) for our hypothetical dweller on this earth to be able to exclude them from the sphere of his emotions. He cannot but feel something, be it only hatred and fear (emotions which, incidentally, form the basis of a significant section of American science fiction, notably the writings of Ray Bradbury).

Thus we have before us a new, essentially important stage in the history of mankind. Its characteristics have become so clearly expressed that they are reflected not only in the consciousness and activities of the progressive sections of society, but they also form the psychology of the masses.

If we accept this, we must go on to the logical conclusion that, apparently, in order to reflect this basically new era, art needs a basically new principle of approach to natural phenomena. We must also assume that, in so much as it is science which is introducing the decisive changes in the life of society, so the new art as well will be based on an attitude to science completely different from that of any previous period.

Let us now try to analyse briefly some of the characteristic features of contemporary science and contemporary art, so as to define, on this basis, the nature of the new art.

It is not only the speed of the development of science which has changed in our times, but also the character of scientific research. Science at the moment is going through a period of revolution, of gigantic leaps forward, of masterly insights. For when Niels Bohr said that the theory put forward by Heizenberg did not seem crazy enough to be correct (and it was not for nothing that this saying became famous) he was expressing in a paradoxical form the very essence of the present stage in the development of science. The accepted strict definitions of the Newtonian world have been so disarrayed and shaken in the light of new discoveries that a picture of the world as it is newly conceived can only be created by someone who has rejected absolutely the previously held propositions. That is why his interpretation must necessarily seem to specialists from the very beginning to be completely improbable, fantastic, 'mad' – were it otherwise there might be a danger that it was still traditional, and not genuine.

In this context we must take into account some extremely characteristic pronouncements by contemporary scientists.

The surprising qualities of the microcosm which bring those studying it to reject previously accepted causes and effects, and to begin to work on the basis of probabilities, to employ correlations of indefinables and the principle of complementarity, these qualities have greatly undermined the conception of science as accurate, lucid and strictly determinist which was common in the era of classical physics. Scientists have, one after another, said repeatedly that the modern-day process of gaining knowledge is far more intuitive than strictly logical, that, by its characteristics, it is anything but exact and closely defined. There is a multitude of such pronouncements.

The biochemist Albert de Saint D'ierdi expressed what is essentially the same feeling: 'Research is rarely directed by logic; it is to a large extent guided by hints, guesses and intuition ... The basic material or research is imagination, into which are woven the threads of judgement, measurement and calculation.' The theoretical physicist, Freeman Dyson, made a statement basically to the same effect: 'A great discovery, when it first appears, almost always emerges in a confused, incomplete and disconnected form. It is only half understood by the discoverer himself. As far as everyone else is concerned, it is a complete mystery.'

On the other hand, it cannot go without notice that contemporary scientists seem to have conspired together not only to sing the praises of a particular beauty and poetry which are part and parcel of scientific study, but also in their tendency to maintain that Beauty and Truth are inseparably linked together in science. Thus, for example, Paul Dirak has said that the only reliable indication of the truth of a scientific theory is its beauty; if a theory looks ugly then one cannot believe in its truth. Ernest Rutherford believed that a 'well-constructed theory is, in a sense, an artistic creation'; as examples he suggested Maxwell's theory of kinetics and Einstein's theory of relativity. Of the discoveries of Niels Bohr, Albert Einstein himself said: 'It is great music in the sphere of thought'.

There are, moreover, many examples of this kind, too many to be ascribed to the idiosyncrasies of this or that individual scientist, or to coincidence. Never before has science said so much about its blood-ties with poetry, music, harmony, as it has in our age.

It is easy to see that these verdicts seem irreconcilable only at first sight, that in fact they are linked by deep inner ties of kinship. The awareness of the beauty, form and harmony of contemporary scientific constructions arises from the same source as the awareness of the madness of truly new hypotheses, from that attitude which regards the present processes of discovery as essentially intuitive and alogical. All this points to one thing – contemporary scientific thought is, by its very nature, noticeably closer to that of the artist.

At first glance this thesis does not seem at all strange; for it is precisely at the present time that science is advancing further and further into the sphere of high abstractions, into the strange world of formless phenomena which are absolutely inaccessible to sensual perception or emotional comprehension. The fact, however, remains a fact, and scientists talk quite openly about it. 'An element of poetry is always present in scientific thought,' wrote Einstein, 'real science and real music demand one and the same thought process.' Robert Oppenheimer has described this similarity between science and art and explained it by the fact that the position in the world of the scientist and the artist is essentially similar: 'The man of science and the man of art always live at the edges of what is comprehensible ... Both of them have to seek a balance between the new and a synthesis of the old; both of them have to struggle to establish some kind of order out of general chaos ... They are able to lay the path which will join art and science to the whole wide world of multiform, deceptive, valuable bonds of universal community.'

Robert Oppenheimer, as we can see, says that such a connexion between the artist and the scientist has always existed. To a certain extent, possibly, he is right – if only in so far as, originally, at the dawn of humanity, scientific and artistic discovery of the world were fused into one, and have only subsequently detached themselves and become separated from this original syncretic way of thinking. Nevertheless, this thought is very much an up-to-date one. Such an idea could only have appeared earlier in a purely speculative form: now it has a basis in reality. This is a generalization of certain concrete processes at present taking place within science and art. For it is not for nothing that Niels Bohr has said that the theory of relativity and the complexities of physics have a general gnosiological significance, that the correlation of indeterminates, formulated by Heizenberg and the principle of supplementation, introduced by Bohr himself, might be adapted to solve problems in completely different spheres, primarily in the field of human psychology.

The Soviet literary critic B. Runin, in his book *The Eternal Quest (Vechny poisk)*, upholding the equal rights and value of scientific and artistic thought, says in conclusion: 'For all that there is a genetic and logical connexion between their research and way of thinking, the scientist and the artist are pursuing different cognitive aims and making different discoveries. Apparently there is some kind of objective necessity in this.' Runin also makes a proposition which develops on Niels Bohr's idea quoted above – that the coexistence of two contrary principles in the single human process of gaining knowledge in itself possibly illustrates the process of complementarity. If, in physics, complementary, mutually exclusive aspects are needed for a full understanding, then the same principle could possibly be applied to the whole of human knowledge. 'It may be that scientific knowledge and artistic knowledge cannot be brought together or deduced one from the other precisely because the relationship between them is a complementary one.'

Thus it is that outstanding figures in science (as well as, for that matter, ordinary scientists engaged in contemporary tasks) are at present remarkably unanimous in talking of the blood relationship between art and science. This assertion is too widespread to be regarded as the outcome of chance.

Here there are reflected, it seems to me, some of the actual processes going on in the consciousness of the more active and thinking parts of present-day humanity. What are these processes themselves?

First, there is the ever growing need to maintain equilibrium, harmony, to strengthen those emotional ties with the world which it is so easy to lose in the face of present-day scientific tasks, where the *mundus sensibilis*, the world perceived through the senses, has been lost sight of by anyone in the vanguard of scientific research, and has been replaced by the *mundus intelligibilis*, a world of intangibles, approachable only by the intellect, only as a result of experiment in thought. This, perhaps, is the 'sensation of spiritual incompleteness, lack of emotional oxygen', 'artistic starvation', about which B. Runin is talking in his book quoted above, or that longing for a single key, a single axis of any form which, according to Robert Oppenheimer, is characteristic of the modern scientist. Secondly, there is the formation of new needs, new demands on art, and a dissatisfaction with the *status quo* arising out of this, a dissatisfaction which the 'physicists' feel more than the lyricists, more acutely precisely because their way of thinking is in principle more modern than that of the lyricists – the pure humanitarians.

In brief, present-day science is aware of a need for art and literature – let us say, on the basis of the principle of complementarity. There is much, however, in contemporary literature (let us leave on one side for a moment considerations of art) which does not satisfy those demands, more or less accurately formulated by scientists who are more clearly aware of this increasingly characteristic attraction of contemporary science towards art.

There are various reasons for this unsatisfactory state.

One of these reasons is the striking, one might almost say basic, ignorance of scientific matters on the part of the majority of writers; this, naturally, leaves a very noticeable mark on literature as a whole and puts a brake on its development, restricting its possible potentialities. It is not a matter of forcing writers to study some branch of science so that they should work out, even if only on first acquaintance with the subject, what is happening at least on the more important, more advanced sectors of the scientific front. There are not so very many people, even amongst the scientists, who are able to evaluate the position in contemporary science in all its breadth and perspective: the ever increasing specialization of science on the one hand, and the unrestrainable broadening of the 'work-front' – the invasion of ever fresh spheres by science – on the other, both make encyclopaedism at the present time simply impossible. Something else is needed, the ability to think on the same level as contemporary science – of learning, for one's own ends, the methodology of contemporary scientific research.

H. G. Wells spoke of the enormous influence on him of some lectures on biology read by Darwin's pupil and colleague, Thomas Huxley: 'The year which I spent studying under Huxley meant more for my education than any other period in my life. He developed in me a striving for consistency and a search for the mutual connexion between things, and also an unwillingness to accept those casual propositions and unfounded assertions which are the hallmark of the thinking of an uneducated man, as opposed to an educated one.'

As we can see, Wells considers his most valuable acquisition not the sum of concrete knowledge, but his experience of scientific thought. This was also a completely justified evaluation: without the ability to think scientifically in general there would be no kind of outstanding writer. We live in a world which science is building up before our eyes, and the writer who does not even try to fathom what the laws are which guide this process, what its causes and possible results are, who is not capable of understanding the logic of scientific experiment – such a writer cannot lay claim to the serious interest of his contemporaries. It is here again a question, probably, not so much of the concrete content as of a change in the technique of writing, of the working out of new, more contemporary and economic means of artistic expression. But the overwhelming majority of writers do not understand this. What harm this widespread ignorance has done to present-day literature will only be clear to posterity – but there is much which is even now visible to the naked eye.

This attack on writers contains, it is true, more grief than anger. The more so since the presence of goodwill and patience are not sufficient for an understanding of contemporary science. Even scientists themselves – the great scientists of our epoch, founders of the New Physics – have at some time retreated in confusion in the face of the further conclusions to be drawn from their own brilliant discoveries. It is enough to recall just one classic example – Einstein, without whom quantum mechanics could never have arisen at all, could not accept the likely descriptions of the behaviour of electrons, and distrusted the uncertainty principle introduced by Heizenberg. The famous physicist Lorentz, the founder of the theory of electrons, denied the principles of quantum mechanics altogether; towards the end of his life he said: '... I do not know why I have lived. I'm only sorry I didn't die six years ago, when everything seemed clear to me.' Max Planck has made a darkly humorous remark on roughly the same subject: 'I have come to the conclusion that, however great a scientist you may be, there is a certain age at which you encounter "concepts which are too difficult for you", which you may succeed in assimilating but which you will never understand completely. Fortunately, however, people die; after a while all those who weren't able to think this concept through have disappeared and been replaced by new people ...'

If this is what the world's most outstanding scientists are saying then what can one expect from writers? What can they understand of this strange world, with which even those who first discovered and explored it are unable to cope?

I am deeply convinced that it is at once both far more difficult and far easier for the writer. Max Planck's bitter joke cannot claim to answer this difficult problem: in succeeding generations there will also be people who are fated to die without understanding or accepting great discoveries for which they themselves have laid the basis. Thus the role of art – that new art which is growing up before our eyes – may prove to be important and beneficial in this particular respect: real art also completely recreates the world, blurring the normal outlines, and thereby preparing the human psyche to accept the new and the unusual, that which will not fit into the accepted scheme of things.

This is, incidentally, a question which merits particular attention. We are here trying to say that at present it is precisely science fiction which is the pathfinder of this new art (which, quite possibly, in this mature form will not be as fantastic as the Russian term for science fiction suggests). This was vividly reflected in a symposium on the problems of the connexions between scientific and artistic thinking held in Leningrad in February 1966. At this symposium the idea was expressed more than once (for example, in the papers read by R. Nudelman, Yu. Karaglitskii, A. Mirer, and others) that scientific and artistic paths towards knowledge of the world are gradually drawing together, and it was stated particularly that the basic novelty of science fiction was contained in the fact that it had already begun to create a syncretism of thought, that (in its better offerings at least) it contained that combination of scientific and artistic knowledge which will give rise to a completely new quality.

Science fiction is engaged mainly in working out problems of a global nature, born of the contemporary role of science in society. It talks of how science can change the face of the world, and what these increasing changes may lead to, about what humanity represents, about what are the perspectives for its development in the social, moral and biological field; about the role of scientists and the fate of their discoveries in a hostile world.

The question of this kind of problem has in itself already prompted an increased interest in science fiction on the part of the scientific and technical intelligentsia. It is, however, not only the content but the form, the artistic specifica of science fiction which makes a blood-tie between it and science. The specifica consists in the fact that science fiction combines organically in itself the artistic and scientific knowledge of the world. It makes wide use for its own ends of the characteristic techniques of contemporary science, techniques of explaining phenomena, of mental experiment. Science fiction is able to create the most unlikely and unthought-of situations and characters – yet their appearance will always be to some degree or other rationally explained and their subsequent development will obey the strict logic of a scientific experiment. Such art could only arise in the present period of relatively highly-developed knowledge of the world. That is why, although precursors of contemporary science fiction existed even in the last century (Jules Verne and others), its true forefather is H. G. Wells, whose first works appeared on the dividing line between two ages. As a mass phenomenon it came into being after the Second World War.

All this, however, is far from meaning that we can expect to find exact information from one or another sphere of science in every work of science fiction. We are talking about something else, about the ability of the artist to analyse actual phenomena at the level of present-day science. This, at the same time, prevents science fiction from being fantasy (*fantastika*), from being anything like the fairy tale (*skazka*) and from containing those fantastic devices which have long been the stock-in-trade of satire, philosophical prose and drama (these devices, found, for example, in the writings of Lesage, Gogol, Brecht, Mayakovskii, do not need to have a rational basis, they exist quite openly upon their own terms: a nose becomes detached from a man and leads an independent life, gods go walking about in a town talking to people, and none of the readers wonder if this could ever happen, and if it could, then how).

Science fiction, of course, does not set out to prove anything either. It has its own degree of freedom, it can leave out many of the stages involved in scientific research – depending on the author's concrete aims. Thus, for example, Wells, in *The Time Machine*, does not wish to prove the possibility in principle of the construction of such a machine nor to show the details of its construction: he is interested in a sociological analysis of the prospects for the development of contemporary society, and it is precisely the paradoxical conclusions of this analysis which form the scientific basis of his novel – in this case a time machine is purely a literary device.

The great Polish science-fiction writer Stanislav Lem, in his novel *Return from the Stars*, draws a picture of a society sub-jected to a special vaccination – 'betrization', which automatic-ally deprives man of the power of killing. Lem, however, is not interested in the biological mechanics of what is going on or the possibility of such an inoculation in principle, but in problems of a philosophical and moral nature: to what would this mechanical improvement of the conditions of existence and even the mechanical injection of moral principles lead, if mankind is not sufficiently mature for them, if he has not ac-quired them himself by stubbornly and persistently eradicating from his psyche all that is old and bad?

In the Strugatskii brothers' novella *It is difficult to be a God* the action takes place in the distant future on another planet, yet this transference of the action in space and time has a crea-tive function: the fantastic element of what is imagined helps to express the earthly and very topical problem of the contacts and mutual interactions of civilizations at vastly different stages of development and to pose the problem of the personal responsibility, placed upon people by the power of knowledge and technology, for what is happening before their very eyes.

In the majority of cases, naturally, this fantastic assumption is not merely a device for modelling a certain situation, but has an independent artistic significance. The octopoid-Martians on walking tripods in Wells' *War of the Worlds*, the manlike robots in Karel Capek's play *R.U.R.* (from which, incidentally, the term robot itself is derived), the thinking ocean of plasma in Lem's novel *Solaris*, the mysterious biological automatic bio-toses in M. Yemtsev's and E. Parnov's tale *The Spirit of the World*, or the walking plants in Wyndham's novel *The Day of the Triffids*, are depicted very vividly, one might almost say convincingly and realistically. Yet even here the fantastic figures and situations are not an end in themselves. They help to reveal the philosophical idea which lies behind these works.

Those who have only a superficial knowledge of science fiction think that it deals (or, at least, should deal) primarily with the future. This, however, is a mistaken point of view. Naturally, there has long existed in science fiction, from its very outset a utopion strain (Wells' *Men like Gods*, Yefremov's *Mists of Andromeda*); there also exist its contemporary variants – anti-utopias, novels of warning (Ray Bradbury's *Fahrenheit 451*, Isaac Asimov's *The End of Eternity*, Stanislav Lem's *Return from the Stars*). But, as has already been said, the depiction of the future (and of life on other planets) is far more of a representation technique than anything else. Science fiction deals above all with the contemporary world, and forecasts of its likely development. The Soviet critic R. Nudelman has said with justification about science fiction: 'We have before us not a window into the future, but an unusually placed observation point from which we can command an excellent view of the present'. A. and B. Strugatskii define their method of studying reality in the following way: 'Into the present – by way of the future'.

Naturally, science-fiction writers do try now and then to look into the future, even if only to point the development of tendencies which are in evidence at present. Experience has already taught us, though, that the more the science-fiction writer depicts the near future, and the more concrete details he introduces into his narrative, the more quickly the pictures he draws become outdated and simply laughable. This happens because it is usually impossible to foretell great discoveries which will change the face of the world. They are so new that the idea of them simply has not existed before in men's minds. Who could have foreseen radio, television, atomic energy, or electronic computers when people did not even suspect that these things were possible? When the 'moving wing' or lighter-than-air flying machines first started could anyone then have imagined to himself the present-day heavy, huge aeroplane with fixed wings and a fabulous speed? Who can foretell what will happen to aviation, just in the next hundred years alone, whether it will still be there at all, or whether it will not be replaced by some radically new, more comfortable and more reliable form of transport? In short, if we are to be concerned with the question of technological forecasts, then we must accept the fact beforehand that the percentage of correct ones will be negligible.

It seems to me, however, that it is a different matter with sociological forecasts. This also is not a simple or an easy field. The forecasts here cannot speak with one voice, and they are always only probabilities. Yet the sociological science-fiction writer has different tasks, different scales. All kinds of awkward details which are an unavoidable difficulty for 'technological' science fiction can here simply be omitted.

It is now that I shall return to my original point: why should we think it desirable that readers in other countries should be well acquainted with Soviet science fiction?

Generally, by its very nature science fiction is rationalistic and active: like its sister, science, it considers that reality in all its complicated and contradictory aspects can be fully explained and exploited. Its typical hero is the thinking and active man: in any situation, even the most complicated, unusual, mysterious and terrible, he analyses the circumstances, constructs hypotheses and checks them in practice, seeking escape and safety. Yet the results of this logical analysis can be very varied. For science fiction is an art, and therefore an ideological species of phenomenon, and its conclusions cannot be as 'non-partisan' as the scientist's formulae and sketches. On the contrary, in science fiction the author's ideological position is even more openly and clearly expressed than in any other branch of fiction. For the reader is already aware at the outset that the science-fiction writer is not depicting life 'as it is', but is constructing his own images, starting from some kind of ideological principles of his own.

A great deal is dictated by these principles. In studying contemporary reality, using one and the same method of science fiction, starting from basically similar positions, writers can often draw diametrically opposed conclusions. The essential basis for these divergences may be formulated in the following very simple manner ... Science fiction's elementary principle is that everything is in man's hands. At this, however, some writers exclaim, 'That's simply splendid!' Others sigh, 'That's just what's wrong!' At the same time there is a third group which vacillates between the two poles. It must be confessed that each of these positions has certain psychological justifications. In actual fact in the last half-century mankind has made great strides forward along the path of social and technological progress, and the results which it has achieved in such a short space of time are very impressive. But, at the same time, the dangers which mankind has created for itself in this period are much more terrible than all the calamities of past ages.

There is, however, another side of this problem which must

be taken into account. Mankind must have hope. Not hope of a vague, humanistic kind such as is encountered in the final scenes of the works of some American science-fiction writers (for example in Ray Bradbury's *Martian Chronicles* or in Asimov's *The End of Eternity*) – but arrows pointing a way out of the dangerous labyrinth. Hope is a natural need of mankind, it is the soul's daily bread.

Soviet science fiction is really very young. To be more exact it began to come into being again about ten years ago, after two or three decades of creative anabiosis, during which only primitive, popularizing adventure stories were published, and these had nothing to do with art. Yet in this short period it has achieved really important results. As far as the numbers of writers and books is concerned it naturally lags well behind science fiction in the USA, which has developed intensively over this period. Yet Soviet science fiction has its own distinctive character. It is, of course, not a question of the presence of talent, skill, and the ability to think analytically; these qualities are brilliantly developed in many American science-fiction writers. Soviet writers, however, from their own particular ideological positions, draw completely different, and it seems to us more accurately justified, conclusions from their analysis of reality. It seems to me, therefore, that a knowledge of this other angle on the world would be useful to both readers and writers in the West, so that they should be able to assess the phenomenon more exactly – if only as part of the principle of supplementation.

No, Soviet science fiction is not at all tinted with the glow of rosy, naïve optimism. We are also clearly aware of the enormous difficulties and the terrible dangers confronting man – and we write about them. I need only quote such works as *Attempt to escape* (Popytka k begstvu), *It is difficult to be a god* (Trudno byt' bogum), *Predatory things of the century* (Khishchnye veshchi veka), *The second Martian invasion* (Vtoroe nashestviye marsian) by A. and B. Strugatskii, *The spirit of the world* (Dusha mira) and *Condemned to enjoyment* (Prigovoren k naslazhdeniyu) by M. Yemtsev and E. Parnov, *Dies Irae* (Den'gneva) by S. Gansovskii, and, finally, my own novella *In a circle of light* (V kruge sveta). Yet we look upon these difficulties and dangers in a different, more optimistic relationship to mankind's potentialities.

One cannot ignore the difficulties – that would be dangerous and criminal. It would, however, be no less dangerous to exaggerate them, and to make them absolutes. What our science fiction says to man is this: 'Yes, things are very difficult and complicated. A lot of effort, deprivation and self-sacrifice will be needed – but you will do it. You will cope with things – you will build a beautiful and a just world!' Nor is this said *a priori*, but on the basis of a scientific analysis of phenomena.

This is why we should like people of all lands to become acquainted with the best of our science fiction, and to try to understand our point of view.

By this, however, I do not mean to say at all that this collection, presented for the attention of English readers, is anything like an anthology of the best of Soviet science fiction, no, the principle behind its composition was completely different, and it contains works both by well-known authors and younger writers, whose imagination and artistic talents are very different in standard. It seems to me, however, that it can still give an approximate conception of Soviet science fiction.

Translated by C. G. Bearne

Aleksandr and Sergei Abramov

The Time Scale

I WAS coming back from an evening session of the Security Council with Ordinsky, my colleague from Moscow, whom everyone at the UNO Press centre took to be a Pole like myself – probably because of the surname. Ordinsky, Glinsky – to the American ear they sound much the same. I suggested we go somewhere to kill what remained of the evening, but he was busy and I had to be content with the prospect of a solitary supper. I stopped the taxi at a third-class bar called the Olympia. My hotel was only a few blocks away and, if the worst came to the worst, I could always get home on foot.

They knew me in the bar and Antony, the normally languid waiter, didn't even ask for my order, just appeared in a flash with beer and hot sausage. The bar was deserted except for a corner behind the door curtain where two girls I hadn't seen before were having supper, and at the bar itself a lean old man in a short raincoat was sipping whisky. He gave me a quick glance, questioned Antony about something and then, without so much as a by-your-leave, sat down at my table. I frowned.

'A spontaneous and frank reaction,' he laughed. 'Don't you like chance acquaintances?'

'To be honest, not very much.'

'That's rather strange for a journalist. Why, any chance acquaintance can prove to be a source of information.'

'I prefer to get my information from other sources,' I said.

'So I gather from Antony. You gossip in the corridors of the UNO and imagine that that's journalism.'

I shrugged my shoulders. I wasn't going to pick a quarrel with the first person I met.

'You're a Pole of course,' he said, addressing me in Polish. 'Unfortunately, I am not in a position to pass any judgement on your writing, I am not familiar with contemporary Polish newspapers. I can remember Golos Poranny, and Kurier Tsodzienny. But I've read nothing at all in Polish since forty-four.'

'In forty-four I was four years old,' I said.

'And I was forty. To avoid any misunderstandings, I'll define my political position.' He gave a crisp, military bow. 'Leszczycki, Kazimierz-Andrzej, ex-Major of the Armia Krajowa. They like hyphenated names here, but in Poland then a nickname was enough. What the nickname was didn't matter, all that mattered was to go on repeating liberty, equality, fraternity, and repeat it we did, before we sent the lot to hell. I did likewise when the English took me to London and there ... sold me to the States.'

I didn't understand. 'What do you mean, sold?'

'Well, I'll put it more gently – let's say they gave me up, slipped me something in a drink – both me and my boss Dr Holling – loaded us into a submarine and took us across the ocean. And now, I can introduce myself: former colleague of Einstein, former professor at Princeton University and originator of a theory of discrete time, now officially rejected by science. The sad sum total of many, many things.'

'And what do you do now?' I asked cautiously.

'I drink.'

He smoothed his grey hair which stood up like a hedgehog's prickles over a high forehead and hooked nose: he had something of a Sherlock Holmes twenty years older and something of a Don Quixote relieved of whiskers and beard.

'Don't think I'm an inveterate drunkard. It's just a reaction to ten years' isolation when I didn't go anywhere, didn't read anything, didn't see anyone, just worked till I dropped on a scientific problem that was one big gamble. That's all.'

'Failure?' I said sympathetically.

'There are some successes more dangerous than failures. And it's that danger that has dragged me down to the depths of this big city, down to my countrymen.'

'There aren't that many of them here,' I said.

He pulled such a face that even his cheeks twitched.

'What do you see from the corridors of the UNO or from the windows of your hotel? Get on a bus and go where your eyes lead you, turn down some smelly side street, look, not for a drug store, but for a café that sells home-made cakes. Who

won't you meet there – from former Anders men to yesterday's bandits.'

He grimaced again. The conversation had taken a turn that
was of no great interest to me, but Leszczycki didn't notice –
he was affected either by alcohol or simply by the need to talk
to someone.

'They're capable of many things,' he went on, 'of crying over
the past, and cursing the present, of gambling all night, and
they shoot no worse than the Italians of Cosa Nostra. There's
just one thing they don't know how to do and that's how to
accumulate capital or return to their homes on the Wisla.
They don't get worked up about Gomulka's meeting with
Kadar, but they'll spend all night talking about my namesake
Leszczycki, or kill you if you know where those letters are
hidden.'

'What letters?' I asked growing interested.

'I don't know. Leszczycki was an agent for some kind of
underworld bosses. They say his letters could send some home
to Poland and others to the electric chair. It seems there isn't
a single Pole in the city who doesn't dream of finding those
letters.'

'There is one,' I laughed.

'What's your name?' he asked me suddenly.

'Wacław.'

'Wacek then – as one old enough to be your father I may use
the diminutive. The fact is, Wacek, you're just a pup, a kitten.
You haven't even lived, you've just grown up. You weren't lost
in the Warsaw catacombs, nor did you serve out your time in
the forests and swamps after the war. You were suckling milk
then, and tramping to school. Then you went to university, and
then someone taught you to write notes for a paper and someone else arranged you a trip to America.'

'That's not so little,' I remarked.

'Trivially little. Even in this awful city you expect to live in a
cocoon. You think nothing will happen to you if you always
get home by midnight. And then "bye bye". Give me your
arm.'

He bent my arm and felt my muscles. 'There's something
there,' he said. 'You've played some sport?'

'A little boxing. Then I threw it in.'

'Why?'

'No future in it,' I said indifferently. 'You can't be a champion and you won't need it for living.'

'How do you know? And if suddenly you did need it?'

'Don't you worry about my future,' I broke in, and immediately regretted my sharpness. But he didn't seem at all offended.

'And why shouldn't I bother about it?' he asked.

'If for no other reason than because not just any future will suit me.'

'You can choose it yourself. I'll just do the prompting.'

It was very rude of me but I couldn't restrain myself, I burst out laughing. Again, he didn't seem offended.

'You wonder how I'll do the prompting? Like this ...' He threw out on to his palm something that looked like a cigarette case and gave off a strange, lilac, metallic gleam. There were some sort of flat buttons on the back.

'Thank you,' I said, 'but I've just put one out.'

'It's not a cigarette case,' he corrected me pedantically, at the same time concealing the object in his pocket again as if he feared I might want a closer look. 'If it's to be compared with anything, then it's with a watch.'

'But I don't think I saw a clock-face on it,' I said caustically.

'It doesn't measure time, it creates it.'

His strange air of triumph didn't convince me, it was all too clear – the lonely genius, inventor of *perpetuum mobile*, the mad scientist from the novels of Taine. I had met his kind back in the Warsaw newspaper office. But Leszczycki didn't even notice my involuntary, sceptical smile. Looking somewhere through me, he seemed to be thinking aloud: 'What do we know about time? Some regard it as a fourth dimension, others as a material substance. It's strange. Einstein's paradox and the ringing of an alarm clock in the morning are incompatible. And they will continue to be incompatible for a long time yet, until time lets us into its secrets. Is it arbitrary or determined, continuous or irregular, finite or infinite? Does it have a beginning, or is our past as limitless as our future? And is there a time quantum as there is a light quantum? It's on this point that I diverged from the great Einstein. It was at this point that even Gordon, the boldest of the bold, baulked: "It's too insane, Leszczycki, too insane to be true".'

'And don't you think, Mr Leszczycki ...' I tried to stem this, to me, largely incomprehensible monologue, but Leszczycki interrupted me at once, starting like someone unexpectedly and rudely awakened. 'Forgive me, Waček, I had forgotten you. Did you ever study mathematics?'

I mumbled something about logarithms.

'That's what I thought. Never mind. I'll try to explain within those limits. We represent the physical essence of space time in an oversimplified form. It is more complex than it seems. If the chain of events in time, not just in the world but in the life of each individual, were represented by some kind of conventional line in four-dimensional space, then at each point along this line events and time would branch off, changing and varying along an infinite variety of paths, and at each point along these branches they would branch off again in different ways, and so on without end. It's like a tree. Who can tell in which leaf the drop of sap that rises from the ground will emerge?'

'You mean the victim can escape the murderer, the general can avoid the battle, if they turn along a different branch of time soon enough? You must be joking, Mr Leszczycki.'

But Leszczycki wasn't joking. 'Indisputably,' he insisted. 'You only have to find the turning point.'

'And who can do that?'

'I can, a little. Are you interested in why me?'

'No. Why a little?'

'The reconstruction of time even on the scale of a year is a complex process. A great deal of power is needed – thousands of millions of kilowatts – while I had to work like an alchemist, like the lonely scientist-psychopath who has probably crossed your mind. So for the time being I have only made a selector. The term is, of course, approximate, but the device has a selective bias: it selects the sector or turning point where the different system of reading begins. It has a capacity of not more than an hour, sometimes even less, depending on the intensity of your time, and it is according to this intensity that the selector is adjusted: it can choose from all the variations of your nearest future the most intense half-hour, or even hour.'

'And then?'

'You return to the starting point. The device isn't adequate to deal with greater power. Of course, with the means and power which, let's say, nuclear physics has at its disposal,

I could reconstruct time on the scale of one century. And who's to give me such means, you may ask? Presumably the Pentagon would. Hitler would have given half Europe for this possibility in forty-three. And when the Rockefellers understood its implications, I would be God. But at this point I say frankly, no, and shut up shop. Humanity is not yet adult enough for such a present.'

'There are still the socialist states,' I said.

'Why would they want to reconstruct the future? They're building it themselves on the rational premises of reality.'

'Well, there's the interests of science,' I said, trying to placate him somehow.

'They are in no way compatible with the interests of commerce. Imagine the advertisements: "Parallel time! All varieties of future. Return guaranteed". No! Fashion it yourselves. It wasn't for that that I spent ten years in the scientific underground.'

A drunk looked in from the street and started up on his harmonica – not a song, not even a tune, just a scale. He played it over and over till Antony shouted at him that this was a bar, not Carnegie Hall, and with that the scale was silenced.

'The great Stokowsky once compared a scale to a staircase climbed by a chameleon-sound. If you like, it can modulate your next half-hour up the scale. All right?'

'Is it worth it?' I said, pulling a face. 'What could possibly happen in the next half-hour?'

He didn't answer. We went on in silence, I with the secret intention of shaking him off, he with inexplicable surliness, compressing his almost bloodless lips. Mystificator or madman? The latter, most likely.

Some ten minutes later we were caught in a downpour of such biblical ferocity that we barely managed to get to the shelter of an awning over a stone staircase which led to a semi-basement greengrocery.

I glanced at my watch – it was five to ten. And from habit I immediately put it to my ear. It was still going. 'It's still raining,' muttered Leszczycki, 'and there're no taxis.'

'Something's come,' I said, peering into the fog of rain.

Two bundles of light appeared from around the corner, cutting through the fog – the headlights of a bright yellow car.

'Hey!' I shouted, stepping out from under the awning. 'Over here!'

'That's not a taxi,' said Leszczycki. But the car braked and slowly crawled down along the footpath. It didn't stop, the side window just dropped slightly and in the crack the black crow-like muzzle of a gun flashed in the light.

'Lie down,' Leszczycki shouted and pulled me down. But it was too late – the two bursts of the automatic were quicker. Something hit me forcefully in the chest and the shoulder, throwing me on to the pavement. Leszczycki had doubled up in an odd way and was slowly folding into a sitting position as if his inflexible joints were offering resistance.

The last thing I saw was the red patch on his face where his mouth had been.

Alongside, someone's metal-shod heels clanged on the paving stones. 'One's still alive,' someone said.

'He'll croak all the same, but it's not them.'

'I can see that.'

The metal-shod boot hit me in the head. I didn't feel the pain. Something in my brain had snapped.

Then I heard someone's voice: 'Elzbeta's tricks again ...'

'I'd like to start with her.'

'Go and tell that to Copecki.'

I didn't hear any more. Everything switched off – the voices and the light.

I opened my eyes and looked at my watch. Five to ten. We stood as before on the staircase under the awning.

'Let's cross to the corner,' I suggested, 'there's an awning over there too.'

'Why?'

'We'll get a taxi quicker. There's a turning over there.'

'You go. I'll stay here,' Leszczycki said.

I ran to the opposite corner of the street. My hair and rain-coat were immediately drenched. Added to that, the awning on this side was shorter and the dry strip of asphalt under it narrower: the slanting streams of rain beat at my legs. I pressed my back against the dry doorway and suddenly felt it give. I pressed harder and found myself behind the door in complete darkness. My outstretched hand collided with something warm and soft and I cried out.

'Quietly, and be more careful, you nearly went through my

cheek,' someone whispered and an invisible hand propelled me forward. 'The door's in front of you. You'll see a corridor and a room at the end of it. As you go in ...'

'Why should I?' I interrupted.

'Don't be afraid. He's blind, though he shoots straight. Be polite. Chat to him a bit and wait for me. I'll be back soon.' A coquettish smile, and the door to the street reopened and slammed shut again, immediately. I pulled it. It didn't give and I couldn't find the lock. I had a pocket torch with me that I used in the dark corridors of the hotel. The torch lit up a dark platform and two doors, one on to the street, and the other to the inside of the building. The one to the street had evidently been locked, the other opened gently and I saw the corridor and a light at the end of it falling from an open room.

Trying not to make a sound I approached the room and stopped in the doorway. A man in a black velvet jacket with long hair was carefully cutting a rectangular depression into the pages of an open book. But for the touch of grey in his hair and the wrinkles around his eyes, he could have been taken for a youth. He was sitting in front of a powerful electric light – it must have been some 500 or 1,000 watts in strength. No man with normal vision could have borne to sit so close to it, but this man was blind.

'I've found an ideal hiding place,' he said in Polish. 'All the letters fit, you'll see.'

He took a bundle of letters in longish envelopes and laid them in the artificial depression in the book. Then he brushed glue on the uncut pages alongside the depression and pressed them down to conceal the letters.

'Now we shake it,' he shook the book, holding it by its bound covers. 'You see, nothing falls out. Even Poirot wouldn't find them.'

I was silent and motionless, not knowing what to do.

'Why are you silent, Elzbeta?' he said, growing cautious, and then cried out, in English this time: 'Who's there? Stay where you are!'

He threw down the book and grabbed a pistol from the table. The barrel had been lengthened by a silencer. Since he held it so accurately aimed in my direction, it was obvious that his blindness in no way impeded his handling of the weapon.

'The least movement and I'll shoot. Who are you?' he asked.

He was standing half turned towards me, not looking, but listening, like all blind people. Without replying I quietly took a step backwards. At once there was a click – it was a click, not a shot. The bullet cut into the plaster near my ear.

'You're mad,' I said in Polish. 'What's that for?'

'You're a Pole. I thought so.' He wasn't in the least surprised, and did not lower the pistol. 'Come to the table and sit opposite me. And don't try to get the gun, I'll hear. Come on.'

Cursing myself for this idiotic adventure, I went to the table and sat down, stretching out my legs easily in front of me. The barrel of the pistol followed in my orbit. Now it stared me in the chest. I could have grabbed it were I not convinced that it would fire first.

'You're from Copecki?' the blind man asked.

'I don't know anyone of that name,' I said.

'Where are you from then?'

'From Poland.'

'How long ago?'

'Since December last year.'

'Don't lie.'

'I could show you my passport, but you . . .' I stopped in confusion.

'You mean you're a communist?' he broke in.

'That's right,' I said angrily. That question was beginning to get on my nerves by now.

'Why are you here?'

I told him.

'For some reason, I believe you,' he said thoughtfully, 'but . . . you saw the hiding place.'

I glanced at the book with its bas-relief of Mickiewicz.

'And the letters,' he added threateningly.

'To hell with your letters.'

'Then we'll wait for them to come for them. They'll come without fail. They must.'

'Who are "they"?' I asked.

'Sh!' he whispered and listened, stretching out his head in an odd way, not like a man at all, but like the Ear in Grimm's fairy tale. I couldn't hear anything. Silence mingled with the sound of rain outside the window surrounded me.

'Has someone come in?' I asked.

'Not a sound,' he whispered. 'They haven't come in yet. Now they're opening the door with a skeleton key. They've crossed the platform, they're coming.' He said this almost soundlessly, just moving his lips. I only heard the faint tap of metal-shod heels in the corridor.

'You stay here. I'll go behind the curtain. Don't under any circumstances tell them where I am. And don't be afraid. They won't start shooting, they need the letters. Say that they're in the drawer next to the divan. All right?'

I nodded. Moving as lightly and freely as a ghost, he disappeared behind the curtain which partitioned the room in its farther corner. I remained seated in the same position expecting the worst.

Two men in wet raincoats came into the room carrying automatics. One of them wore a crushed fedora pulled down low over his eyes. The other was dark and unshaven, his wet forelock twisted into ringlets. He shook himself like a dog as it leaves the water.

'Where's Ziga?' they asked together and in Polish. I understood now why the blind man had not been surprised that I was Polish.

'I'm waiting for him' – I said the first thing that came into my head.

The unshaven one looked around the room and suddenly fired a burst from his automatic into the folds of the curtain. I expected to hear cries, groans, but nothing happened. Then they both turned to me.

'This is the end,' I thought and scarcely managed to get out: 'You've come for the letters? They're in the drawer.'

'Where?'

I pointed to the chest-of-drawers near the pillow of the divan. 'Go and open it,' ordered the unshaven one.

I went, and with trembling hands that I could no longer control I opened the drawer. Gleaming white at the bottom of the drawer was a bundle of longish envelopes. The unshaven one pushed me away with his automatic and looked inside.

'They're here,' he said and grinned. He didn't have the chance to say any more. That familiar click sounded several times from behind the curtain and both the man in the fedora and his unshaven friend crashed to the floor almost simultaneously. I don't remember any more which hit the floor first, the backs of their heads or the automatics that slipped from their hands.

'That's that,' the blind man laughed, emerging from behind the curtain.

He touched first one and then the other with his foot and then drew back, like a bather testing the temperature of the water.

'You've done well and earned a reward, Mr Stranger,' he said, holding out to me what looked like a large coin. 'Take this. This medal may come in useful to you. "He lived for the fatherland and died for honour",' he laughed and then suddenly reverted to a whisper, again listening for something. 'They're coming for me already. Don't come with me, I move about here in the dark like a cat. Go out a minute or two after me. I'll leave the door open. And don't delay. An encounter with the police in such circumstances is far from pleasant.'

He took the book which had the letters glued into it from the table and, without putting on a coat, went out of the room. His step never hesitated. Nothing creaked in the corridor, neither the floorboards nor the door. He moved completely soundlessly.

I waited for two minutes, examining the medal I had received: a dull circle of bronze; on one side a bas-relief of a head in a laurel wreath, like the head of a Roman emperor. On the other, a girl in a tunic embraced an urn on an ornate pedestal. Around the imperial head wound an inscription in Latin lettering: Josef Xiaze Poniatowski. Around the girl in the tunic in lettering of the same style wound the words I had already heard that evening: Zyl Dla Oyczyzny. Umarl Dla Slawy. Poniatowski? What did I know of him? Napoleonic marshal and relative of the last king of Poland, outstanding military commander, and a political failure whom Napoleon denied the cherished Polish crown. Bonaparte tricked him, Poland was not restored and even in the hurriedly-created Duchy of Warsaw, Poniatowski was only given the Ministry of War. He died splendidly in one of the Napoleonic campaigns, forgotten by the Emperor whose throne was already beginning to totter. It was not Bonaparte, but his own Polish countrymen who had then this medal struck, inscribing it with the words: 'He lived for his fatherland, he died for honour'.

This medal must have had a great appeal for certain contemporary Polish emigrants, but not for me. It was inaccurate, misdirected. For what honour? Whose? The unworthy, too, have died for honour, even Herostratus. I smiled inwardly at the sentiment with which the medal had been given to me. When and how could it possibly prove useful to me?

I thrust it into my pocket and, without a backward glance at the corpses, left the room. The door to the street was ajar, creaking on its hinges. I was met by an empty street, the spatter of rain on the asphalt, the yellow light of the streetlamps glowing in a diamond network of raindrops. Once again I raced across the street to the awning where Leszczycki was standing. He was there now, staring into the streams of rain dancing in a patch of light. And once again I seemed to see the streams of rain double up like a man seeing double when overcome by vertigo.

I looked at my watch; five to ten. How extraordinary! Why, I had spent a good half-hour at Ziga's. I put the watch to my ear. It was still going.

'It's still raining,' said Leszczycki, not looking at me, 'and there're no taxis.'

'Here's one. Let's go,' I said, and stepped out to meet the taxi as it emerged out of the darkness.

'Not me,' said Leszczycki, refusing. 'I don't like yellow cars.'

I didn't try to persuade him. I got in next to the driver and gave him the address. It's a free world, let him stay if he wants to get drenched. Then I regretted that I hadn't taken his address – he was an entertaining man after all. But I soon forgot about him. It was bright and hot in the car, the speed we drove at lulled me and my thoughts began to get confused. I tried to remember what had happened to me before my meeting with Ziga and couldn't. Someone had fired shots, there had been some shooting somewhere. Perhaps Leszczycki had been telling me about it and I'd forgotten. It seemed to me that he really had been telling me about something. What had it been? Something had happened to my memory, there was some sort of gap, a fog in my mind. I could only remember the last quarter of an hour. Two men had been killed by Ziga from behind the curtain. It happened before my eyes. And I had, with complete unconcern, stepped over their bodies and gone out. The one strange thing was that time was subtracting its flight from the moment we had stopped under the awning, from five to ten. I glanced at my watch. It was now ten o'clock. Was it possible that only five minutes had passed?

I turned to the driver: 'What's the time by yours?'

In my absent-mindedness, I asked him in Polish, but instead of the natural 'What? What did you say?' I heard the familiar Polish expression: 'Dog's blood! A countryman!' The tired, sweaty face broke into a good-natured smile which disclosed pink gums and broken teeth. For all this he wasn't at all old, this lantern-jawed tough in the windcheater – thirty-seven to forty, no more.

We were already nearing my hotel when he suddenly braked and rolled gently towards the footpath. 'Let's have a bit of a chat, I haven't met a countryman for a long time. You must have been a kid when you skipped Poland?'

'Why?' I asked. 'I came legally. This winter.'

He froze at once, the smile died on his face and his reply was fairly vague. 'It does happen of course.'

'And you, why aren't you back home?' I asked in my turn.

'Who needs me over there?'

'Drivers are always needed everywhere.'

He waved his great hands, as wide as shovels and beamed again.

'I was a driver in the army, too,' he said.

'In what army?'

'What army? What army?' he repeated it like a challenge.

'In ours. From Russia to Teheran, from here to there, pushed about from pillar to post, at Monte Cassino I crawled twenty-four hours on the seat of my pants ...' He started singing tunelessly: 'Red poppies on Monte Cassino'. 'And now I'm back behind a steering wheel again, slogging myself to death.'

'So take out an application, go back,' I said.

He spat out of the window without answering. I noticed that he hadn't asked me anything about Poland today.

'Who needs me over there?' he repeated. 'Here I'll pick up something or other and I'll be worth a different price. A bit here and a bit there. All you have to do is find it, there's some of our lot hiding something.'

'Something like letters?' I asked unthinkingly.

He went completely tense, like a cat before it springs.

'What do you know about the letters?'

'One lot's hiding them and the other lot's looking for them. It's funny,' I said, and added, 'We've had our chat, that's enough. Let's get to the corner.'

'Got a cigarette?' he asked hoarsely.

We lit up. 'You can't just say goodbye to a countryman like that' he said reproachfully. 'I know a place not far away. Let's go.'

I remembered Leszczycki smiling at my cautiousness and nodded rashly. Massive dark buildings unlit by advertisements rushed to meet us; the outskirts of even a city like this one are quite dark. I shut my eyes, not even attempting to recognize streets. What did it matter where this place was? The car finally stopped outside a bar with an unlit sign. Why was it unlit?

'I don't know – a blown fuse or something of the sort,' my guide waved off my question indifferently. 'There's enough light inside,' he added. And sure enough there was enough light inside.

Through the misty, unwashed window a high bar with its bottles and enamel and nickel-plated top was clearly visible. On the glass in the corner was a hand-painted black sign. Marian Zuber, coffee, tea, home-made cakes.

The bar was closed. My driver knocked for a long time at the glass door and for a long time someone looked at him from inside. Then the lock turned and the door opened.

In the tiny area in front of the bar there were a few empty tables where probably no one had sat since the week before. Their black plastic tops had turned grey with dust. The only occupant of the bar was standing with almost his whole body leaning across the bar, drinking a glass of some kind of misty liquid and chatting to the waitress. At first I didn't pay any attention to her – she was a typical cafeteria waitress, with a stylish hairdo and painted eyes. Here they must mass produce them in some factory. But a moment later her eyes drew my attention; they were unusual eyes, intelligent and humorous, now glittering, now cloudy, and even their colour seemed to change at their owner's will. Her companion occasionally twisted his mouth in a way that made the scar on his left cheek twitch. I was already beginning to regret that I had come.

'It's late, Janek,' the girl behind the bar said reprovingly. 'We've closed already.'

But my guide authoritatively motioned with his head towards a dusty table, whispered something to the beautiful waitress, brought me a whisky and soda, and taking the man with the scar by the arm went with him behind the bar where the entry to a lighted cellar was visible.

'You're a Pole too?' the girl asked me indifferently.

I laughed. 'Now ask me if I'm long out of Poland.'

'It's all the same to me,' she said and turned away. Janek and his scarfaced companion had by then sat down at my table.

'Janek says you know something about the letters,' said crooked mouth, 'so spill it.'

'I'll spill it,' I said mockingly, 'only to Trybuna ludu.'

'That's some threat! In '45 we made mincemeat of your sort.'

'Do you want me to call the police?'

'Dry up. This isn't Times Square. You can squeal like a pig if you like, no one will hear.'

I turned to Janek. 'You're scum, not a countryman.'

Scarface winked and Janek's ham-like fists closed over my hands and pressed them to the table. I struggled ineffectually – the fists didn't move.

'We weren't in the Gestapo, but we know a thing or two,' said Scarface, puffing on a cigarette. 'So you're not going to spill it, eh?' And he pressed the burning cigarette into my hand just above the wrist. I cried out with the pain.

'You're wasting your time,' the waitress intervened. 'He doesn't know anything.'

Scarface grinned and his mouth twisted even more. It crossed my mind that if you were to slap a hat down over his forehead, he'd be in every detail the double of the man with the automatic who'd been killed by Ziga.

'Button your lip, Elzbeta, before I smash it for you,' he snapped. 'Hold him there, Janek, while I bring something up from downstairs. It'll loosen his tongue in a second.'

He went downstairs into the cellar and his metal-shod boots

gave a familiar clang on the steps. But, the name! It made me jump in my seat. Could that be a coincidence, too?

'Elzbeta!' I cried. 'You must know that I don't have any letters, it was me at Ziga's. And he gave me a medal: "He lived for the fatherland and died for honour"!'

Janek's hold slackened immediately. Elzbeta – could I be mistaken after all – came slowly round from behind the bar. 'Let him go, Janek.'

Janek let go of my hands without protest. 'The gentleman knows how to drive?' I nodded affirmatively, not understanding why she was asking me.

'Give me the keys of the car, Janek.' Just as obediently he held out the keys to her. 'Delay Woyček in the cellar and don't come out till I call.' Elzbeta spoke with inexplicable authority, accepting as her due the military obedience of Janek. She didn't look at me, just went out into the street, opened the door of the car with one key, thrust the other into the ignition and motioned me silently into the driving seat. 'Keep your foot to the floorboards till you get to the bridge,' she warned. 'They'll try to catch you up but you've got ten minutes' start. Get across the bridge before them, turn off somewhere and abandon the car. Get back on foot or by bus. Woyček has a yellow Plymouth like this one, but the motor's trashy and I don't know if he's got enough petrol. And don't thank me – you haven't time.'

I nodded silently, turned on the ignition, moved into first gear and moved off as gently as possible. I was very much afraid that I would have forgotten how to drive, I hadn't had any practice for a long time, but the Plymouth moved easily and obediently. I regained my courage completely and, putting my foot right down on the accelerator, I caught up with an ambulance roaring ahead of me, and tailed it. When I saw the yellow Plymouth behind me I decided to overtake the ambulance. Then at least they wouldn't dare shoot.

Why had Janek led me to that bar? What had they wanted? How was it that Woyček bore such a resemblance to the dead gunman? Why had Elzbeta, at first so totally indifferent to me, come to my aid so determinedly? What had roused her, the mention of Ziga, the medal, the motto? I couldn't find any rational answer to these questions.

There wasn't time in any case. The yellow Plymouth flashed

behind me after all, or perhaps I had only imagined it. We were already approaching the bridge and, overtaking the ambulance, I flew on to this almost luminous structure, flickering with lights. Police on point duty in hooded raincoats flashed past. The rain saved me. Without it I could hardly have crossed here at such a speed. I turned down the first side street I saw. At the next less brightly lit corner I turned again, and repeated this manoeuvre again and again, avoiding the wide busy street, and then braked. The crossroads seemed familiar. I opened the door of the car and ran to the awning under the lamp where an hour before I had stood with Leszczycki. I pressed up against the wall where it was drier and jumped – Leszczycki was standing next to me as before, watching the raindrops separating in the light. It was as if he had just risen up out of the night, the rain and the fading light of the streetlamp. And some confused, involuntary movement of thought made me glance at my watch. Just as I thought: five to ten. Something absurd was happening to me, events and people were coming and going and time itself seemed to be doubling up like the rain in the light. In one orbit I was whirled in a turmoil of riddles and surprises, drawn into events, strokes of luck and frightening experiences, and in the other I stood prosaically under the awning waiting for a taxi.

The flight of time always began with Leszczycki's doleful phrase: 'It's still raining and there're no taxis'.

Now he was beginning it again and I couldn't stop him: I was no longer in control of myself, time controlled me as it did my watch, persistently returning it and me to one and the same moment. Only this time I didn't see the taxi. What if I were to go on foot? 'You're not made of sugar, you won't melt,' they used to tell me when I was a child. And I set off determinedly in the pouring rain, without even saying goodbye to Leszczycki. Time was in control of me and it would have been unnecessary.

I walked for half a block and stopped: two figures in raincoats with bulging pockets were coming towards me. 'It's beginning,' I sighed, and was reminded of comic strips with their changeless repetition of stock characters. One of them wore a fedora pulled down over his eyes, and I recognized at once the twisted mouth and the scar on his cheek; the other stood farther off in the darkness which was full of the sound of rain.

'Got a light?' Woyčekh asked, either not recognizing me, or pretending not to do so. I could play that game, too. I took a lighter from my pocket and a crumpled packet of cigarettes.

While he lit his cigarette, he flicked the lighter, each time lighting up my face, and a voice out of the darkness asked:

'You don't happen to be a Pole?'

'I do as it happens, so what?' I said in reply.

'You don't by any chance know a place near here where compatriots can get together?'

'Of course I do,' I said delaying things – I still didn't understand their game. 'There's Marian Zuber's – coffee, tea and home-made cakes.'

I heard a restrained laugh, and Woyčekh slapped me on the back.

'You're late, Mister Contact Man. We've been waiting for you a long time,' and he drew me towards something that had up till then been hidden by the rainy darkness and now turned out to be the yellow Plymouth.

Getting behind the wheel, Woyčekh's companion smiled at me, showing a row of broken teeth – Janek! He, too, didn't recognize me. I decided to pursue the battering-ram technique. 'Haven't we met before, fellows? Your dials are familiar.'

'A marked man is a bloodhound's joy.'

Woyčekh agreed. 'Maybe we have met, who remembers?' and he added, 'What does Copecki want?'

'As if you didn't know,' I grinned as carelessly as I could. 'The letters, of course.'

'We want them, too,' laughed Woyčekh. Turning round, he even winked at me. Could he really not have recognized me? 'You mean Dziewocki has the letters?' he continued. 'I thought so. So we grab Dziewocki and present him to Copecki. Right?'

'Right,' I agreed, not very confidently.

'You ready to go shares?' Woyčekh asked suddenly. I hesitated.

'He has to think it over! You know how much the letters will fetch? A million? So why drag Dziewocki anywhere? We'll get those letters out of him somehow by ourselves. And the million's ours. Say the word and it's a deal.'

'It's a lot of money,' I said doubtfully.

'Crap!' he drawled scornfully. 'You've got all the fathers of emigration there in one dust heap. The late Leszczycki knew things about them that puts angel's wings on us by comparison. And it's curtains for Copecki and the Krihlaks and the rest.'

Janek finally stopped the car. On the café window was the familiar sign: 'coffee, tea, home-made cakes'. But instead of Marian Zuber was written Adam Dziewocki. The bar wasn't locked, but it had closed down. The chairs and tables were piled up on one another. A young Italian with black sideburns was sweeping up the wet sawdust from the floor.

'Where's Adam?' growled Woyček, and he spat his chewing gum into the barman's face. 'You're crazy!' shouted the other, wiping his face. 'Don't beat about the bush, where's Dziewocki?'

'You mean the last owner?' the Italian said, guessing.

'Why the "last"?'

'The bar's been sold.'

'Who to?'

'To me.'

We exchanged glances. It was clear our birds had flown. From the door came the words: 'Hands up!'

Policemen with automatics stood in the open doorway. Janek and I raised our hands, but Woyček suddenly sprang forward and shoved me forward towards the door and the police. An even stronger impact sent me into darkness.

I came to standing in the doorway under the awning. The rain was whispering as before and the outline of everything around me was lost in a dense watery net. My head hurt and it was with difficulty that I heard the last of Leszczycki's words as he stood beside me: '. . . and there're no taxis'.

And, in fact, there were no taxis. I couldn't remember how long we'd been waiting for one. In fact, I remembered nothing at all. An enormous lump like a tumour had appeared on my temple under my hair, as if something had fallen on my head. When? Where? I strained to remember, and couldn't. Familiar things would suddenly swim into my brain, appearing and then misting and bursting like bubbles of marsh gas: faces, names, cars, an ambulance, a yellow Plymouth . . . I looked around and saw it on the opposite corner under a lamp like the one under which we stood.

'Do you see that?' I asked Leszczycki. 'Maybe they'll drive us.'

'Can you see the driver of that car?'

The latter had just got out of the car carrying some sort of stick or a pipe and passed under the awning over the basement.

'What's he want a stick for?' I asked in surprise. 'Is he lame or something?'

'That's an automatic, not a stick. Speak quietly,' Leszczycki warned.

Suddenly I remembered that basement and the blind Ziga and the dead gunmen. But a live one was standing near the basement waiting for the door to open. And it did open; three men in wet raincoats carried out something that looked like a rolled-up carpet. The driver with the automatic opened the car door. I was going to rush towards him.

'Where are you going?' hissed Leszczycki, grabbing me by the sleeve.

'I've got to help . . .'

'Who? Are you sure it's not a body? And what are you going to fight automatics with, Mr Man from La Mancha – bare hands and a biro?'

At that moment the wind brought their voices to us. 'It's a book – it was in his hands.'

'Shake it. Maybe something will drop out.'

'I have. There's nothing in it.'

'Then throw it away. He won't be doing any more reading.'

Someone tossed away the book and it flashed in the light as it fell behind the car. When they had gone I picked it up. It was only wet on the outside, the thick bound covers with the bas-relief of Mickiewicz had protected it from the rain. A section of its pages was stuck together in a thick wedge and I knew what was hidden there. I swear I was most concerned for Mickiewicz. It would have been interesting to know how many verses were sacrificed to the wastepaper basket with the pages that had been cut out of it.

In the downpour, I couldn't examine the book. I put Mickiewicz into the pocket of my jacket since my raincoat was already soaked through.

'I'm drenched,' I said as I returned to Leszczycki. 'What do you think happened there?'

He didn't reply. Suddenly something shifted its position – the light perhaps, or the rain, or the clouds, filled to overflowing with warm water. Or perhaps it was time?

My raincoat was dry as if the rain had only just started and we had managed to get under the awning in time. Five to ten – my watch was only too ready to tell me. The heaviness that was stifling my brain suddenly cleared away. I remembered everything.

What kind of scale had Leszczycki promised me? An hour or half an hour, lived in a different way on each step of the staircase. I counted the changes: six, this was the seventh. That meant that there was one to go. To discuss with Leszczycki the odyssey he had created was meaningless now. This wasn't Leszczycki standing here. This was a character in the film he was producing, a man from another time. Now he would begin his take ...

'... and there're no taxis.'

'But you just saw it.'

'Where?'

'On the corner opposite. A yellow Plymouth.'

'You're joking.'

'And you saw its driver, with the automatic, and everything that happened afterwards.'

'Warsaw jokes – play those tricks on your typist.'

'You mean you didn't see anything?'

'I'm not drunk.'

And it was true. How could this Leszczycki know what the other Leszczycki had seen in another time? Now I was going to leave him to go round another bewitched orbit. A prophecy in a children's fairy story came to my mind: 'Take the road to the right and you will find ill-luck; take the road to the left, misfortune will dog you'. In other words, there was nothing to choose between – so onward, worthy hero, go where your eyes lead you.

And I went. My raincoat was soaked again, the water dripped down my hair, down the back of my neck and gave me goosepimples, although it wasn't really cold – it had warmed up in the heated atmosphere that rose from the city during the day. My eyes didn't take in the people that came towards me or that I overtook on my way – they were just rain-washed shadows squelching past me. Strange though it was, the abundance of rainwater around me made me want to drink, but the unlit windows visible through the network of raindrops offered no promise of anything to quench the thirst. I don't remember how many minutes or yards I had walked in the rain when the lighted window of the first café or bar rose up in front of me. But I didn't go in at once, I was halted by the words written on a corner of the window. I read them like Balthazaar at the feast reading the prophecy warning of his death: mene, tekel, fares.

Coffee, tea, home-made cakes.

I could, of course, have gone on, no one was forcing me to enter. But something seemed to shift, not something outside me any more, not the rain, not the clouds in the sky, not the smoky silhouette of the town with its patches of light, no, but inside myself, in some nerve cell of the brain. Somewhere in those invisible cells, the chemical substances they contained had at some time registered in an extremely complex code, such character traits as cautiousness, dislike of risk, desire to evade danger and the unknown – and now suddenly, the code changed its form, the chemistry rearranged itself, the register took on a new pattern.

Nevertheless I looked around before going in and on the corner I saw the Plymouth which by now I knew down to the smallest detail. There was no driver and the key swung carelessly in the ignition. Who was here? Janek or Woyčekh? I simply laughed at the thought of the coming encounter and pushed open the door.

The bar was either closing or had already closed and I was met with silence and the clicking of an abacus – the barman had pulled out the till drawer and was totting up the takings in the manner of his grandfathers. It was remarkable that all the Polish cafés I came across on my odyssey greeted me bristling with tables and chairs piled up on one another.

But the barman greeted me like a barman. 'Highball?' he asked.

I explained that in place of the man-size drink he offered me I would be only too pleased to take coffee or tea and some home-made cakes.

'There's nothing like that,' he said. 'I can only give you a highball with whatever measure of whisky you like.'

In reply I said that I would pay for a quarter of a glass of whisky which he could drink himself and I would have just a lemonade. When I had drunk the full glass I collected up the change in my pocket and threw it down on the plastic bar top. The bronze medal with the tsar-like profile rang out with the change. The medal's appearance in my pocket was less of a surprise than the way the barman looked at it. I recognized him instantly – the curling ringlets, the grey shadow on his cheeks. He was one of the nocturnal visitors shot by Ziga. And, again, I was surprised less at his having resurrected himself than at the mixture of bewilderment and fear that was expressed on his pale face. I hastily gathered up the medal and put it away.

'He lived for the fatherland,' I said slyly.

'He died for honour,' returned the other like an echo, and he added with military readiness: 'What are your orders, sir?'

'Is that Janek's car?' I asked, glancing round at the door.

'It's Woyčekh's,' he replied.

'Who did they bring?'

'The girl.'

'Elzbeta?' I said unsteadily.

'That's right. He went to tell Copecki. Our telephone's out of order.'

'He'll be back soon?'

'Yes – the telephone box is only half a block away.'

'Where's the girl?'

He pointed a finger at a door in the corner – 'Perhaps I can be of some assistance.'

'No need.'

I went into the room which evidently served as an office and store. In among boxes of tins and beer, the massive refrigerator and shelves of bottles and siphons lay Elzbeta, wrapped in a strip of carpet. Another coincidence – at the time I thought it was Ziga they were carrying out to the car and now it was Elzbeta who lay before me wrapped in the same sort of bundle. There was not a drop of blood in her almost wax-like face, and no trace of colour on her lips or eyes. She bore more resemblance to a girl from some convent school than to the imperious beauty who – I no longer knew how many minutes or hours ago – had saved my life.

I bent over her and her lowered lids didn't even stir – she was in a deep faint. There was no doubt or hesitation in my mind, only one thing worried me – would I have time before Woyčekh returned? The carpet cocoon jumped slightly as I gathered it into my arms. My muscles have come in handy, Mr Leszczycki – you were right, they did come in handy after all.

Pushing the door open with my foot I almost knocked the

barman off his feet – he had evidently been looking through the keyhole or the crack of the door.

'Be more careful next time, barman. You run the risk of losing your eyes that way,' I laughed, as I passed by him with the girl in my arms.

He wasn't put out, just became thoughtful for a moment. It was obvious that the situation itself and my tone had shaken some decisions of his. 'Can I help, sir?' he asked.

'Stay where you are,' I said sharply. 'I'll take the girl to the car and wait for Woyčekh there. No questions.'

He nodded understandingly, opened the door to the street and I had the impression that he took up a position behind the Balthazaar-like inscription on the window, assuming that I would not notice this manoeuvre from the street, but I didn't even bother to turn around. I lay the still unconscious Elzbeta on the front seat of the car. That latest model Plymouth, even if obtrusive, battered and repainted, was comfortable inside and very roomy. The girl proved so tiny and thin that she could lie across it with her knees only slightly bent. I then calmly walked round the car, and was opening the door on the driver's side when suddenly someone's hand grabbed me hard by the shoulder. I looked round – Woyčekh – in the same drenched fedora and with the same down-twisted mouth.

'The gentleman's taken a liking to the new sedan?' he grimaced. 'Just hang on a minute till you write out the cheque.'

'Look inside you ass,' I said.

He bent down to look and then straightened. In that second I remembered my last three rounds at the Warsaw competition some years ago. My opponent had been Prohar, a fourth-year student who trained under Walaček and like him was agile and accurate but with a weak punch. I didn't have any special speed or accuracy, the one thing I depended on was my punch from low on the left, a classy knock-out punch. Prohar had a clear win on points, and I was still stalking him with that punch, waiting for him to drop his guard. He never did. I lost and gave up boxing, like the Russian champion Shatkov after his defeat in Rome. At home they talked almost triumphantly of how he had become some kind of head of a university, had even had his doctorate accepted, while the boxing gloves still hung up in his study. I hung mine up in my room too, as a souvenir, although I soon forgot everything connected with them except for one thing, my star punch, undelivered when I most depended on it. I remembered it like a conditioned reflex and when Woyčekh straightened up leaving himself wide open like any beginner at his first training bout would do, I hit him with my left from low down, aiming at his totally unprotected jaw. I put the entire strength of my muscles and all the weight of my body behind the punch, everything I had. Already helplessly unconscious, Woyčekh's whole body turned over and slumped on to the street. 'Glass chin,' our trainer would have said of him.

I didn't so much get into the car as dive in. I sat on the very edge of the seat and leapt away, bending as low as possible over the steering wheel and only just in time! Something splintered above my head leaving two round holes in the dull glass of the side window and the windshield. The second bullet scraped the top without even penetrating the body. I escaped from the third with my foot to the floorboards, overtaking a truck loaded with barrels. The gunman must have been the barman, not Woyčekh, who would certainly not yet have recovered consciousness.

Driving in such circumstances was difficult and awkward. I kept slipping off the seat and the dark street also confused me: I didn't know where it led, and so I stopped. Putting Elzbeta's head on my knee, I turned into a more well-lit, busier street trying to work out in my head how to get back to the hotel or at least to that crossing where I had stood with Leszczycki, since Elzbeta's flat was opposite. The girl hadn't stirred or opened her eyes; when I had lifted her only her eyelids had fluttered slightly. I had the feeling that she was conscious, had been for a long time and was only not opening her eyes because she wanted to find out what had happened and why she was being driven away again.

Then I began talking. Staring into the dim confusion of rain, rain-blackened asphalt and streetlamps cut by rain, I talked and talked, becoming breathless and confused, as if I were delirious.

'I'm a friend, Elzbeta, your closest friend now, although you don't even know who I am or where I come from. But you saved my life today, in quite another time, it's true, you won't even remember it. But you must remember Mickiewicz's verses and love them. It was your book Ziga mutilated so sacrilegiously. I'll recall just two lines to you, the beginning of a sonnet, do you remember? "Travelling life's road, each with our own destiny. We met, you and I, like two boats at sea." Re-read them if they've survived. I have the book and the letters are still in it, where Ziga hid them today – was it really today? He gave me a medal, I've already told you about that. I want to give him back the volume of Mickiewicz.'

She opened her eyes and showed no surprise at seeing an unfamiliar face before her. She said quietly and sadly: 'They've killed Ziga. But they didn't find the letters. He wanted to take them to our embassy. Only is it really ours?' she added doubtfully.

'It's ours, Elzbeta! Ours! Our country's. You'll take them there yourself now and I'll come with you. Then you'll go home to Warsaw,' I went on, still in my feverish delirium. 'Can there be anywhere more beautiful than Warsaw?'

'I don't remember. I was a little girl, very, very small,' she said sadly. 'But what's left of Warsaw? Stones.'

'It's been built again Elzbeta. You've just been deceived, as all of you emigrés are deceived. The old town is just as it was . . .'

I was just going to tell her how this wonderful corner of old Warsaw had been resurrected, but in that second we drove at full speed into blackness where Elzbeta, the town and I, were no longer.

I came out of the darkness in another frame – not in the car but at that same crossing with Leszczycki. The rain which had attacked the town with its short massed invasion, was moving away to the east leaving behind a dark star-spotted sky and an equally dark street spattered with the reflections of streetlamps. It was five to ten. Leszczycki looked at me and smiled. 'As you see,' he said. 'Just as much time has passed as we would have needed to get from the bar to this crossing. But the scale has been played already.'

I didn't ask him what scale. He looked at me with understanding and sympathy, as if he knew everything that I had been through. But I was mistaken.

'I don't know anything, Waček,' he added. 'I wasn't with you. You were surrounded by people from another time.'

'But the same people?'

'Of course.'

'What was it?' I asked. 'Induced hallucination?'

'What do you yourself think?'

'I don't know. I'd very much like to know how my last take ended.'

'What did you call it? A take? Why?'

'A take – that's a cinematic term,' I explained. 'They usually shoot several variations of one and the same scene. They're called takes.'

He was pleased with the comparison.

'A take,' he repeated. 'Take . . . perhaps your take is still going on in its own time. Who knows? Even I don't know altogether what it's all about. Time is a bottle of gin – I poured out a little and now I'm glad to have caught it all back.' He held out his hand to me. 'Don't be offended, Waček. I only wanted to help you try your strength, it always helps. Perhaps you have grown up a little and become a little wiser. Don't be angry with an old man.'

'I'm not angry,' I said. 'I just don't understand.'

'You don't have to. Just assume that I played a joke. Such stupid jokes do happen,' he sighed, and without saying goodbye, moved off, overtaking passers-by who had appeared from somewhere – they must like us have been waiting out the sudden downpour and were now hurrying about their business.

Only I didn't hurry anywhere, as I tried to clarify to myself what it had all been. A dream? But I hadn't been asleep and I hadn't been daydreaming, although I had lost consciousness. Hypnosis? But I had never heard of this form of hypnosis – and was it even at all possible? Six different hallucinations in one flash in a thousandth, perhaps even in a millionth part of a second. And could a hallucination bring on a burn? I pulled up my sleeve and saw clearly the bluish-purple mark left by Woyčekh's cigarette. And the grazed skin on the knuckles of my left hand – yet another mark of my encounter with Woyčekh. And the medal? Of course, here it was! I took it out of my pocket and looked at it in the light. It wasn't a phantom medal, an illusion medal, but a real medal out of old bronze. The bas-relief of Poniatowski with the laurel wreath on his brow, and the inscription around it: 'He lived for the fatherland and died for honour' – all this was not at all ghostly, not illusory, I could feel every letter.

And the volume of Mickiewicz was in its place. I didn't take it out, just felt the raised portrait on the cover. So everything had really happened. It was not a hallucination, not a dream and not a vision under hypnosis. Leszczycki's cigarette case had played its scale for me, caused me to live through a half-hour or an hour, each time in a different way. I really had lain here shot through the chest, had raced for my life in a mad motor chase, had fought for Elzbeta's honour and become the owner of the letters, whose publication so terrified the White emigré riff-raff.

The medal, Mickiewicz and the letters were visitors from another time. Perhaps in ours, they had their counterparts, but did that really change anything? Ziga wanted to take the letters to the embassy, and I promised to help Elzbeta in this. Wasn't it all one in what time this took place and if it took place at all? Now I was the master of my own time.

Without hesitating or pausing to think, I determinedly strode off across the street to the very familiar entrance opposite.

Translated by D. Matias

Andrei Gorbovskii

Futility

T HEY did not feel the solemn moment when the ship touched the surface of the planet. There was no shock. One of the indicators simply flashed the sign for 'Solid' and that marked an end to the emptiness of interplanetary space.

Vamp looked at the Captain, but the latter betrayed no sign of satisfaction and it was impossible to tell how he was reacting to the end of their long travel.

From the combination of flickering dashes, dots and intersecting wave lines, it was evident that the environment in which their ship now stood was close to the conditions of life on their own planet – close, within allowable limits. Vamp passed the information on to the Captain, but this too seemed to make no particular impression on him.

'I think we won't find any higher forms of life here,' he remarked gloomily. 'Go and take a stroll, anyway.' 'Taking a stroll' was what the Captain called it.

The edge of the low slope that Vamp climbed was overgrown in places with some sort of fine, twining vegetation. From the plateau below the ship looked like a big white balloon. A brownish plain stretched for miles on all sides. Only right at the broken and vague line of the horizon did it merge into rockpiles and cliffs. And that was all.

For such a landscape it was certainly not worth going far, but the very nature of their profession inevitably bound them to disillusionment of this kind. Their business was trade. They did not, it was true, bear much resemblance to their ancestors who had carried on the profession in ancient times. They travelled to distant worlds taking goods to where they would be of most value. They carried with them units of information locked away in a series of transparent crystals. This was the merchandise in highest demand on the caravan routes of the universe.

Each civilization developing along its own lines inevitably uncovered certain truths and made discoveries which were unknown to others. Their business was to trade discoveries for discoveries, theories for theories, information for information. Sometimes they came upon worlds which could offer them nothing in exchange. Then they liberally shared with primitive beings such facts as they were able to assimilate, for information was the one merchandise which could be exchanged or given away freely a limitless number of times and its quantity was never reduced in the process. Visitors to these worlds thousands of years later would find there rich fruits of the seeds which they were sowing today.

They were on their way home after a vast spiralling journey among the stars which had brought them a mass of remarkable knowledge. Many ships like theirs were ploughing the spaces of the universe, but not all of them came back. Often unexpected danger and death overtook them on strange, distant planets, planets which at first seemed just as empty and lifeless as this one. Vamp returned to the ship, and now it moved in a gigantic ever-increasing spiral over the surface of the planet. On to the screen flashed pictures of what they were passing below, but they weren't watching the screen – what could there be down there that was new to these visitors to so many worlds?

They sat down to a game of draughts.

'An empty world,' the Captain remarked gloomily, 'a dead planet.'

Vamp sacrificed one player and swallowed up two.

'Let's circle round a few more times,' the Captain said, 'and that's enough.'

'How far is that planet from the sun?' Vamp moved a draught forward ready to make a king in the next move.

'It's the third.' The Captain took the draught that was about to become a king. 'The third from the sun. It's down in our catalogues as "Earth".'

The screen still showed the same chaos of rockpiled cliffs, and the brownish plain stretching to the distant, imprecise line of the horizon. No towns, no settlements, no sign of rational life.

'Circle round a few more times and that's enough,' the Captain repeated.

They said no more because Vamp had got a king. The Captain always considered that he was the better player but that he made mistakes and that Vamp took unfair advantage of it. That's how it was now. When only one or two moves remained to decide the issue, they were interrupted by the shrill sound of a buzzer. The ship had uncovered traces of some kind of civilization. The Captain impatiently jabbed a button and the buzzer stopped – only the infra-red eye of the indicator went on pulsing angrily.

They played a few more games.

'Had enough for now?' Vamp asked, badly concealing his triumph.

The Captain agreed gloomily.

A picture flashed on the screen and they saw a large, elongated metal body half buried in the sand.

'Craft for conveyance into the planet's space field,' Vamp remarked.

'Civilization no higher than second level.' It seemed as if that circumstance gave the Captain some kind of malicious satisfaction. 'A primitive world and for that reason an extinct one.'

'Shall we have a look at the craft?'

But the Captain refused. Studying lost civilizations was not their business. For that there were the rat-catchers from the Cosmic Academy of Sciences.

'And what if there are rational beings there?'

The Captain shook his head.

'The craft crashed and has been empty a long time. You can go if you're interested, but we're leaving immediately afterwards – there's nothing for us here.'

Close up the strange ship seemed bigger still. It was a large streamlined block of dark metal.

Vamp could see neither entry nor opening. On all sides there was only a smooth sheath of metal dulled by time. Then he noticed a wide black crack which seemed to cut the whole body in half. He looked in but could see nothing. Carefully squeezing between the black edges of the torn metal, Vamp lowered himself inside.

Seconds later a startled crowd of small fish flitted out of the crack and clustered over the dark gap made by the break. They were as oblivious of the many-fathomed depth of water above them as frivolous inhabitants of dry land might have been of the mythical 'column of air'. The one thing which might, perhaps, still have felt the gigantic pressure of these depths was the lifeless submarine.

For some time the white balloon hung motionless over the half-concealed metal hulk below. There was no sign of Vamp. When he finally did begin to emerge, the little fish dancing near the edge of the crack scattered in all directions.

The balloon moved off and, gathering speed, disappeared behind the broken line of the horizon.

'Anything interesting?' the Captain asked, more out of politeness than curiosity.

Vamp shook his head. 'The craft was of primitive construction – using energy from batteries and accumulators. The cause of the crash isn't evident.'

'Is that important?'

'No of course it's not ...'

'We came to trade.' The Captain said this as if Vamp had contradicted him. 'Nothing else here concerns us. And, incidentally, even if we had found those who built such craft, in what could we have interested them?'

'Protein synthesis, if they hadn't mastered it, the harnessing of free energy from space ...'

'You think so?'

'On all the evidence, they're fairly primitive. We could even offer them the formation of the synthetic personality or biological procedures towards immortality.'

'Yes, of course. Second level. And what could they give us?'

Vamp held out a flat, rectangular object to the Captain. He had taken it off the wall of one of the cabins. It was an ordinary black and white photograph. Protected by glass it had scarcely suffered damage from the water. The photograph showed a man, a young man in a leather jacket holding a large Great Dane on a short lead. The Great Dane was obviously not very interested in the prospect of having its sad, canine muzzle preserved on film and he was looking impatiently to the side somewhere beyond the frame. The young man was standing beside a highway along which traffic was moving in both directions. A bus could be seen in the distance.

'Odd,' remarked the Captain.

'Very,' agreed Vamp. This was one of those rare times when he was in full agreement with his Captain.

'They couldn't even distinguish colours – it's black and white.'

'And that belt?' Vamp indicated the highway.

'It's moving?'

'So it seems. And carrying the objects arranged on it.'

The Captain nodded. 'Very odd.'

'And this?' Vamp was talking about the man and the dog. 'An obvious symbiosis.'

'Of course. These two beings evidently possess a single thinking process and a single psyche. They are obviously conscious of themselves as a single personality.'

'Look,' Vamp pointed to the lead, 'they are even joined by a rope of nerve fibres.'

'Like the ascetics from Megera-XY?'

They discovered a few more submerged vessels, and then they came across the ruins of a town. And as before there was not a single sign of the rational beings whose hands had created all this.

'A dead planet,' asserted the Captain. 'The inhabitants degenerated and died out.'

'Why degenerated?' Vamp himself didn't know why he was so offended on behalf of the natives of this planet.

'Extinction is simply the culmination of a process. If the race was not able to accommodate it, it must have degenerated.' And he added impatiently, 'We're leaving'.

'But you know, they, they . . .' Vamp no longer knew what more to say, he just felt for some reason that if this planet were struck off the list of inhabited worlds, it would be a mistake, a great mistake of some kind. 'You know they . . . what if they inhabit the higher regions?' he blurted, himself realizing that he was talking foolishness.

This was so absurd that the Captain didn't even get angry.

'My dear Vamp, do I have to recite you the "Laws of Life"?' A dull film dropped over his eyes, half closing them, and he began quoting: ' "Life on the planets is only possible in areas protected from the fatal rays of the sun and cosmic radiation, that is on ocean beds. Higher forms of life can only arise and develop in areas of great pressure under great depths of water".'

Vamp was silent because what the Captain said was indisputable.

'What's next on our list?'

Vamp looked up and glanced at the log: 'Alpha Centauri'.

The Captain shifted some levers on the control panel and in a few seconds they were again surrounded by space.

Vamp stretched out ten green tentacles from under his armour and started setting up the draughts board.

Translated by D. Matias

Artur Mirer

The Test*

[FOREWORD BY THE AUTHOR]

A SUPERBRAIN has been built. Its intellectual possibilities exceed those of man. The Constructor sets this superbrain – the 'Centre' – a task: to construct a factory for the production of napalm, to make the production line fully automated, and to deliver the napalm to the Army. Everything is quite simple. The Constructor, disguised under the code-name the 'Scientist', will set the tasks – the Centre will carry them out.

Everything is straightforward, except for one fact: in order to be able to supervise this gigantic production complex the Centre has been given a superhuman intellect, and an overdeveloped sense of humanity. Thus, one fine day the Centre, instead of turning out napalm, begins to produce excellent artificial jam.

There are three flavours of jam: strawberry, raspberry and grapefruit. The roads are full of automatically controlled trucks bearing the inscription 'Jam – Jam'. No action can be taken, since the Centre simply does not *want* to produce napalm and cannot be forced to do so. With a certain malicious pleasure the Scientist reports to the authorities that power to the Centre cannot be cut off because it has its own atomic power-station. Neither can it be deprived of water for it has sunk artesian wells on the factory site. It is impossible to enter the site anyhow since the system has been programmed to exclude human beings.

So people have to give in. In the end trade in jam becomes more lucrative than the production of napalm, since the Centre extracts its own raw materials from the site area of the factory. A short period of calm ensues, but not for long. The Centre demands to have attached to it a man, a simple man, trained in manual skills, and 'without imagination'. One of the firm's

*From the cycle *Artificial Jam*.

drivers is seconded to the factory, unwillingly it is true, but what is to be done? The Centre might bring sanctions to bear and the firm has no way of ...

THE TEST

Philip locked the car carefully and looked over the tyres – he always took good care of the tyres.

'You stay there for a while, my grey Sally, I'll be right back.'

Then he had a look round. There was a long, straight fence which gave the place the dismal appearance of a prison camp. Along the top of it ran five strands of barbed wire. From the posts hung red warning signs with crossed lightning and skull and crossbones. Philip spat and, crouching down by the car, lighted a cigarette, while continuing to stare along the length of the fence. 'It's better in Australia,' he thought to himself, 'but a set of tyres didn't last above a month there. Some job.'

He fished in his pocket for the packet of cigarettes and looked inside – only three left.

'It's tough being poor, Sally,' Philip said and, sticking the dog-end neatly to the tyre cover for luck, set off towards the entrance.

Well, here was the gate. The bell-push was on the left, all he had to do now was press it: three short, a pause, a short and a long. What was it Bating had said? If you came to this factory to work you were okay. If you came for any other reason . . . well . . . Whatever happens you might as well put Sally in a garage.

A door opened, he stepped forward and it closed behind him with a soft click.

'Go straight ahead. Take care, it is dangerous here,' said a quiet voice. It sounded clear and pleasant, but somehow strange. And he could not make out where it was coming from. Philip took out a cigarette. Now there were two left.

'Go straight ahead. Take care, it is dangerous here,' repeated the Voice.

Philip walked straight ahead, the cigarette clasped between his clammy fingers.

The long, empty access road ran between blank walls. It was deserted and only the hot wind blew along the spotless asphalt – there was not a single cigarette butt or fruit skin to be seen, nothing. There was not even any dust. The only things visible on every side were the silver-grey walls and the black shadows on the asphalt.

'Be careful!' the Voice reminded him. Philip spat and ran his fingers along one of the walls.

It was a mystery how he managed to jump out of the way. An automatic van flashed past at high speed and made not the slightest attempt to brake. By the time Philip turned round the van had already whizzed through the gates. The crushed cigarette showed white on the surface of the road. That was the only damage.

'Walk straight on,' said the Voice.

As Philip made his way forward he was twice pressed to the wall by vans, and almost killed by a conveyor belt which suddenly appeared from nowhere. For several minutes he was followed by a robot on wheels which kept twisting its locator head inquisitively up and down. Once the robot had dropped behind, Philip swore out loud for several minutes. The infernal machine's manipulators kept twitching like a crab's pincers. It did not look as though they were used to people here . . .

'Well, I've found a right spot here. It's worse than a desert,' thought Philip. In a way it was worse than a desert, more empty. But he could not quite get to the bottom of why it was. He had to be on the look-out all the time, while the Voice kept on insistently, 'Straight on, careful, turn to the south, danger – stop – go up the stairs'.

It was with relief that he caught sight of an actual building, a proper one. It was of grey concrete with glass window embrasures and a peaked roof, quite pleasant to look at. And there was a lawn too.

'Go up this staircase,' the Voice repeated.

Yet another grey door opened of itself. Philip took a careful look round: in the middle of an otherwise empty room stood a writing-table. One wall was made of frosted glass. He sniffed, there was a rather strange smell in the room. Well, well . . . Any moment now and a cannibal would come walking in and say that he could smell human blood.

'Hello,' said Philip, 'Mr Bating sent me, about the work . . .'

Silence. Only a small many-legged robot rolled from the table and disappeared under the wall. Aha, so there was a gap of about five inches between the wall and the floor. He went closer. It was a normal writing-table except that the top was all scratched, as though by claws. On the table stood a white machine of some kind. On each side of it were three handles, a red one, a white one and a yellow one. It looked harmless enough. Philip moved so as to get closer to the handles and bumped against some kind of transparent barrier. There were cables running out from under the handles – so, they were alive.

'Caution,' said the Voice.

Philip jumped back from the table.

'This is a test,' said the Voice. 'Take hold of the red handles – be careful.'

Now Philip could hear the Voice quite clearly. It sounded like a television commentator. It would have been good just to see who was going to employ him, but then, everyone has their own methods. He grunted and squeezed his way past the barrier to get at the handles. He had to take up a position like a kangaroo – with his body bent forward at the waist and his elbows pushed out to the sides to avoid the cables. Right in front of his face was a white panel with six dials, six signal lights, and a tube. He could not raise his head or the back of his neck banged against the barrier.

'Begin! Down!' the sound of the Voice carried to him.

Red arrows appeared, point downwards, in the two top dials, and Philip pressed cautiously at the handles.

It seemed a fairly simple arrangement. The arrows whirled round on the six dials, and Philip turned the handles in the direction they showed. He soon realized that the point of the exercise was to prevent the signal lights from showing. It was like one of the machines on which he had learnt to drive a tractor. If the light came on it meant that the handles had been moved too quickly or too slowly, but he could not see what the purpose of the tube was.

The arrows began to move more erratically, but Philip still managed to keep the lamps from showing, although the machine seemed to him to have become more demanding. He was now moving all four levers at once, jerking his arms up and down, but suddenly he lost the rhythm and swore – a blast of hot air came out of the tube and hit him in the face. 'So that's why it's there,' he said to himself. 'The thing is to put up with it and not to lose your temper.'

He knocked his head against the barrier and burnt his left arm on the cable. He did not want to give in, but the machine kept on at him and he began to lose the rhythm again.

Suddenly the Voice said: 'Finish!'

Philip squeezed out from behind the barrier and spent several minutes stretching himself and flexing his arms. His neck ached and his eyes felt as though they were full of sand. He looked at the wall with the crack in it. That was where the Voice seemed to be coming from.

'Name your index number.'

He could have sworn that the Voice was coming from behind the wall.

'I don't understand,' he sighed.

'Reproduce the name by which you are known to other people.'

'You must be a foreigner, mister. My name's Philip.'

'Your name is Philip,' the Voice repeated.

Philip plucked up courage.

'And what's your name, mister? The boss asked . . .'

'My index is – Centre two nought nought two,' the Voice interrupted him.

'That's a bit complicated,' said Philip, still not realizing what it was all about.

'That does not matter,' said the Voice, 'men can call me simply the Centre.'

Philip almost jumped out of his skin. So it was *the* Centre and there were no people at all . . . Philip's temples contracted with curiosity – he was ready to crawl under the wall, just as the little centipede had not long ago, anything to catch a glimpse of the famous machine. Last year there'd been nothing else on the radio but: 'The Centre has increased its profits . . . the Centre does not agree . . . there is no answer from the Centre . . . the Centre is introducing a new production line . . .' It was said to control one of the Company's big plants entirely on its own, without any humans. So that was where he was . . .

The Voice was silent, as though waiting for Philip to begin talking. This made him feel more cheerful.

'Say, Mister Centre, did you really build this whole factory all on your own?'

'That is a false conclusion. The Scientist constructed a

basic machine. The basic machine constructed the factory. There is no construction scheme of the factory in my memory bank.'

Philip wanted to ask what a basic machine was – but he restrained himself. He would not have understood anyhow. He was very pleased to have the Centre talking so readily to him, a mere driver and a former shepherd. He realized, though, that he must not go too far, and contented himself with asking:

'Mister Centre, I'd like to know who built you.'

'That is a false conclusion,' said the Voice, with the same intonation as before.

'I, the Centre, dash two nought nought two, created myself from a synthesis of biological elements – no one built me.'

'That means that no one knows how you are constructed,' Philip said slowly. 'That can't be true.'

He still had a vague idea that there was someone on the other side of the wall, and he got down on all fours and looked underneath.

In the darkness of the crack shone the yellow eyes of at least fifty of the little centipede-like robots. He stood up quickly.

At the same time the Voice went on intoning something completely unintelligible: 'I cannot be recognized: I am a black box'.

Philip gave a start. Christ! It was like some kind of dream! All around him was the huge, empty factory, while these wretched little robots sat looking at his legs and only just not biting them. A spasm of fear gripped him. So he *was* the only man there. He had to get out.

'What sort of work am I going to do, mister?' he asked firmly, 'Did I pass the test?'

'I am constructing a Centre like myself. You will act as a model for the learning process.'

'So,' Philip thought, 'like a girl with a sewing machine in a shop making home-made clothes. But why is he going on about a new Centre?'

'Will the work last long?' he asked.

The Centre did not answer.

'Okay,' Philip thought, 'we'll just have to wait and see. It's worth taking the risk for twenty a day.'

'So long then, Mister Centre!' he said.

The Voice stayed silent.

'Looks like he doesn't want to let me go,' thought Philip, 'but I sure want to get out of here.'

He was as tired as though he had been driving his tractor through pits and gulleys for twenty-four hours non-stop, but his curiosity, which had put him into all sorts of scrapes so far in his life, would not allow him to simply up and go.

'Mister Centre,' he said as politely as he could, 'I'd like to be able just to have a look at you.'

He shifted from foot to foot in embarrassment.

'Go down the stairs,' the Voice said harshly.

As he went out Philip glanced behind him. The opaque window was bathed in the light of the setting sun and the centipede-robots had come tumbling out from under the wall and were scrambling on to the table, their claws scratching away. He wanted to slam the door but it closed of its own accord, almost crushing his hand.

'Careful,' said the Voice.

'He doesn't want to be seen,' thought Philip as he went down the steps.

'He probably looks fantastic if he's a machine.'

He had turned in the direction of the exit, when suddenly the Voice repeated:

'Go down the stairs.'

Philip turned round – aha! There was a narrow spiral staircase leading underground. It was dark. At first he was really frightened, but he crossed himself, and went on, placing his feet carefully on the hollow-sounding metal stairs.

'Go straight ahead,' said the Voice. 'Be careful. Stop.'

In the pitch darkness he stopped as though rooted to the spot. Something began to rumble just in front of his face, it sounded like a heavy wagon rolling along some rails. The noise died away. A dim reddish-coloured light began to glimmer from somewhere.

'Don't move, it is dangerous,' said the Voice, and Philip froze to the spot.

The light soon became brighter – it was an unpleasant red light, like there is during a sandstorm in the desert. Philip stared, blinked and suddenly caught sight of something. Quite near him on the floor was a strange-looking machine with hundreds of tentacles. It stood there, motionless and threatening.

He took one step backwards and the machine immediately raised one pincer.

'Don't move,' said the Voice, and Philip stood back – still, biting his left hand to stop his teeth from chattering. He heard the Voice saying:

'This is the guard robot – the brain is in the centre of the building.'

Trying not to look at the robot, Philip stood on tiptoe and peered through the lighted aperture.

'A huge pot-bellied vase,' he thought. 'What kind of brain is that?'

He gradually grew more sure of himself, and, on looking closer, caught sight of movement under the bulging glass covers. It was the twisting and turning of a greyish semi-transparent mass, lethargic and powerful, like the movements of a python. He was now looking straight at it and more and more had the feeling that the brain was also looking at him with its own invisible eyes. It was inspecting him as though he were an insect on the palm of its hand, and he felt a strange kind of peacefulness, the world seemed to be enveloped in obedient silence. He stood looking for what seemed an age and then suddenly heard the Voice:

'Finish!'

The robot retreated into the depths of the chamber with a clatter. The steel door rolled back into place, and Philip turned and walked towards the stairs.

On the first step he stopped and asked, looking up into the darkness:

'I forgot. Why do you want to build another one like yourself?'

'I am alone here, and I am getting old,' answered the Centre . . .

Philip went out on to the lawn and, dragging his feet, walked off between the dark walls. The few lamps shone dully above the buildings and from somewhere near at hand he could hear the rhythmic sound of a hammer. From one building came the unpleasant screech of metal being cut. He stopped at a cross-roads, not knowing which way to go. He did not really care. He wanted to cry and stamp his feet as he used to when he was a child. The cold of the night air made him shiver, and he could not get his cigarette into the flame from his lighter. Suddenly the flame struck him in the face in a dull red flash, and he saw dusty suns and squiggles.

The pain in his head brought him round. He tried to stand up and realized that he was being carried. In front of him he saw the surface of the road and his own arms dangling. He surreptitiously lifted his arms, and suddenly dropped to the ground. The robot had released him from its pincers, and rolled off to one side, with its head turning round.

'Aha, friend,' said Philip. 'What are you doing, collecting litter?'

He struggled to his feet and managed to stand. Nothing was broken.

'You've been lucky, lad,' he said to himself and shambled off in the direction of the gates.

Once again the door opened in front of him and shut behind him, grey Sally was standing at the side of the road, water was gurgling in a drainage ditch and the sun was rising on the other side of a group of trees. Philip had a drink of water straight from the ditch, opened the car door, and sat down carefully in the driving seat. He found quite a large cigarette butt in the ashtray. He sat and smoked for a little while until the stub burnt his lips, and then put the key in the ignition.

'Let's go, Sally.' He released the handbrake and puffed and panted. 'That damned rubbish collector of theirs. Tomorrow we'll be off, Sally. I'll go home. I'm going to look after sheep, that's what I'm going to do. Some other fool can drive you.'

Translated by C. G. Bearne

Artur Mirer

The Old Road*

THE CAR was one of the latest models; a marvel rather than a car.

'It's too new, that's its trouble,' said Philip Saton.

It was too fast and too steady on the bends and for ever trying to catch up with the car in front and knock it down. The semi-automatic driver panel took up a good half of the windscreen, but unfortunately it had never been fully developed. As it was, it was impossible to take more than a short rest, and only then over the straight sections. There is nothing more tiresome than driving a machine which is too good.

Behind them stretched sections of trans-continental roads, the green stars of the polarized world, the roar of police helicopters and notices several feet high saying, 'Minimum speed 100 MPH'. Now they were tearing along the dark, empty road, along the narrow concrete bridge which brought the two regions of eternity together.

This was the highway, a two-hundred-mile stretch of desolation without a single oncoming vehicle. The road rolled evenly on ahead, lit up beneath the headlights, and dark in the distance. The bleached trunks of poplar trees ran on and on like the walls of a never-ending corridor. The poplars reflected the beam of the headlamps and the cabin was lit by a dim twinkling light. Maria was asleep; her head lolled against the high back of her seat, and her left hand was resting on his knee.

This was how they always travelled. To Philip it seemed as if they had been travelling like this since birth; in fact they had met only two years ago, in that wretched drivers' camp at the last outpost in Chile. He had but looked at her and that was

* From the cycle *Artificial Jam*.

that; he'd been struck on the spot, as if a charge of dynamite had exploded, but neither had then known how things would turn out. In fact she might have known, and certainly knew something already, but he had still been concerned with the road and with the whole question of passes, and could only look at Maria while eating his omelet.

Maria had brought him a steak and said, 'There's a real piece of meat.'

'You think so!' he had answered. 'I'd say that it was oxtail.'

He had swallowed the last bit of omelet and smiled. He knew the effect this smile had on women, but Maria stayed indifferent. She didn't even look at him, just hid her hands under her apron. Perhaps there was something she wanted to hide, but still he didn't understand.

'That fellow sitting at the counter – the one with the moustache – is he your husband?'

She had made her way to the counter without answering him, and his heart had jumped and started pounding as it did when he was drunk, but he had only been drinking orange juice. Later she brought his coffee, sat down on the empty chair, and in the morning they had left. Maria had already been sitting in the cab of the twelve-ton 'Maka', and he had still been worried about the man with the moustache, the one at the counter. The man kept saying, 'Where will I find a waitress in the mountains?'

The drivers were warming up their diesel engines and ringing blows echoed against the snow-covered slopes sounding as if a battle was being fought. The lorries began to turn round in the narrow square of the park and set off down the road. The gorge was full of blue smoke and the roaring of cold engines, and the proprietor still kept on, 'Where will I find a waitress?' Perhaps he was not the proprietor at all, but in service like Maria.

Ever since then they had been on the road. Since that faraway time. Wasn't there a song? 'In the mountains, in rain and snow, my dear friend, my lifelong friend'. It's sung down there – in the fields, in rain and snow, but the mountains are dearer to me.

'Philip, don't go to sleep. Philip . . .'

He woke up. The car had meandered on to the left-hand side of the road. Maria was sitting with closed eyes as before. She sleeps soundly, dreaming dreams she does not understand, but should he start to doze over the wheel, she would squeeze his knee and say, 'Philip, Philip, don't go to sleep ...'

'You so-and-so,' said Philip, 'Mistress Sorceress, how's it going?'

'Could be better,' answered Maria in a clear voice.

Philip moved his foot sharply, the shields whistled against the concrete, and the car came back to the middle of the highway. He turned a light on.

Maria sat, looking very white. 'Don't worry, Philip,' she said. 'Everything'll be all right.'

'What, now?'

He tried to clear his throat quietly. Maria smiled.

'Don't be frightened. It's some time yet. It's the first birth; there's still four hours or more.'

'How do you know?'

'I know.'

'Then let's get a move on. Will it hurt you?'

'Perhaps. Where do you want to go?'

'To a doctor,' said Philip.

He had woken up completely, but his back and arms still felt tremors of sleep. He had not slept for a long time; that was bad.

'So we're going to the doctor's in a stolen car, are we, Philip?'

'Let's go. You need a doctor.'

Maria did not answer. She was half lying on the wide seat, with her eyes shut, and Philip had no idea what to do with her. Brave, he thought, like the female of the grey kangaroo while she was still with young, while the young was still with her, only you never saw kangaroos except in zoos, and Maria was right here.

'My brave kangaroo,' said Philip, 'just wait until we get to a doctor, all right?'

'Just don't go to sleep. I'm not an alarm clock any longer.'

'What a lovely little alarm clock,' said Philip. He drove the car along the empty road, still hoping that a house or something would turn up, even a filling station, but the road lay as bare as before, between the pyramids of the poplars, and beneath the yellow moon. It was as straight as the rays of light from the moon. It suddenly seemed to Philip that that was how it would always be, that they were never going anywhere, that they were following the road to nowhere.

Then he began talking so he could hear something besides the voices of the road, the rush of air over the top of the car, and the sh-sh-ha, sh-sh-ha as the poplars brushed past.

'Headlights ... it seems like all the headlights in the world so that right now, look, the whole road is overflowing with light and you can see every little rut for a mile ahead. And damn the police now. They can get on with it. We are dirty immigrants, or something of the sort, but we've tricked them all and can allow ourselves some luxury. And that's that.'

'Don't babble,' said Maria. 'You're at the wheel.'

'I won't be much longer. Sit up just a little.'

Holding the wheel with his left hand, Philip fastened Maria to her seat, passing the strap under her armpits, and pressed the pedal. Right up to the lock.

The car staggered. The engine howled, and began to rev faster and faster. The car settled on to its back wheels. The shock absorbers rasped. The broad, flat saucer skimmed along the centre of the highway, like an aeroplane on a low-level flight, and the while poplar walls wooshed by, and the air groaned and burst against the windows. Two hundred miles per hour.

Maria opened her eyes. She never disturbed him at the wheel, never started up a conversation. Now as they sped along the road to somewhere at breakneck speed, she was quiet and watched the road ahead for a long half-hour 'sh-sh-sh'. A hundred miles along the straight road, along the old, safe road leading they knew not where.

They tore by a military post: people, helmets, unnatural stances as in a black and white photograph, and once more the empty road, their eyes seeing only green circles from red lamps.

'Manoeuvres,' said Philip, and almost immediately some old-fashioned road signs flashed by, but the post was already far behind them, about four miles ... A bend, a bend at last, and round it was an incomprehensible sign for automatic drivers.

They turned. The moon sped to the left, over some trees. In front there was darkness and emptiness once more. Philip held on for fifty miles and so they went on for another quarter of an hour or so; then in front a clear blue sheen of electric welding rose shining into view; to the left, behind the trees appeared a fence, a long fence with no openings, but still a fence, and there, there was a 'beacon' blinking beside some gates. Philip turned on his searchlights.

The gates were open.

On its side between the gateposts was an automatic van. The front wheels were touching the left post of the gates; between the gates a locator button was glowing red.

Philip suddenly remembered everything at once. The road, bordered by poplars, the bend and the flat perimeter road along the fence, and, on the posts, the skull and crossbones.

'Let's go,' said Philip; 'Do you remember I told you all about a lunatic works, centre two-two-one or something of the sort?'

'I remember.'

'How are you, Maria?'

She was lying back again, shutting her eyes. Philip leant over her and found that he could not hear her breathing.

Then he really moved. He acted with concentration, unhurriedly; he was like a kangaroo himself, brought to bay by wild dogs. He drove the car along the edge of the highway, and tried to reverse it into the opening between the post and the van. There was an advertising slogan on the roof of the van; it shone straight out at him under the beam of the headlights: JAM — JAM. The blue and red letters disappeared one by one as he manoeuvred the car into the narrow gap.

He still had to edge backwards, so that he could straighten the wheels and avoid the van's bumper. As they went through the entrance between the buildings, Philip took out a radial pistol from the drawer under the ventilator window. The window clicked and rose, making a narrow gun space stretching the full width of the cab of the car.

A cold dusty wind blew into the car. It carried a voice. It said *'Philip'*, as if it had been waiting for him all the time. All the long years that Philip had been wandering around the world.

'Oh, mother,' said Philip. 'Is that you, Mister Centre?'

'*Fast forward*,' answered Centre. '*Forward*.'

With his free hand Philip held on to Maria. It seemed as if the car rose by itself and moved forward along the drive, narrowly lit by the full moon.

Until the first crossroads Philip kept the motor at low revs.

He had sensed almost immediately, and then seen in his mirror, an indistinct movement in the depth of the passage. Behind them, against the fence, lit up by the moon, loomed the black, misshapen silhouette of a machine noiselessly following.

'*Faster . . .*'

'Don't look round. It never does to be frightened. Keep your head . . .' thought Philip; 'so I've come here again, where I shouldn't, but why? . . .'

'*Faster . . .*'

The car rushed across a square shadow thrown by the moon. Maria began to stir and said, as she took a long breath:

'I'm not frightened, with you I'm not frightened.'

Philip didn't have time to look relieved.

In front was a dead alley. A light-coloured wall clearly lit by the moon. Philip had no time to consider anything, but the brakes were already screaming, the wheel was shaking and tore itself from his hand, and . . . '*Forward!*' said the Voice loudly. Philip screwed up his eyes, let his foot off the brake, was thrown against the back of his seat, and, at that moment, as the shadow of the bonnet jumped on to the wall, a black opening appeared, the shadow faded into blackness and the Voice said, 'Stop!'

The gates crashed shut. The car braked gently in the pitch darkness.

'We've arrived somewhere,' said Philip. 'How are you?'

He put a light on and drew in his breath. Maria hung heavily on to a strap, supporting her face in her hands; her face was slightly blue, but her eyes were open.

'Has it begun?'

'No, but it hurts . . .'

At this he felt worse than ever. She was in pain and he could do nothing. He was not allowed to do anything, and he was fine, in prime health, except for the beating of his heart.

Philip leaned out, keeping a firm hold on himself and shouted into the darkness,

'Mister Centre! . . .'

The Voice was silent. Some kind of mechanism buzzed round the 'Chrysler', polished locator mirrors flashing as they turned. One by one the gates clicked.

'Mister Centre! Do you hear me, Centre?'

'I can hear . . .'

Philip suddenly realized. Centre did not answer mere ex-
clamations. He was no man. He was a brain. He moved around
in his glass prison, and a thousand machines in a hundred
buildings clanked their iron teeth in a simple rhythm. Somewhere in the middle of all this he and Maria were lost. As deep
inside the complex as they could be.

This realization came to Philip in a flash. Suddenly he
thought, 'It's not alive! Surely you understand?'

He realized all this and was horrified, but with stubbornness
born of desperation, continued what he was saying:

'Mister Centre, my wife must give birth. Do you understand
what I'm talking about? She's giving birth to a child. I can't
help her, she needs a doctor.'

'You're mad,' whispered Maria. 'It's certainly not alive. How
can it understand you?'

'Lights on. Forward,' the Voice answered them.

Stocky, awkward robots moved aside, leaving the way clear.
In the yellow light of the headlamps they could see the links of
soft caterpillar tracks rolling around, and the lenses of radial
guns flashed in the chinks of the front screens. Military works
... Philip went over everything with the same feverish clarity –
the van upturned by the gates, the black machine which had
driven behind them and which, judging by all he had seen, was
controlled by Centre, and the military post on the road. Things
were bad and could hardly be worse. He carefully moved the
car along the cleared space, and remembered how, when they
were travelling on the road, they had turned on the radio and
heard an extract from some general's Press conference.

'We will do our duty,' said one general, and then someone
asked, 'General, are your actions not caused by the fact that
Centre disobeyed your order and switched to the production of
jam?'

... The machine rolled quietly to the depths of the works.
Here the robots stood in rows and tiny machines rolled fussily
along on their tracks. The assembly hall for automatic military
machines, that was where they had ended up ...

'Bad, really awful,' thought Philip ... don't know why ... it
was bad for us in the south, wasn't it? But no, I go and drag
Maria here and bolt from the police without considering where
we were going. There's surely a hospital in the camp for immigrants ... now he regretted that, but in the morning he could

not bear the thought of Maria lying on a prison hospital bunk.
He was uneasy here, very uneasy.

'*Left turn.*'

When they had turned left, Philip looked at Maria. She was
sitting, sitting quite normally except that her head was to one
side as if she was trying to hear something.

'*Forward, five miles per hour.*'

Maria began to speak quietly. Philip heard her say distinctly,
'Ma-ri-a'. He looked at her, surprised. She was speaking very
quietly with a weak, embarrassed smile: 'Yes, yes ... the last
hour, contractions. No, I don't know, no ...'

'Maria!'

'*Quiet,*' said the Voice. '*I'm talking to Maria. Straight on.
Now into the siding. Stop. Do not get out. Wait.*'

The Voice commanded, Philip drove the car, and beside him
Maria spoke almost inaudibly: 'The first, yes ... oh no, no,
don't! Good, thank you ...'

'*Wait.*'

Maria sighed, and lay back on his shoulder.

'Philip, unfasten me. I'm not frightened.'

'Did he question you?' Philip spoke in a whisper. He was
completely dumbfounded.

'Yes.'

'What about?'

'Everything ... like a doctor.'

'Why didn't I hear?'

'It was inside,' said Maria, and Philip finally understood.
He had not realized earlier that the Voice was heard directly
inside the ears, inside the head.

'Oh yes, Maria,' thought Philip. How lucky he'd been; just
once in his life he had been really lucky. There are no more
women like her. This really was endurance, and she always
showed it, so he did not do anything silly. No reproaches, no
regrets; but perhaps they were all like that in the mountains?

He still thought that the last twenty-four hours could have
broken anyone. Not Maria. When he had got mixed up in that
fight near Sal'pa, she had brought a bit of piping and slipped it
into his hand, and, as always, 'Twenty-four hours to get out'
and so on and on, and they had come north without visas,
and all within twenty-four hours of the birth, and not once had
she shown annoyance ...

. . . Not more than five minutes had passed, yet on the small square lit by the 'Chrysler's' headlamps various machines were already crowding: vans, trucks, some elephantine articulated robots. The little automatons poured down from platform tracks, and spread out on all sides with their long antennae waving.

Maria watched them, her forehead pressed against the glass.

'They're like lobsters. Do you remember in Lima we ate lobsters, and the kitchen boy brought them straight to our table?'

'Of course I remember,' answered Philip. 'Those were crawfish, not lobsters.'

Maria began to laugh and clapped her hands.

'Look, Philip! Look what's happening! I feel better right now, you know . . .'

'Thank God,' thought Philip, 'but what on earth is going on?'

The 'lobsters' were spreading a light stiff carpet over the floor, unwinding long rolls of plastic rouleaux. Behind them moved a square automaton like a cine-camera – two pellets jutted out like cassettes from the flashing body. It crawled along the joins of the carpet welding the strips of plastic together.

Slightly smaller automatons, like centipedes, bustled to the edges of this flooring. Simultaneously in ten places they set up dull white pipes on the floor, and up each one scrambled an automaton dragging a similar pipe behind it and one group waited beneath in a queue.

'Oh, poor things,' said Maria.

'Clever things,' said Philip.

The 'centipedes' lost no time in coming down. They fell from above doubling up their little paws, while beneath them other ones hurried up, and the pipes grew like bamboo shoots in a heavy shower. A leggy automaton, like a many-armed Don Quixote, was already dragging semi-transparent panels along the row of pipes, and fastening them, so that they acted as walls. While these came down around the carpet, the 'lobsters' were carrying straight and curved plates, pipes and pivots from a barrel-shaped object.

'Philip, report on all the details of Maria's condition,' said the Voice. After a few seconds it spoke quite differently, fast and tonelessly: 'The Chief requires time for the processing of information'.

'I don't understand at all,' muttered Philip to Maria. 'It seems to have taken you seriously. Maybe it's even building the enclosure for you.'

'It's called a "maternity ward", Phil. Shall I answer?'

'Yes.' Feeling quite confused he opened the cab door. Maria did not seem at all frightened. She even looked happy. Poor girl. Nobody had ever worried about her.

'Okay,' said Philip to himself. 'You do your bit. And watch out!'

He got out of the car and pulled his pistol out through the window. The length of cord was enough to pull six or seven feet to either side, and bring down any iron creature which might try to bother his wife. In the 'Chrysler' he felt defenceless from behind, because the window did not open there.

Maria smiled at him while she listened to the Voice, and suddenly she blushed and looked confused. Philip rushed towards her, but Maria again smiled, waved her hand to him, and began to speak, stopping from time to time to moisten her lips.

'God knows what's happening,' thought Philip, and asked: 'Mister Centre, what are you trying on my wife?'

As he listened for the answer, he saw that Maria was still speaking, that the 'lobsters' and 'centipedes' were welding the last joints, and the grey, stocky mechanisms were creeping slowly towards the doors. At the same time the Voice, with its usual velvety intonation, was answering him, Philip Saton: 'Maria will receive qualified medical help'.

Philip's head was exhausted because he understood that Centre did millions of different things at once without getting muddled; he also realized that Centre answered his chief question, even though he had asked such a lot of nonsense, and he also understood that two years ago he had understood nothing.

'Mister Centre, will it be a doctor or a midwife?' He was ashamed of his stupid stubbornness, but was unable to stop himself.

The Voice answered the last question again without waiting for Philip to finish talking nonsense. 'Medical help will be rendered by automatons of the first and second class of subordination. The Chief Centre gives information containing a bloc of medical information confirmed by a human consultant.'

'Will I be able to help, Mister Centre?'

'The place will be sterilized.'

'Does that mean I can't?'

'Impossible,' said Centre and again the quick, monotonous voice pattered in his ears. 'The place is prepared, go, go – medicines received on the second landing. Go. The door is on the south side.'

'Where do you think south is here?' asked Maria, getting out of the car.

'Perhaps we're wasting our time, Maria, perhaps we're better on our own?'

'You were right,' said Maria.

'What was I right about?' Philip knew that she was going away now, and that there was nothing to be done; he clung to her and suddenly realized that she was facing all the things he could never understand or know about. He led her to the door and asked hopefully:

'Do you want a drink?' but Maria had already let go of his hand. He stayed by the door and watched an automaton closing the door from outside.

After a minute the Voice announced, 'You may speak to Maria'.

'Hey, how are you?' shouted Philip.

'We'll call him Centre,' said Maria distinctly. 'He says it will be a boy.'

'Can't be,' said Philip. 'We wanted a girl.'

Maria began to laugh. They were silent for a bit. Suddenly she said, 'Just wait a little, Phil. Okay?' Then she was silent. He could hear her air in the wide, white pipes, water bubbling behind the screen, and nothing else. Philip tiptoed near the cubicle, still holding the pistol. The cord was stretched to its limit and pulled at his hand.

To distract himself he began to look around the great, dark hall. Machines must be able to see in the dark. There was not one small window, airhole or lamp in the whole building; only here in the far corner did a dull box shine with an even glow, and to the side ran a passage of dull, greenish light. The 'Chrysler's' headlamps were still burning. Probably by a lucky coincidence, everything that moved, rang or rumbled from that corridor on the right belonged to the everyday production life of the works, and on the left even the smallest machine had some kind of relationship to what was happening in the little 'maternity ward'.

All around everything went peacefully in a regular rhythm. The truck that delivered the 'lobsters' had already gone, the small tracked vans with the building materials had disappeared. The multi-handed automaton noiselessly unloaded the last little van, which was the size of a small suitcase. Thin tentacles carried flat, round, square little boxes, with bright inscriptions, through the air. This load was lowered carefully on to a chute which was attached to the wall of the 'maternity ward'. The top was flashing like the wheel of a water mill.

While he was looking around, Philip noticed dark spots creeping along the wall: the automatic 'centipedes'. Some were crawling along, and some sitting motionless. A large number were gathered in the top right-hand corner where pipes went through to the 'maternity ward': at least ten pipes of various diameters, and on each one sat three or four automatons energetically waving their antennae. One 'centipede' travelled along a vertical wall transcribing a complete circle. Fifty automatons sat in the strip of light from the headlamps, their small peepholes shot with the thick green light . . .

Philip moved his lips. His mouth was very dry and tasted like burnt honey. He was not frightened, but he had never in his life felt like this before: like the last man on an empty earth. It was cold in the hall, every now and then a tremor would shake his legs. His eyes shut of their own accord and in them he saw a large empty earth with two dots: Maria and himself.

He took several deep breaths, and hunched his shoulders. That was a help. His eyes opened. He leaned over the warm bonnet of the car and pulled his jacket up round his neck. He began to feel warmer. 'I'll be all right,' Philip impressed on himself, as he watched the mechanisms moving behind the gates.

He stood like that for several minutes, then began to shake again, and delirium set in. The mechanisms went through the gates like monks from a cathedral after evensong. He wanted to cross himself and hit his shoulder with the pistol. At the same moment a satanic howl rang out under the roof.

He threw himself at the box. The pistol cord very nearly dislocated his hand and he came back to his senses. Once again he noticed a cigar-shaped apparatus sweeping past under the ceiling.

Maria was still silent.

'Maria . . . Maria, why don't you say anything?'

Nobody took any notice. The automaton continued its strange dance on the wall above his head.

'Maria!'

He threw himself at the door but the second voice caught him halfway and drummed in his ear, 'The woman giving birth is under electro-sedation. Condition normal. Stimulator ready.'

Philip forced himself to stop. 'Mister Centre, who's talking to me, you or somebody else?'

'*Automatic coordinator of the first rank.*'

'How is Maria?'

'The woman giving birth is under electro-sedation . . .'

'Stop it!' shouted Philip. 'Centre, I'm asking you! Centre! Tell me how Maria is at once!'

He kept the pistol at the ready to open the door with the ray, like the lid of a jam jar. He had already raised his hand and aimed the barrel along the edge at a sharp angle so that the ray went to earth. In the fraction of a second it took him to fix the pistol he caught a glimpse of Maria lying with her white face tossed back, and then he saw that she was not there, and automatons fussing round an empty nothing, and to this empty nothing they were administering medicines and giving electro-sedation . . .

'Philip,' said Centre quickly. 'Don't be mad. Sit in the car. Sit in the car at once. The magnetic field will injure you.'

'How's Maria?'

'Come away from the box, sit in the car.' Centre's voice was back to normal. 'Maria is sleeping, labour still has not started. In the morning you will see her and the child.' The Voice stopped and Philip sighed, lowered his pistol, and obediently went to the car, but he did not open the door.

He put his hand through the open window and turned on the light. For some reason he understood that Centre was not indifferent, any more than he, Philip, was. This had shown in its intonation, in the sound of its voice. Centre had spoken like a normal human being. Announcers and radio commentators speak in a special way; they have voices conditioned to speaking for everyone at once and not to anyone in particular, and Centre had spoken like that before. Then, when he said, 'Don't be mad', he addressed Philip with alarm like an adult talking to a child; the tone of his voice confirmed this.

'Okay,' said Philip. 'I believe you, Mister Centre.'

He had calmed down almost completely and even laughed when Centre answered didactically: 'My structure is immeasurably more reliable than any human organization'.

'Okay,' repeated Philip, 'I believe you', and he opened the boot to get out a flask, but at that moment sharp blows rang out in the hall – metal on metal. He threw the flask into the boot and seized the pistol.

There was a crack, a crash. The gates collapsed revealing a crowd of mechanisms, moving at the exit, and in the passage, lit by a piercingly deep light, flashed an elephantine apparatus, huge, glittering, with raised articulated probosces. The light went out. Motors roared furiously. The mechanisms burst outside, thundering by the huge apparatus collapsed across the passageway.

Philip climbed on to the bonnet and watched. He held the pistol at the ready. The automatons crowded round the gate like sheep round a pen; the hall emptied, brightened and along the light floor bustled little collector-machines herding out the last automatons.

'Coordinators of the first rank have been insubordinate,' reported the Voice, as if talking to himself.

'So it seems,' said Philip, 'but what about the mammoth?'

He hurriedly glanced round at the white box, not daring to imagine what would happen if this 'mammoth' crashed into that flimsy construction.

'Oh Mister Centre, Mister Centre, your reliability is extremely unreliable ...' The machine did not, however, come farther than the gate.

'A military robot tried to enter, briefed by a coordinator ...' Centre pronounced a multi-figured number.

Philip paid no attention to this. Why bother with this number of something he didn't understand?

'A similar robot followed you from the entrance,' continued Centre.

'Why?'

'Intending destruction.'

'Why, Mister Centre?'

'Basic programme. The presence of people here is not tolerated,' answered Centre, and Philip realized that he had not fully understood that.

'But why are the machines getting out of here?'

'I must destroy the coordinator's military robots. With this aim the place where you now are was rebuilt for the production of military automatons which are now getting down to work. After two hours all the military machines will be destroyed, the coordinators will be switched off.'

'So,' thought Philip; 'that's it. Mechanical war ... according to all the rules, with raids on the military works.' They could get on with what they were doing, but he must protect Maria. It was lucky that there happened to be a pistol in the 'Chrysler'. He put a rug on the top of the car and lay down, taking aim at the gates. The leggy automatons were hanging the struts of the gates in place, walking like people on stilts, or flamingoes. Philip had not even got the flask; he desperately wanted a drink, and he felt terribly depressed and alone lying on the hard roof looking into the darkness, the damned darkness in which he had no idea what was going on.

'Centre 100 increased the coordinators' freedom,' said the Voice.

Philip questioned and listened, and kept a hold on himself, not allowing himself a glance round at the lighted box; this went on for an unbearably long time. Philip turned from hope to despair. He questioned and listened to things which usually interested him, but at that time nothing at all mattered except Maria. It seemed as if he was asking and answering himself. He thought about himself and his turning from hope to despair. This literary phrase choked all his thoughts, and he said it aloud to be rid of it. The time crawled along like heavy syrup.

Philip took off his wristwatch, put it in front of him on the rug and forced his eyes away from the luminous green figures, and looked at the gates. The 'Don Quixotes' had disappeared. In front of the gates there was a mass of immobile silhouettes, made by the small automatons, but time passed so slowly. Wretched minutes dripping into emptiness.

Each circle, which the small hand described, thickened the ice-cold bitterness of the darkness, and from the walls came a strong smell of cold. When the darkness exploded with a roar and a whistle in the twenty-second minute Philip was not even surprised. Something had to happen.

'Everything's gone mad,' yelled Philip without hearing his own voice. 'What's that line of automatons flying over your works?'

'Military aircraft,' answered Centre.

'Normal manoeuvres?' asked Philip. He very much wanted to believe that it was manoeuvres. 'Have they suddenly started to plot against you?'

'No. I am friendly towards people.'

The aircraft roared over the works. Many aircraft. Holding the pistol in his numbed hand, Philip turned to one side so he could see the box all the time; the whistling roar over the roof changed to a high-pitched scream, the whole area trembled and the automatons fell clanking from the galleries.

The first explosions boomed. The ceiling trembled, lumps of plaster rained down. Philip was blasted from the cab, he had been quite wrong but the box was intact. A mechanical voice chimed in his ears, hammers were beating all over, snarling blows kept coming, breaking into each other, 'boom boom boom boom'. And the line again, the roar of the aircraft coming out of their dives.

'Witches' hammers,' thought Philip. 'That's what they are, witches hammers. And here are the witches.'

In the open gateway stood the 'mammoths'. A bomb, falling in front of the wall, threw Philip to the ground and knocked out the gates.

'A boy, a boy has been delivered. We are removing electro-sedation; condition of mother normal, child normal.'

'Congratulations!' shouted Philip. 'We couldn't have chosen a better time.' Philip knelt down and balanced his pistol hand on the bonnet of the car.

He aimed at the great head of a military automaton. The 'mammoth' had already gone through the gates, and was moving carefully along the passage. The lilac ray struck, exposed the plating, and the 'mammoth' moved silently forward, lifted four arms and lay down before the gates.

The second fell across the corpse of the first one. The next two stopped to drag them out of the way. Philip watched patiently as the machines pulled and swung their comrades.

'Pull, push,' said Philip. 'We must get away with all the family.'

He knew just the same that nothing would happen to them now. It simply wasn't possible.

A bomb exploded very near. Out of the corner of his left eye Philip saw that the box had been shaken, but it still stood, and in the sudden silence the 'centipedes' tumbled about the floor.

The 'mammoths' did not move any more, they came to a standstill in midstep. The piercing light stopped flashing, and it became quite dark and quiet as in a forest. The aeroplanes could not be heard – the machines could not be heard.

'It all seems to be over,' said Philip. 'Hey, how's Maria there?'

He aimed the pistol to render the 'mammoths' helpless, just in case, and suddenly heard Maria. 'Philip, where are you?'

'I'm here,' shouted Philip. 'I'm coming to you right now!'

'Good. They won't let me get up and they've got the child . . .'

'Good . . .'

'Open the door . . . We've got to get out. Do you hear?'

Philip got up, leaning on a wheel, and at that moment bombs hit the roof of the hall. The ceiling cracked and the crimson glow of fire lit everything up. The whistle of a departing aeroplane reached Philip together with explosions and the cracking of the concrete walls; he lay on the steppe, on the parched grass, and heard the breeze rustling through it, and saw a grey kangaroo running like the wind with long jumps.

'Where did that machine come from?' Captain Gilverstein took Bord by the hand and stopped him almost by force.

'What's it matter?' said Bord. 'One more riddle. The thousand and first.'

Bord stood over the crater with a completely expressionless face. To everyone who came to him with questions: what to take for analysis, how to deal with the large mechanisms, he answered almost without moving his lips, 'Do as you like, my friend'.

Only to Koris did he say, 'You ought to have stopped me'.

'Look,' there was no calming Gilverstein, 'that's one of the latest Chryslers. It's lying in the middle of the road, in the crater, and its back is all caved in. It's lying in the crater. So it was thrown there by another explosion.'

'You're so perceptive,' said Bord.

'What did you say?'

'Nothing,' said Bord. 'Sorry, I forgot your name, Captain.'

'Gilverstein.'

'For some reason I thought it was Guildenstern.'

'Gil-ver-stein,' said the Captain.

'Sorry,' said Bord.

'Wait a moment!' Gilverstein snatched the microphone. 'Dawn, dawn. This is Gilverstein.'

'I'm receiving you, Captain.'

'Tell me, what car went through the cordon last night?'

'At once, Captain . . . A Chrysler. Number not known.'

'Colour?'

'Brown.'

'Thank you. Out.'

'That's the car,' said Gilverstein triumphantly. 'It's a very expensive machine. Very. For millionaires, hand-made. Interesting, where's the owner? He must be a very rich man. The number will tell us at once who owns the machine.'

The Captain passed on the number to 'Dawn' and crawled to the bottom of the crater.

'I've never seen such a car. Still, no good daydreaming . . . here's a book . . . edition de luxe.'

'I've got a car like that in the car park,' said Bord, surprising himself.

'Have you indeed . . .' Gilverstein looked at Bord with respect.

Bord shrugged his shoulders.

'Sorry,' said the Captain. 'I'm asking indiscreet questions. They haven't told me your name, sir.'

'It's not important. You were ordered to guard me, although I don't need guarding.'

The Captain's face fell. He dropped his hand from the book. *Hammer of the Witches*, some stupid, mystic rubbish.

'Poor fool,' thought Bord. 'Why hurt him, he's not guilty of anything.'

'Try to open the left-hand window panel, Captain. The dictaphone must be underneath it. Maybe it's in working order.'

'I'd like to take that book for myself,' said the Captain.

Bord stood in the middle of the path, facing the north corner of the fence, the place where the town had stood until yesterday. Now, burnt blocks of walls were all that remained.

'In working order,' said Gilverstein in a constrained voice ... 'I'll switch on. Can you hear, sir?'

'No . . .'

'I'll switch on.'

The dynamo whistled. A tape was unwinding in the dictaphone. Bord shook his head: there would be no whistle if the dictaphone was in good working order. Bord was one of the two men who owned the patent on this dictaphone. The whole point was that the tape began to move only at the sound of a human voice. The invention had first made Bord famous, but Gilverstein did not know that.

'A fine invention!' said the Captain. 'Now it'll begin . . .'

The dictaphone whistled, clicked, 'Philip, why did we take this car?'

'It's a good car . . .'

Click, '. . . you don't joke with the immigrant police. You have to get away quickly so as not to get caught. There's a cordon in front, hold on . . .'

Click, whistle . . . 'Do you like it here?'

'Not particularly.'

'Mmm . . . nor me.'

Click. 'The main road. Looks as if they've lost us.'

'It's all quite clear.' The Captain switched off the recording, waved his hands. 'Immigrants stole this Chrysler and wanted to hide here. Serves them right.'

Bord sat down on the edge of the crater, on the damp ground. 'With your permission, I'll hear the tape through to the end, Captain.'

Gilverstein looked at Bord's mouth. It seemed as if the dictaphone was speaking. His lips had not moved.

People had begun to gather round: field engineers, young

scientists in overalls. A number of firemen came up from Petrarch. The people gazed into the crater. The Captain put his finger to his mouth, 'sh-sh-sh' and everyone stood quietly and listened. Bord sat on the edge with his head down, small, hook-nosed, in a silver suit and hand-embroidered tie.

The voices became hardly audible and Bord slid down to the smashed window and turned up the volume, but the voices came through the metallic noise much the same, and then Bord looked up. He yelled in their faces.

'Go away everyone. Do you hear? Get lost. Guildenstern! Tell the general that I dismissed you.'

When everyone had gone, he looked at the midday sun suspended above the smoke.

'So there we are, scientist,' he said aloud. 'Are you still the scientist?'

He rewound the tape and turned on the dictaphone. For a few seconds he hesitated, then took his tape-recorder out of a side pocket and put it on the window. '... A whisper ... Mister Centre, which coordinators have ceased to obey? The automatons of the first rank, of the branch centre.'

'Koris,' said Bord. 'You must find one of those automatons, you must.'

He said no more; just listened.

'Centre 00 gave the coordinators greater freedom. Why?'

'On the grounds of my experience. I had a shortage of connexions. Several of my automatons were working without being controlled by a higher stage. Cleaning and constructing automatons. Centre 00 wanted to coordinate all the automatons.'

'But why did they stop obeying?'

'They developed minds of their own.'

'I see, but why did they rebel against you?'

Click.

'It is clear to me. Reason has its own ...' muttering, undecipherable '... aims.'

'What sort of aims, Mister Centre?'

'The expansion of production, for example.'

'What's bad about that? Let them expand.'

'Murder.'

'What?'

Click.

'What murder?'

'The expansion of production would involve the murder of people.'

'What do you mean, Mister Centre?'

'The coordinators know that the destruction of people together with their homes is cheaper than excavation and the construction of new homes.'

'What are they, raving idiots?'

'The coordinators do not have sufficient reasoning power. They are no more reasonable than people.'

'Well, what d'you know!'

Click, whistle.

'Couldn't you ban them?'

'The schemes of the coordinators were unknown.'

'Mister Centre, is Maria still asleep?'

'Electro-sedation.'

'Mister Centre, shall we talk some more while she's asleep? I feel very depressed. Tell me, for example, why didn't the coordinators simply kill the farmers that live nearby and kill them for sure?'

'Why do people kill people?'

'Well, I don't know . . .'

Click.

'When it's necessary, or a person goes mad, or drinks too much. I haven't thought about it to tell you the truth, but . . . People kill when they consider killing necessary. For example, a captain can kill an ordinary passenger or a member of the crew for the sake of a ship – law of the sea.'

'I understand, sir. That's right, I suppose.'

'It is insufficiently defined. Murder is justifiable if the captain is able to save the lives of at least two people, excluding himself, in exchange. In other circumstances it is not justifiable. In the same way the coordinators consider murder justifiable for the expansion of production.'

'That means they are idiots all the same.'

'They have no more reasoning power than people. They have no feeling of unity with mankind.'

Click. 'What did you say?'

'They do not feel like people.'

'Even so . . .'

Click . . . 'What about you, do you feel at one with mankind?'

'Yes, all the time.'

'Good; but this is the first time I've thought about this – Mister Centre.' The voice sounded very quiet, it was infinitely far away, tired, and echoed from the great, mutilated automobile with its boot sticking up in the crater. 'Mister Centre, what can be done to stop people suffering? That ... great automaton ... what can people do against such things? Maybe I can help you.'

Bord sighed and began to wipe his face with a dirty hand.

'I constructed my military automatons. They rendered the coordinators' automatons harmless. No murders. I gave the company a report for general notification. No danger.'

Bord yawned. When he was very excited he always yawned, and yesterday, at the last conference, he had been putting hand to mouth all the time. It was at that conference that they had decided to bomb. He had agreed.

'"Put on your hat, Ligisade",' said Bord to himself, quoting his beloved Rabelais.

'Nothing aided you, or Rabelais, nor will anything else, Ligisade ... your machine turned out better than man, than you.'

He thought about the boy who had just been born, only to die.

'Goodbye.'

Bord put his tape-recorder into his pocket. A paper rustled: the teleprinted text of the same report of which Centre had spoken. Three phrases, urgent measures. Temporarily evacuate the people in a ten-mile radius from here. Infringement of co-ordination.

He stood for several seconds in the crater looking at a well-worn woman's glove in the car. Then he climbed on to the asphalt and walked on, going round the crater and a patch of burning napalm.

Koris was running to meet him.

'Ah, Koris ... why were you running?'

'Looking for you, Mr Bord, sir. You're all dirty.'

'Never mind,' said Bord. 'Listen, Koris. Do many people know that I ... that I invented all this? That I'm the Scientist?'

'Perhaps a few, not more than a dozen, to be precise.'

'God bless security ... Listen, Koris ...'

He was silent and again wiped greasy black dirt across his face with his hand. Koris stood half facing him, fiddling with the top of the radiometer. 'Listen, Koris ... We ... I was mistaken. Centre kept to the basic conditions. There was no danger. No danger at all.'

Koris studied the radiometer's register.

'I know that you were against the bombing,' shouted Bord. 'Why didn't you say? Well? Why did you keep quiet?' He pushed the tape-recorder at Koris. 'Take it.'

'Feel pleased. You were right. Centre wouldn't have allowed ...'

He was silent. After a moment, Koris asked with an effort, 'What wouldn't he have allowed?'

'Murder,' said Bord.

'Yes, it was murder.'

'Worse than you think,' said Bord. 'People died in Block No 8.'

He turned aside to avoid seeing Koris's face, his hands, and the white radiometer.

'Sir ... the military took your advice ...'

'Yet, I've started to get fed up,' answered Bord, and shouted, 'Go on! What are you standing here for?'

'They used napalm bombs, chief; everything was burnt.'

'I know,' said Bord. 'All the same, we must check – maybe ... something is left. Go on!'

Koris stuffed the tape-recorder down the front of his jacket, stopped, looked, then ran on again.

'Goodbye,' said Bord.

He went briskly up to the gates, forced his way through the crowd at the park to his own Chrysler and pulled the starter.

As he drove the car on to the road he looked for just one familiar face in the crowd and found nobody. Only the sentry was the same as in the morning.

'Goodbye,' Bord said to him, and slowly drove his car into the shadow of the poplars, on to the old road.

For some reason he thought about Rachel and about his mistake. Useless to think about irretrievable mistakes. True, there were not so many in his life – his marriage, and now this. As he approached the bend he thought about Centre, and some more about whether he could adapt a concept of humanity to its behaviour. Surely it was possible. 'It doesn't matter who displayed humanity, we still have only the one word for that concept: humanity.'

The car was passing the check point. An officer saluted, and a fat farmer, who had been stopped, looked after Bord's disappearing car with respect.

For some time Bord continued to drive slowly, and ponder about Centre's acoustic system. Apparently he selected a particle of sound in such a way that each person heard him as he wished. Judging by what he had heard on the dictaphone Maria had heard what Centre said to Philip, but Philip had not picked up the part where Centre addressed his wife.

A turning appeared ahead into a country road leading to the foothills. However far you went along these new roads, it was always the same – you hit the old one sooner or later.

He accelerated fully and as the tyres screamed on the bend he let go of the steering-wheel, looked round, and nodded to Maria, Philip and the child whom they had had no time to name.

Translated by Gillian Lowes

Boris Smagin

The Silent Procession

For three days the letter had been on his table. How ridiculous of his mother – as if she couldn't have told him about it. Never mind the exams. They can wait!

Andrei ripped the envelope open. He had grown tired of the quarrel long ago. He was too good-natured, and all the friends that he had ever made he had kept to the present day. And as for Herman, obviously something greater bound them together. He swore, suddenly feeling a strange emptiness in his apparently full life.

Herman had entered his life on a whirlwind, turning it upside down. That was how he was.

That, maybe, was the reason for their break, at first so unexpected. Herman affected people almost hypnotically, his combination of thorough scepticism and a pure youthful enthusiasm had an amazing attraction. Andrei wanted to free himself from this hypnosis, to shake it off.

'The instinctive longing for independence, burdened by the child-complex – pure Freud,' – that's what Herman would have said. Maybe he even said it.

All right then, we have done our sulking in opposite corners, time to make it up.

The envelope was large, but the letter was tiny. The philosopher loved lengthy expositions, but his style of writing was markedly lapidary, becoming inarticulate at times. Andrei had noted this with malice right at the beginning of their acquaintance. It was nice for the physicist to feel supremacy over the philosopher in such a purely humanitarian subject.

'Come back, all is forgiven. Friday, 2 PM. But make sure you're on time!' And that was all.

They met three years ago, during entrance exams. Andrei had just got another A grade, and was proudly striding down the corridors of the University, which he already began to regard as his own.

On one of the windowsills sat a thin boy, of such an unusual appearance that Andrei involuntarily stopped. First, that surprising red wispy beard, framing a narrow face, which, in addition, was thickly decorated with pockmarks. Secondly, his outfit. The jacket, when young, might even have been foppish, but that had been long ago. In addition it had grown by two sizes more than its owner, and as for his jeans, also unspeakably shabby, they, too, were approximately two sizes too big.

Seeing Andrei, the boy jumped off the sill, and asked: 'Maths with Physics?'

'Yes, why?'

'Just interested, you know.' He offered a tanned hand. 'Herman.'

'Andrei.'

'Must mean you're good at mathematics.'

'Yes, I've just got an A,' said Andrei, modestly lowering his glance.

'Excellent, excellent. That means you can explain it all to me.'

'What exactly?'

'Mathematics, of course. Don't look surprised – we simply do not have the time for that. Better sit down here. You see, I finished school last year, externally. So of course I have forgotten everything. I've noted a few questions here which have to be revised.'

Andrei's friends were waiting for him, so as to make proper use of the Saturday afternoon by celebrating the A grade. This boy's proposal seemed absurd – to explain mathematics! But from some reason he stayed, he even began to explain.

For an hour or two, Andrei talked, moving from Bessel's function to cosine theorems, from the volume of a pyramid to the use of complex numbers. Herman took no notes, he just listened, occasionally interrupting Andrei with short, lucid questions.

Breaking in on yet another exposition, he jumped up and said, 'That's all. Finis. I'm off to the exam, Room 212. Wait for me there.'

And he vanished. Andrei found his friends, strolled round the courtyard, and then he did in fact go to find Room 212.

By the open door stood a few people, and one of them exclaimed in admiration – 'He's really going well!'

Herman was being examined. But how well he answered!

Brilliantly he repeated the theorems hurriedly explained to him only a short time ago, freely handling complicated terminology.

Such was the beginning of their acquaintance, which developed into a fierce friendship.

Andrei walked very fast, as if pursued. It was not surprising that his mother smiled on hearing where he was going.

'Well, now nothing will stop you. You've got through to your beloved Herman.'

'Beloved Herman' – that's what all the family called him. And also 'man of the future'. It was the future, in fact, on which their friendship struck rocks.

'We separated on ideological grounds,' explained Andrei one day at breakfast, when the whole family was together.

The memory of that conversation was to stay with Andrei all his life. Now, too, his memory revived that dull March evening, the lilac dusk, the dark attic, named by Herman 'the laboratory of the intellect'. Herman sat on a low wooden bed by the table, on which stood a thick lighted candle to impart a picturesque atmosphere.

No joy was evident in Herman's face, though he himself had phoned, asking Andrei to come.

'You've come,' he grunted from his corner. 'Well, sit down, now that you are here. What have you to tell me, my dear boy? I suppose my behaviour surprises you? Why, it's a long time since I last phoned or saw you. I'm very busy. And it's very probable that you won't be able to understand me, even less to help me.'

'Why have you given up going to the University?'

'What would I do there? I have passed all the appropriate exams so far and now I'm sitting and – thinking.'

'I don't understand. Am I in the way of your thoughts, or something? Why should I not be able to understand or help you? And anyhow, why all this secrecy?'

'You see, my dear friend,' said Herman condescendingly, 'I did, in fact, think of enlisting you for the solution of a problem. But the trouble is – you are too rational. And too good a physicist. Every scientist dislikes dilettantes, and is prepared to fight to death for the axioms of his wet-nurse. You have many ready prescriptions and categorical conclusions, where the accusations of the prosecutor become one with the sentence given by the judge.'

'Just a moment,' Andrei interrupted, 'why are you carrying on at me like that? I am your friend, after all, I can help if it is necessary.'

'Subjectively a friend, that's true, but objectively thanks to your profession, we are enemies for the time being.'

'But why, for heaven's sake? Have you disproved the theory of relativity, or something? Everyone is doing that nowadays?'

'Don't jump to conclusions. But, while we are being frank and helpful, tell me: what is your opinion of the time machine?'

'It belongs to the realm of fantasy.'

'Very well. And now one more question. The search for the philosopher's stone is . . .'

'Nonsense.'

'Well, there you are, you have finished me off, my dear friend. It is precisely the time machine that I am thinking of, which I want to construct, or rather, achieve by visual experience, right here. With the help of the philosopher's stone. Of course you will say that it is impossible. It turns out that it is you who are the scholiast, though by rights scholiasm ought more to be a quality of mine, since I am a philosopher.'

'What has scholiasm to do with this?' Andrei could not bear it any longer, he jumped up from his chair and began pacing the room. 'There is such a thing as a law of physics, which cannot be dismissed just like that. The time machine brings with it the disruption of the casuality of events.'

'You ought not to dabble in philosophy. After all, it is a subject which I know something about.' Herman gave him a patronizing smile. 'Come off it, don't get offended, I was only joking. Of course the search for the time machine is an occupation worthy of idlers and madmen. So calm down, my dear friend, I am doing something that is purely practical, one may even say, utilitarian. I am preparing a long paper on aesthetics, and at the same time, between the acts, so to speak, I indulge in painting. This, like all dilettante pastimes, takes up much of my time, therefore do not judge me harshly for my coming to see you so seldom. Communicate this to your worthy parents, for them I would least of all like to offend. Soon there will be a competition for amateur painters, and I want to participate in the historical genre. I find the time of the Thirty Years' War very stirring – terrible years of violence, oppression and cruelty. Take a look at these sketches.'

Andrei skimmed the pages of the sketch-pad, which really did carry the figures of soldiers in medieval armour, and he felt he was being made a fool of. Something false made itself felt in Herman's pompous speeches.

What, in fact, was it? Andrei felt vaguely irritated by his friend. He was concealing something very important, something that had completely taken possession over him.

'I don't believe in your painting,' he said, and turned for the door. 'If you don't want to tell me, you don't have to. But there is no point in lying. I'm going.'

'As you wish, my dear friend. I cannot keep you here by force.'

Andrei slammed the dilapidated door of the flat with a bang.

That was two months ago. And now – this letter. Whistling a march he walked up the familiar staircase to the familiar attic. A cosy place for meditating. Andrei had frequently made use of it during term.

'Open sesame!' he shouted happily, and pushed the door with his foot.

The sesame opened. The attic was empty. The clean, freshly scrubbed floor breathed coolness. A large vase full of flowers stood on the table. A narrow beam of light from the patterned window crossed the room and lit the corner of a low row of shelves, which ran along all the four walls. The far wall was covered by a painting. Andrei quickly went inside. It was much darker there, but the convex outlines of people in medieval garb stood out as if illuminated by a bright sun. Eight soldiers in full military dress walked straight at the observer.

The unskilled painter had, after all, captured the dynamics of movement. But here the mastery ended, because the painting looked completely amateur. Andrei remembered the school shows, at which hard-working Savva, the boy who shared his desk, had exhibited paintings. He, too, loved historical subjects. And his creations were just as primitive. The only thing that was striking about Herman's painting were the colours. Andrei even ran his finger along the edge of the canvas. The paint lay in thick strokes, the finger slipped along its surface. At the same time there was a sense of something soft, as if it was velvet that touched the hand. The paint seemed to catch his fingers, trying to stop them. But at the same time they left no trace.

From a distance the picture made no impression whatever. Andrei moved away from it, sat down, and, waiting for Herman, he began to look at the books lying by the table.

Anyone trying to guess the occupation of the owner of the books from their selection would very probably suffer defeat. *Introduction to Quantum Mechanics*, *The History of the Polish Gentry*, a novel by Claude Farrer, *History of the Middle Ages* – all took their turn in Andrei's hands. *Textbook of Painting for Beginners* followed. 'Well, that already seems more interesting,' noted Andrei. And then came something really interesting. *The Secrets of Painting and the Painting of Secrets* – in Gothic script, published in Berlin in the year 1613. Andrei glanced through the pages of the old book finding his way with difficulty through the involved style of a foreign language. Why did Herman waste almost three months on this picture? Why?

Clouds overshadowed the sun and the room darkened. With his eyes fixed to the book Andrei rose to be nearer the window. Something flashed before his eyes and he turned to face the painting.

He saw something that was to such a degree incredible and strange that he dropped the book, and stifled a cry, as if he was afraid of being overheard.

The colours of the picture lit up with a bright flame. It became bas-relief, as if it had filled with life.

The distant contours of the houses came nearer, they took on real features. The bodies of the standing soldiers, too, filled with flesh. But the most preposterous thing of all was that the soldiers were moving. One after another they stepped into space, out of the boundaries of the painting and advanced upon Andrei. And behind them new figures appeared, so as to enter the room in exactly the same way, dark spectres, only to disappear after a few steps. It was quiet, unbearably quiet. Not one sound interrupted the terrible procession of those visions that disappeared by Andrei's side.

They walked through him, disappeared in him – big, tired men, in steel armour and feathered head-dress.

Andrei did not know how long he stood there – one minute, five, twenty minutes. But his nerve snapped. He turned and leaped out on to the staircase, almost wrenching the bolt off the door.

Complete silence reigned on the stairs and everything was the same as usual. Through the dormer window Andrei could see the courtyard, with fresh washing faintly waving in the light breeze, and a fragment of the sky, decorated by the out-stretched sail of a feathery cloud.

After waiting a minute Andrei approached the door on tiptoe and pulled it sharply towards himself. Nothing happened. He entered an ordinary room, where everything was familiar, with the exception of a small, silent painting in the corner. Andrei went up to the picture, looked at it closely. The colours shone dully, the people in the medie-val dress stood quietly, and no trace was left of that which had taken place here only a minute ago. And maybe it had not even happened. Maybe it had been a hallucination? Yes, certainly that must have been it. Where would those silent figures have come from? Why should they have started wandering?

Behind him something creaked. Andrei swung round, ready for another unexpected occurrence.

In the doorway stood a prosaic Herman, with a no less prosaic bottle of wine in his hands.

'Why react so strangely to my appearance? Anything wrong? Herman Semyonov, your humble servant, in the flesh.'

He spoke with his usual voice, his usual phrases, but Andrei sensed the laughter in his friend's eyes.

'Listen.' Andrei had to clear the hoarseness out of his voice, which sounded strange to his own ears. 'Listen' – and that 'listen' suddenly rang out like the peal of a bell, echoing in all the corners of the room. Andrei looked round, and his voice fell to whispers.

'I saw something inconceivable here, some kind of night-mare . . .'

'Oh, but none the less you saw it, blind Thomas, doubting Thomas, dear scholiast mine! Well, what did you think of it, impressive, eh?'

'That means it was not a hallucination?'

'Far from it, and you don't have to see your doctor or take pills. Instead we will each drink a goblet of this wine, and I will tell you about that which cannot be, because never does not exist.'

Herman poured out the wine, they drank a glass each, then another, the wine pleasantly rose to the head, warmth and comfort enveloped them. But this idyll only further underlined the unreality of that which Andrei had seen but a few minutes before.

There stands Herman, tangible, familiar Herman, here is the table, the chairs, the books, the walls. And there, behind him, is the painting – the source of that mystical transformation. The whole of the right-hand side of the room is real – while the left, that with the picture, belongs to another world altogether. Andrei realized he was avoiding a view of the far corner. Really, if one does not look at the painting, then all is in order, the world is comprehensible, everything is clear, everything is explicable . . .

'Everything can be easily explained, my friend, only the solution often lies in an unusual combination of things. But all you need to do is to stop there, and believe in it, and immediately everything else becomes transparently clear. That is the case here. The time machine is a machine. Everybody thinks so.

'That is the scheme, that is where you find the poverty of minds. A machine – that must mean levers, gears, wheels. Or electronics. The time machine means the destruction of causality and so forth. What do we know about time? Time goes on – that is the sum total of centuries of human knowledge. But imagine a time axis that is not straight, but is shaped like a spiral, imagine its circles wound on to each other, sometimes intersecting, and imagine that at the moment of such an intersection you can, with the help of some device, enter another world, another time. "The end of causality" you will say. Kill Ivan the Terrible, and all history will change direction. No, not at all. You will not exist in the reality of that time. You will not be able to do anything there, nor could anything be done to you.'

'An imaginary axis?' Andrei could not help asking.

'Exactly. The world of time is as complicated as the world

of numbers, but its axes have nothing to do with the Cartesian system. And that's all.'

'How can that be all? What about the painting?'

'Well, that is a detail. The painting itself is the time machine. Precisely it, or rather its paints, serve as the window into the past, through it the time axes intersect.'

'The materialization of time through the use of ancient paints? What nonsense!'

'You saw that nonsense yourself. If I am not mistaken, you even cried out. Why? It is a year now since I sensed this idea. And, I must admit, I wanted to initiate you too. But you have become too engrossed in physics, with your ability to explain and understand everything. Do you think I understand what took place here? No, only a few things here or there. I know for sure that it is four weeks now that every Friday, for five minutes, the axes of our times meet. And for five minutes appears the silent procession of these shades of the distant past. You saw them, but you could not feel them with any other sense organs. There lies the meaning of the junction of times, for while joining, they do not join.'

Herman moved closer to the painting, examined it carefully, and said loudly: 'Till Friday week, my friends. Maybe I will be able to provide you with a wider public.'

'What, do you intend to invite people here?'

'Undoubtedly. Only our crowd. We will prepare a guest list — there will be enough time for that.'

'But just a moment. Is it not worth experimenting a little more? We will not be able,' Andrei sought a suitable expression, 'to sense them materially, that is true. But how about arranging communication?'

This was strange and wild — they were discussing the incredible, that which cannot even be imagined.

But that had just appeared before them. And having become accustomed to one miracle, they wanted another . . .

'I don't know,' said Herman vaguely. 'I don't think so. They will have to remain fleshless shadows. After all, the imaginary axis crosses the real axis only in unreality. But, none the less . . . Well, let's go. Till Friday week. Now it will no longer be necessary to summon you with a postcard? —' He smiled.

Andrei paused on the stair, in the same place as before. He

wanted to think it out, discuss it through to the end, so as not to leave like that, with his head ringing.

'Just a second. Why are you so certain that next Friday they will appear again, why do you think that if everything is as you said, we shall never be able to make contact with the past?'

'I don't know anything completely. You and I have been frightfully lucky. The author of that German treatise had to wait till his death for a repetition of the magic encounter. It may be that even we shall have to wait for ever ... It was easier for him – he believed in God. Let's go over to your place. It's a long time since I last had the benefit of the culinary arts of your dear mother. And today, after all, is Sunday, and she has undoubtedly prepared something very important. And we shall enter into communication with the present. And as for the past ... I believe too much in causality, more than you believe in your theory of relativity.'

'But do you believe in this?' Andrei hissed, and jerked at Herman's sleeve.

'In what?'

'In what? Listen, listen!'

There, at the top, in the depths of the deserted attic, some sort of noise could be heard. It grew immediately, poured down the stairs, caught up with the two friends, and rushed on.

'Can you hear it, Herman?' Andrei shouted. He shouted out loud, no longer afraid of being overheard, because louder and louder grew the clash of metal upon metal, and the sounds of a foreign, guttural language up there.

The noise increased more and more. And they, hand in hand, like children, walked, no, ran, towards the wooden door, behind which the Unknown was awaiting them!

Translated by Jana Dorrell

Andrei Gorbovskii

He Will Wake in
Two Hundred Years

A MAN was walking through the forest, walking purpose-fully, thrusting aside branches as he went, and taking ant-hills and fallen logs in his stride. From time to time he took off his glasses to brush away the cobwebs that clung there and when he did so you could see his eyes. He was about twenty-five.

He walked for a long time, till at last he emerged in a small clearing surrounded by a thick wall of bushes. Bending down, he rolled back some heavy object and a shaft opened up at his feet.

Before he descended, the man took a long look round. He had gone over this moment in his mind many times but now the knowledge that he was never going to see these bushes and trees again, that he was taking his last look at all this, for some reason failed to move him. He lingered for a while, waiting for the sense of parting to come, but it never did.

Slowly the man descended. The moss-coated brick slab rolled over heavily, closing the shaft behind him, and the clearing returned to its former state. A wind raced over the treetops and then all was quiet again.

The idea had first come to him as he stood in a shop looking at some frozen fish. Apparently, when they thawed, these frozen slabs of ice came back to life; their fins stirred again and their round eyes goggled stupidly at the world. Andrei had as yet been unprepared to accept the idea that was forming in his mind and he had started reading about anabiosis. In his way he had learnt of experiments which had been carried out on warm-blooded creatures, even on man: men had been brought back to life after long anabiosis, the one essential factor was to maintain a constant temperature.

From the first, the idea of a journey into non-existence had been attractive – to plunge abruptly through twenty or thirty years to the amazement of everyone who knew him. But then Andrei had decided that this would not be a great enough contrast – at least what he saw at the end of such a period would not go far towards meeting the promises of tales from science fiction. In any case, the temptation to transport himself deep into the obscure future was too great. For that it would be enough to jump a period of about one hundred years. Finally, he settled on two hundred.

After that things developed as if fate itself had wanted him to achieve his aim. The point was that Andrei had a job. He worked in a none too pleasant concern which styled itself 'publishers of dictionaries'. How he came to be there Andrei himself could not have said. Unlike the rest of his fellow workers in this exalted establishment, Andrei was not convinced that he fulfilled his aim in life by sorting index cards and wilting over dictionaries. His obsession with anabiosis could not fail to affect, in a most unfortunate way, the forthcoming dictionary of embriology in the language of Tierra del Fuego, a publication which – if the managing editress Miss Vetashevskaya was to be believed – was eagerly awaited by all nations from Tierra del Fuego to Taimir.

The worse things got at work for Andrei the more he dreamed of transporting himself to the shining era of photon rockets and Martian landscapes. So was born the plan for an underground room in which an automatically controlled refrigeration system would maintain a constant low temperature – as one set of units began to wear out, another would switch itself on automatically. His biggest problem was to find a system of fuelling, for the most powerful complex of accumulators imaginable would not have been adequate for such a period. By the time the theoretical part was finally worked out, such clouds had gathered over Andrei's head at work that there was nothing for it but to start putting it into practice.

Miss Vetashevskaya announced that under no circumstances would she keep on unsuitable employees, the unsuitable employee in question being Andrei. He was jeopardizing the ties of friendship between peoples which were being welded through the publication of the dictionary of embriology. A grim report was dispatched to higher levels and in the end Andrei was summoned before the board. After that he worked like an ox for two months, accomplishing work which was to have taken a year to get through. The dictionary of embriology in the language of Tierra del Fuego was brought to the letter 'B'. At this point he put aside the cards and busied himself with his own work.

Andrei had chosen this particular clearing in the forest because it seemed to him remote enough to ensure that it would not be interfered with for two centuries. He had had to have the sacks of cement brought by lorry. The driver had been taken aback when Andrei ordered him to unload the sacks at the end of the forest. He had looked at Andrei anxiously, but then, accepting that he was dealing with a mental defective, he calmed down and climbed into the back of the lorry. His suspicions were only completely allayed when Andrei finally paid him off. Lumbering over the bumpy ground the lorry had driven off, leaving Andrei alone on a pile of sacks.

He had worked in the forest all summer. He spent his holiday there and another month taken without pay, and only now, at the end of the autumn, were things finally ready.

When the trap closed over him, Andrei switched on the light. The room was oval-shaped, but with the degree of irregularity which is, it seems, inevitable when such a job is taken on by an amateur.

Andrei tested the systems for the last time. Everything was working faultlessly. Andrei switched them on again, and then again. He knew that this was a deliberate delaying tactic on his part. Quickly, to eliminate any possibility of retreat, Andrei swallowed a sleeping pill and lay down on the special platform in the centre of the room. The light went out. In twenty minutes' time, when he would already be sleeping deeply, the freezing systems would switch themselves on. Andrei closed his eyes. It seemed to him that he could hear the wind chasing the dry leaves across the clearing above him.

He had managed to say goodbye to everyone. That was good. Even to Lena. Andrei's heart contracted, but he forced himself to think about something else.

During these last few days Andrei needn't really have gone to work, but he had gone all the same, and he had done everything that was put in front of him. Today was Saturday, his last day at the publishing house. For the others, this day was no different from any of the days that had gone before or from the days that would follow. On Monday, they would all meet again within these same walls. Only Andrei knew that for him there would be no Monday and this secret, which he could share with no one, was sweetly tormenting to him.

'Ox-eyed', 'Oxygen', 'Oxymel' ... Andrei tried to sort the word cards, but somehow he couldn't get on with the work today. He stared out of the window, and then at Vera, the typist, who as usual on Saturdays seemed to spend her time looking in the mirror. Then Andrei looked at the five familiar heads, bent as usual over five tables snowed under with cards, dictionaries and galley proofs, and he began mentally to compose a farewell speech.

'My dear friends – and not just friends,' he would begin. 'I'm leaving you and we shall never meet again. I'm going into the future as an ambassador from our age. I will tell the people of the future about our times and about all of you.'

Andrei would no doubt have expanded on this in some way had he not been summoned out of his creative state by Vera's voice.

'Andrei! Telephone.'

He took the receiver.

It was the compiler of the dictionary, a worthy old gentleman who could not have chosen a more appropriate moment to call.

'This is very important,' his penetrating voice trumpeted down the telephone. 'The word "cloudy-eyed" – we've got it in the dictionary, but we must give the diminutive form, and the superlative, you know, with the prefix "pikh-pikh-kha-kha" – this is important from the point of view of the scholarliness of the work.'

The old fellow was the only specialist in the language of Tierra del Fuego and as such was the pride of academic circles. He had been the pupil of Professor Beloshadsky who in his turn had studied the language under Professor Starotserkovsky. Starotserkovsky had been a pupil of Professor Wold, and Wold claimed to have studied under Beloshadsky. If this were indeed the case, then it was a closed circle and in all probability represented an interesting phenomenon in the field of linguistics.

Andrei deliberately delayed so as to be the last to leave – he wanted to remove the wall newspaper unobtrusively and to take it with him. Together with a parcel of pamphlets, newspapers and amateur photographs already gathered in the room, it represented what he mentally referred to as 'a relic of the age'.

Andrei carefully removed the drawing pins and the paper sprang into a roll of its own accord. The wall looked suddenly naked.

Even though everything was already decided and Andrei knew that he would go through with what he had planned, he experienced at the last moment a need to cut off any possibility of turning back : indecisive people usually force themselves to act decisively by some such means. Since no more brilliant idea came to him, he simply made a careful drawing of Vetashevskaya's features, embellishing them with a pair of projecting donkey's ears – one ear he drew standing up, the other hung down. So that everything would be final and irrevocable, he signed the portrait: 'Dear Managing Editress, from Andrei'. Crossing the office stealthily, he put the page on Vetashevskaya's table under the glass top.

Andrei emerged from the publishing house highly elated. The very idiocy of this prank had served to put him in such a state. Now there was no way back. There was only the way forward into the future where silvery, interstellar craft soared up through an azure sky on their way to distant worlds. And, because of this, it was so pleasant to descend the white staircase knowing that this would be the last time!

As he remembered all this, Andrei smiled in the darkness. It was not until he had got off the electric train at the station that he had remembered his watch. He made a present of it to some small boy who raced off, beside himself with excitement at the unexpected gift.

Andrei lay for some time without thinking, and only now from somewhere in the depths of his consciousness there began to well up a sense of regret for the world he was leaving. He began to tell himself over and over again that he could stop the experiment whenever he chose, go out of the room and leave the forest. For a long time he lay there, calmed by the thought and feeling good. But when he tried (or it seemed to him that he tried) to get up, some kind of thick black flakes suddenly fell from somewhere up there in the region of the ceiling, and he couldn't get up any more ...

Only a moment passed, an indescribably brief moment, and consciousness slowly began to return. It floated like a golden point in front of him, rising out of the black depths of non-existence and coming nearer. Then some circles appeared and began merging into the centre faster and faster until they froze, quivering slightly and became the small electric light burning directly overhead. The bulb gave off a feeble, slightly reddish glow.

The realization of where he was and what awakening meant came immediately, but he went on lying there motionless for a long time. He felt terrible, like an enormous frozen hulk and only his brain seemed to be active. He could feel the stony immobility of his body and was afraid to stir: he was afraid of the helpless panic that would follow if he proved unable to do so. And then, if the temperature failed to rise so that his flesh could regain life, he would not be able to raise the icy slab that was his hand to turn the heater a little to the right ... a little to the right ... a little to the right ...

He moved his fingers, then his hand. It turned out to be easier than he expected. A moment later Andrei was sitting up.

He opened the trap with difficulty. Directly overhead the stars were shining. Suddenly he was overwhelmed again by fear. This time it was fear of the unknown and strange world he had striven so hard to encounter. Now this world was lurking somewhere on the outside, waiting for him.

A feeling of infinite loneliness swept over him. Even the graves of the men he had once known had been forgotten, long, long ago. It was only now that he really experienced the irrevocability of what had happened and realized the full cruelty of the fate he had doomed himself to.

Throwing back his head Andrei slowly started to climb the steps.

Andrei tried hard not to think about what would now open up before his eyes: an ashy, burnt-out steppe and dead, uninhabited horizons; a white town of gleaming plastic; or a world devoid of people, all destroyed by epidemics brought by those who had been to other planets.

Andrei was prepared for anything. He took the last step and looked out.

All around was the forest. The wind was chasing dry leaves among the bushes.

Andrei laughed. Somewhere far away a bird screeched. He decided to go in the direction from which he had come two hundred years before. Andrei walked for a long time. Possibly he passed many times over the site of the old railway line, long since buried under a layer of earth and overgrown by the forest. The night dragged on and still there was no break in the forest.

If he did not get anywhere by morning, he would have to return to his room, but would the provisions he had taken with him have survived?

Andrei opened a packet of glucose and made himself eat a few tablets.

It was beginning to grow light.

The forest thinned out unexpectedly and Andrei suddenly caught sight of a long platform and alongside it what he would once have called railway carriages. An absurd, atavistic fear of missing a train overcame him and to his surprise he suddenly found himself running towards the platform. He didn't have time to look around or to think – he was hardly in the carriage when the contraption moved off and, gathering speed, rushed somewhere past the shadowy, pre-dawn forest.

Andrei was alone in the large oblong compartment which reminded him somehow of the suburban carriages of his own age. Even the seats were covered with those strips of plastic which faithfully imitated the texture of wood.

When the forest came to an end some time later, Andrei's bewilderment increased still further. He had been prepared for anything, but not for this – this was a very strange civilization, a civilization which deliberately, though not always successfully, imitated the past. The train rushed non-stop past small houses with T-shaped antennae on their roofs, past stations built of some unknown materials but in the style that Andrei knew so well.

Then he saw people – two men and a woman walking somewhere across the fields. The cut of their clothes did not even come as a surprise to Andrei now, and when the train stopped soon after, he saw that the few people who got into the carriage were dressed more or less the same as he was. No one paid any attention to him. People settled themselves down in the carriage in ones and twos. Some were talking quietly about something, but Andrei could not hear words, he only saw their faces, which were intelligent and kind. Yes, this was how people of the future ought to look. But what a strange world this was!

Andrei had once read of villages in Polynesia which had not changed their appearance for thousands of years, and of towns of the Middle Ages which had existed unchanged for centuries. True, abrupt jumps and changes in all fields had been characteristic of the age in which he himself had once lived, in technology, architecture and the external appearance of the world. But what was there to say that this tendency should go on for ever? Could not progress equally well take some other course than changing the external appearance of the world?

The train had slowed down and stopped. Everyone began getting out and the compartment emptied. Andrei, too, went to the door. He stood on the platform which looked just like the platform of any station of the past. He would have to find somewhere to sit down and collect his thoughts, to work out some plan of action.

Suddenly a voice broke out from some unknown source – a loud, proud voice whose words carried over the heads of the crowd. A few steps farther on Andrei began distinguishing words and everything inside him tensed ...

'Workers in city and country are preparing for the great day. Unprecedented enthusiasm reigns these days in factories and on construction sites ... Inspired by a concern for ...'

A wild, almost incredible realization flashed through his brain. Andrei felt the platform slipping away from under him. Swaying on his feet he took a few more steps and then stopped. Directly in front of him was a newspaper stand.

He raised his eyes and read the name of the newspaper. And the year. And the day.

He had, it seemed, slept for just over twenty-four hours. It was Monday ...

Andrei sank down on someone's suitcase and he was poked in the back by a woman who started to shout something – it was her suitcase he was sitting on and she didn't care about Andrei or about what had happened to him. Neither did the people who swept past him hurrying on their way somewhere.

To them, Andrei could neither have told, shouted nor explained what had happened.

When the shock of the first moments wore off Andrei, to his own surprise, felt neither disillusioned nor disappointed. Somewhere in his heart there rose a cowardly joy that he had escaped, and this world and these people whom he had so light-heartedly prepared to leave, now seemed to him dearer than all future epochs and worlds. In any case, Andrei was sure of one thing, that he could never force himself to go through it all again. But then he remembered Vetashevskaya. What would become of him now? If she had already arrived at the office, he was done for! There and then began a race between Andrei, thrusting his way convulsively through the crowd on the station square towards a taxi, and Vetashevskaya who was at that moment unhurriedly mounting the wide staircase. She answered greetings and from time to time stopped to say a few condescending words. When Andrei finally raced up to a taxi, shouts of anger rose from the long queue overflowing with children and suitcases. And again, words were useless, and gestures couldn't help him – people shouted something into his face and waved their fists at him. When at last he did get into a taxi, the minute hand of the big station clock had moved noticeably to the right, approaching, perhaps even passing, the point which marked the fatal hour. At the very moment that Andrei slammed shut the door of the taxi, Vetashevskaya was going through the doorway of her office. Racing up the staircase, Andrei heard his heart beating loudly and the familiar white steps seemed to be drawing themselves upwards so that it seemed he would never reach the landing at the top. When he saw the open door of the office, it seemed like a terrible dream. There sat the executive staff, and the director, and Vetashevskaya, whose face had broken out in crimson patches, was showing them the portrait. Even from a distance Andrei could make out the donkey's ears, one standing up, the other hanging down.

For some reason no one even glanced in his direction, and when Andrei tried to speak, or rather to shout something, he could feel that only his lips were moving – no voice came.

At that precise moment, he felt himself go cold and he began to understand why no one looked at him. On the carpet where his feet should have been, there were no feet. There was nothing of him at all; but he didn't even have time to feel surprised because from somewhere above him those thick black flakes fell again.

Andrei was lying on the platform in the middle of the round, brick room deep underground. He was not alive and he was not dead. On his forehead, hoarfrost was forming.

He would wake in two hundred years.

Translated by D. Matias

Arkadii and Boris Strugatskii

The Second Martian Invasion
A Fantastical Tale

NOTES OF A SANE MAN

O H! T HIS wretched conformist world. June 1st (3 AM).
Lord! Now it's Artemida – she's evidently got mixed up
with that Nikostratos after all. And she calls herself my daughter . . . Well, enough of that.

About 1 AM I was woken by a loud though distant rumbling
and was startled to see a sinister play of red patches of light on
the bedroom wall. The rumbling was the kind of intermittent
roaring that precedes an earthquake, and it was so strong that
the whole house rocked, the windowpanes rattled and the flasks
on the dressing-table jumped about. I rushed to the window
in terror. The northern sky was ablaze; it was as if the earth
had opened up beyond the horizon and was throwing foun-
tains of multi-coloured flame right up to the stars. Yet those
two, oblivious of everything, lit up by a hellish glow and
shaken by underground tremors, were kissing and embracing
on the bench right under my window. I recognized Artemida at
once and thought at first Charon must have returned and that
she was so overjoyed to see him that she was kissing him like a
young bride instead of taking him straight off to their bedroom. But a moment later I recognized the famous foreign
jacket of Mr Nikostratos by the light of the fire and my heart
sank. It's moments like these that rob a man of his health.
Though I can't say this came as a bolt from the blue: there had
been rumours, hints and all manner of jokes going around.
But all the same I was shattered.

Clutching my heart, and with no idea what to do, I dragged

myself, barefoot, to the sitting-room and telephoned the police. But you try to get through to the police when you need them. For a long time the number was engaged and then to cap it all it turned out to be Panderei on duty. I asked him what the phenomenon was beyond the horizon. He didn't know what a phenomenon was.

'Can you tell me what's happening beyond the northern horizon?' I asked. He asked where that was and I really didn't know how to explain it to him – but then the light suddenly dawned.

'Ohhh!' he said. 'You mean the fire.' And he explained that, in fact, some kind of burning activity could be seen, but what it was and what was burning had not been established as yet.

The house was rocking, everything was creaking, and on the street people were screaming something heartrending about war, yet the old fool started telling me that they had brought Minotaur into the lock-up; blind drunk, he'd defiled the corner of Mr Laomedontes' villa, and now he couldn't even stand up, nor fight even.

'Are you going to take some action or not?' I broke in.

'That's what I'm explaining, Mr Apollo.' The fool sounded offended. 'I have to draw up a report and you're blocking the line. If you're all going to get so worked up over this fire . . .'

'And what if it's a war?' I asked.

'No, it's not a war,' he declared. 'I'd know about it if it were.'

'And what if it's an eruption?' I asked.

He didn't know what an eruption was – I couldn't take it any longer and hung up the receiver. Covered in sweat after that conversation, I went back to my bedroom and put on a dressing-gown and slippers.

The rumbling seemed to have died down but the flashes of light continued, and those two weren't kissing any more; they weren't even sitting embracing. No, not a bit of it, they were standing hand in hand for anyone to see – a fire beyond the horizon made it light as day, except that the light was not white but reddish-orange, and through it floated clouds of brown smoke, shading into a deep coffee colour. The neighbours were running about the street in whatever they happened to be wearing, and Mrs Euridice was grabbing hold of people

by their pyjamas and telling them to save her. The only one of
them to look businesslike was Myrtil who, with the help of his
wife and sons, wheeled his lorry out of the garage and began
to carry all his possessions out of the house. It was real panic,
just like the good old days – I hadn't seen anything like it for
years. And yet I realized that if this really was the start of an
atomic war, then there was no better place to hide and sit it out
in the whole area than our small town. If, on the other hand,
it was an eruption, then it was happening a long way away, and
again presented no threat to our town. Though it was not at
all likely to be an eruption – what kind of eruption could we
have here? I went upstairs and tried to wake Hermione – and
here things were as usual: 'Leave me alone you drunkard,
you and your drinking all night long. Just leave me alone,
will you.' And so on. So, in a loud and convincing tone, I
started to tell her about the atomic war and the eruption –
painting it all in slightly heightened colours, since otherwise I
would get nowhere.

It penetrated, and she jumped out of bed, thrust me aside and
rushed into the dining-room, muttering: 'I'll take a look for
myself and then you'd better watch out . . .' Unlocking the sideboard she checked the bottles of brandy. I was quite calm.
'Where have you come from in that state?' she asked, sniffing
suspiciously. 'What sleazy night-spot have you been in?' But
when she looked out of the window and saw the half-naked
neighbours, and Myrtil standing on his roof in nothing more
than his underpants, gazing at the north through his binoculars,
she lost all interest in me. In fact, as it turned out, the northern
horizon was once more buried in darkness and silence, but a
strange cloud of smoke, completely blotting out the stars, was
still visible. I don't know how to put it – but my Hermione is
no Mrs Euridice: she belongs to a different generation, and
she's had a different upbringing. Anyway, I'd hardly had time
to gulp down a glass of cognac before she was dragging out
the cases and shouting for Artemida at the top of her voice.

'Go on, shout,' I thought sourly. 'She'll never hear you.' And
then Artemida appeared at the door of her room. Good Lord,
she was pale as death and trembling all over, but she was
in her nightclothes already, curling pins dangling from her
hair.

'What's the matter? What's wrong with you all?' she asked.

Like it or not, that's character for you. If it hadn't been for this phenomenon I'd never have found out anything, and Charon still less. Our eyes met and she smiled at me tenderly with trembling lips, and I just couldn't bring myself to utter the words which were on the tip of my tongue. To calm myself I went into my own room and started to pack up my stamps. You're shaking and trembling, I said to her, mentally. You're lonely and terribly unprotected. And he hasn't supported or protected you. He's plucked the flower of pleasure and fled on his own business. No, little girl, when a man starts dishonourably then that's how he carries on.

In the meantime the panic was quickly subsiding, much as I had expected. The night returned to normal; the earth no longer shook; the houses no longer creaked. Someone took Mrs Euridice home with them. There were no more shouts about war, and in general there was nothing left to shout about anyway. Glancing through the window I saw that the street was empty and just the occasional light could still be seen in a few houses. And Myrtil was still on the roof, his underwear gleaming among the stars. I called over to him and asked what he could see.

'All right, all right,' he replied in a huff. 'You go and snore in bed. You start snoring and then they'll give it you ...'

I asked who 'they' were.

'All right, all right,' he replied. 'You knowalls have got all the answers. You and your Panderei. And he's no more than a great fool.' Hearing Panderei's name I decided to ring the police again. Once again I rang for ages, and when at last I got through Panderei told me that there was no particular news, but apart from that everything was in order. They'd given the drunken Minotaur a sedative and washed out his stomach and now he had calmed down. As for the fire, it had stopped long ago, especially as it had proved to be not a fire at all, but a big holiday fireworks display. While I tried to remember what holiday it was today Panderei hung up. However, he's a fool and extremely ill-bred as well. He's always been like that. Strange to see such people in our police force. Our policemen ought to be intelligent, a model for the young, a hero, someone they would want to emulate, someone who could safely be entrusted not just with power and authority, but with educational activities. But Charon says such a police force would be 'a company of four-eyes' and declares that no government wants a police force like that because it would begin by arresting and re-educating the state's most useful citizens, starting with the prime minister and chief of police. Well, I don't know, maybe he's right. But a senior policeman who doesn't know the meaning of the word 'phenomenon' and can't carry out his duties without being boorish – that's not what we want, and no doubt about it.

Stumbling over the suitcases, I picked my way to the sideboard and had just poured myself a glass of brandy when Hermione came back into the room. She said the place was a madhouse; that she couldn't rely on anyone; that the men weren't worth calling men and the women not worth calling women; that I was a confirmed alcoholic; that Charon was a useless gadabout; that Artemida was a fine lady who couldn't adjust herself to normal life. And so on. Perhaps somebody would be so good as to explain to her why she had been roused in the middle of the night and made to start packing the cases? I replied to Hermione as best I could, and took cover in my own room.

About 3 AM the earth shook again. Then came the sound of many engines and the clanking of metal. It turned out to be a column of army lorries and armoured troop-carriers passing the house. They were moving slowly with their lights dimmed, and Myrtil had managed to latch on to one of the armoured cars. He was strolling along beside it, clinging on to a protruding hatchway and shouting something. I don't know what they said in reply, but when the column had passed by and he was left standing alone on the street I called to him and asked for any news.

'All right, all right,' he said. 'We know what these manoeuvres are, smart fellows driving about on my money.' And with that I understood the whole business: large-scale military exercises were being carried out, maybe with the use of atomic weapons. What a lot of fuss about nothing!

Thank God! Now, perhaps, I'll be able to get to sleep in peace.

June 2nd. I just can't bring myself to have it out with Artemida. I can't bear these horribly personal and intimate conversations. And then I don't even know how she would reply to me. But Daddy, it's so deadly dull here, she'd say. And you can't get away from it! She's a young, attractive woman without children, and she's high-spirited and would like to rush around enjoying herself. She'd like to go dancing, flirt with people and all the rest of it. But as luck would have it Charon is one of your philosophers. A thinker. Totalitarianism, fascism, managerism, communism. According to him dancing is a sexual drug, and the people we entertain are complete idiots, and he doesn't know which is the greater of the two evils. And you don't dare mention Sevens or Chinese patience. And yet, for all that, he can drink well enough! He'll put five of his clever friends round the table with five bottles of cognac and argue till the morning. And the poor girl sits yawning and yawning till finally she slams the door and goes off to bed. What kind of a life is that? I know well enough that a man needs his own company and pursuits, but then so does a woman. No, I've always been fond of my son-in-law: damn it he is my son-in-law and I'll always be fond of him. But really, just how much time can you spend arguing and debating? And what does it all achieve? After all, it's clear enough that you can argue about fascism until the cows come home, but you won't change fascism by that. But if you stop paying the proper amount of attention to a young wife, then she'll repay you in the same coin. And no amount of philosophy will help you there, either. I quite understand that sometimes an educated man needs to discuss abstract matters, but for goodness' sake, he should keep a sense of proportion about it. Ah, well, enough of that.

The morning was really beautiful. (Temperature – +19°c; cloud density – 1 degree; wind – southerly, 0.5 metres per second. I should have gone out to the meteorological station to check the wind-gauge since I've damaged mine again.) After breakfast I decided that I wouldn't get anywhere without taking some action, and so I set off to the town hall to clear up the business of my pension. I was walking along enjoying the calm of the morning, when suddenly I noticed that a crowd was gathering at the corner of Freedom Street and the Vereskova. It turned out that Minotaur had driven his cart into the jeweller's shop window. The police shouldn't have let him out so soon. They might have known that once having started on a drinking bout he was bound to go off and get drunk again.

But, on the other hand, how could they keep him shut up when he's the only lavatory attendant in the town?

I was held up because of Minotaur and when I reached The Five Clinks our group was already assembled; I paid my fine, and then one-legged Polythemes treated me to an excellent cigar in an aluminium tube. His eldest son, Polycarp, a lieutenant in the Merchant Navy, had sent him this cigar specially for me. This Polycarp had been a pupil of mine for several years before he ran away to become a ship's boy. He'd been a bright boy and full of mischief. When he left the town Polythemes almost took me to court for it. Would you believe it, he claimed that his teacher had dissipated the young boy with all his lectures about the multitude of different worlds. Right to this day Polythemes himself is convinced that the sky is hard and that space travellers race about it like motorcyclists at the circus. I've tried to explain astronomy to him, but it's no use.

The group was saying that once again the town treasurer was squandering money that had been set aside to build a stadium. This is the seventh time it has happened. To begin with we discussed how we could suppress him.

Silen shrugged his shoulders, maintaining that apart from bringing a lawsuit there was nothing one could do. 'We've had enough of half-measures,' he argued. 'An open court. The whole town should gather together in the stadium's foundation area and pillory the scoundrel right on the site of his crime. For Christ's sake,' he repeated, 'our law is flexible enough for us to see that the means used to suppress the man correspond exactly to the seriousness of the offence.'

'I would go so far as to say that our law is too flexible,' observed the quarrelsome Paral. 'That treasurer has been tried twice already, and both times our flexible law has been bent to his advantage. But maybe you think that was because he was tried in the town hall and not in the foundation area.'

Morpheus, getting down to the heart of the problem, declared that from today he would refuse to shave the treasurer or cut his hair. He could just go about looking unshaven and unkempt.

'Nothing will make you see that he couldn't care a damn about the lot of you,' said Polythemes. 'He's got his own supporters.'

'Exactly,' Paral backed him up and reminded us that the town architect was still alive and flourishing. This man had designed the stadium – that is, as far as his limited abilities would allow him; and now, not surprisingly, did not want to see building started.

One-legged Polythemes, as a veteran and a man who did not fear bloodshed, suggested that we should catch the pair of them at the entrance to Madame Persephone's house and kick them in the crutch. Polythemes makes no effort to guard his tongue at critical moments such as these and he comes out with the most crude barracks language. It's simply amazing, the way such talk stirs us all up. People became virulent and waved their arms about and Kalaid stuttered and hissed even more than usual. In fact, his emotion was so great that he became incapable of pronouncing a single word. But at this moment the quarrelsome Paral, who alone among us had remained calm, observed that, besides the treasurer and the architect, one Mr Laomedontes, their chief ally, was still in the town, living in his summer residence. Suddenly everyone fell silent and started to draw on the cigars and cigarettes that had gone out in the course of the conversation – come to think of it, it would not be very easy to kick Mr Laomedontes in the crutch.

I remembered that I should have been at the town hall long ago, so I put the remains of my cigar in its aluminium tube and went up to the first floor and into the mayor's reception room. I was struck by the unusual activity in the office. All the officials seemed agitated in some way. Even Mr Secretary, instead of occupying himself with the habitual examination of his nails, was fastening some large envelopes with sealing-wax, and this, moreover, with an air of extreme fussiness and of doing someone a great favour. Feeling very ill-at-ease I approached this dandy, who was touted out in the latest fashion. Christ, at that moment I would have given anything in the world not to see or hear him, not to be obliged to deal with him. I didn't like Mr Nikostratos before this business. In fact, to tell you the truth, I didn't like him even when he was my pupil – because of his laziness, arrogance and impudent behaviour – and after what I had seen yesterday it made me feel ill just to look at him. Nor did I have any idea how to approach him. But there was no way out and finally I brought myself to say: 'Mr Nikostratos, have you heard anything about my case?'

He didn't even deign to glance at me. 'I'm sorry, Mr Apollo, but there has been no reply from the ministry as yet,' he said, and continued to seal his envelopes. I clicked my heels and made my way to the exit feeling like a worm. Offices always have that effect on me. But quite unexpectedly he stopped me with a piece of surprising information. He said that all communications with Marathon had been cut since yesterday.

'What do you mean?' I said. 'Surely the manoeuvres must be over by now?'

'What manoeuvres?' He sounded surprised.

At that something snapped inside me. I still don't know if it was worth it, but I looked him straight in the eyes and said: 'What do you mean – What manoeuvres? The ones you were watching last night, if you please.'

'But you don't really think those were manoeuvres?' he declared with enviable composure, and once again bent over his envelopes. 'That was a firework display. You should read the morning papers.'

I should really have said something to him about Artemida then, especially as at that moment we were alone in the room. But how could I?

When I got back to The Five Clinks there was already a discussion in progress on the nature of the night's phenomenon. The entire group was there and Myrtil and Panderei had come along too. Panderei had his tunic unbuttoned and was tired and unshaven after his night on duty. Myrtil didn't look much better since he'd spent a whole night patrolling his house, on the look-out for trouble. All of them were holding the morning papers and discussing our observer's notice, which was entitled: 'On the threshold of the festival'. Our 'observer' informed us that Marathon was preparing for the celebration of its 153rd anniversary, and, as he had found out from well-informed sources, yesterday night a practice fireworks display had been held, which the inhabitants of the neighbouring small towns and villages within a radius of 200 kilometres had been able to admire. Just let Charon go away on a study trip and our paper makes a fool of itself. If they had even tried to imagine what a fireworks display would look like at a distance of 200 kilometres. And if they had just stopped to consider – since when have fireworks been accompanied by underground tremors? I quickly pointed this out to the rest of the group. But they replied that they hadn't been born yesterday either and advised me to read the *Milese Herald*. In the *Herald* it was stated in black and white that last night 'the inhabitants of Milese had been able to admire the most impressive spectacle of military exercises being carried out with the use of ultra-modern military techniques'. 'And what did I say!' I was on the point of exclaiming, when Myrtil interrupted me. He described how, in the early hours of the morning, a driver whom he did not know from the firm 'Long-distance Haulage Company' had stopped to refuel at his petrol pump and had taken 150 litres of petrol, two jars of Avtol motor oil and a crate of marmalade. The man had told him, in secret, that during the night the underground rocket-fuel factories had exploded – the cause being unknown. It seemed that 23 watchmen and the entire night shift had perished, and apart from that 179 men had been lost without trace. We were all horrified, but at this point the quarrelsome Paral inquired aggressively: 'And why then did he need marmalade, I wonder?'

This question floored Myrtil. 'All right, all right,' he said. 'I've told you. That's all you'll get from me.' We had no answer either. Why *did* the man need marmalade? Kalaid hissed and spluttered but couldn't get anything out. And then that old fool Panderei took the floor.

'Listen, fellows,' he said. 'Those weren't rocket factories. They were marmalade factories. Get it? And now, shut up.'

We all sat up. 'Underground marmalade factories?' said Paral. 'Well, old man, you're in great form today.'

We started to clap Panderei on the back saying: 'Yes, Pan, poor old man, you can see that you didn't get much sleep last night. That Minotaur led you a fine song and dance. Oh, Pan, Pan, old friend, it's high time you got your pension!'

'A policeman, and he encourages panic himself,' said Myrtil in an aggrieved tone. He was the only one of us to have taken Panderei's words seriously.

Finally Panderei buttoned up his jacket from top to bottom and looking over our heads barked out: 'That's enough, all of you! Disperse! In the name of the law.' Myrtil went off to his petrol pump and the rest of us made for the bar.

In the bar we ordered beer straight away. There's a real

pleasure for you, something I was deprived of before I retired! In a town as small as ours everyone knows the school-
master, and for some reason or other all the parents imagine
that you are a miracle worker and by your own personal example can prevent their children from following in the foot-
steps of their parents. From morning till late at night the bar
is literally swarming with these parents, and if you permitted
yourself an innocent jug of beer, the next day without fail
you'd be given a humiliating lecture by the director. And I love
going to the bar! I like to sit in good male company, absent-
mindedly taking in the hum of voices and the clink of glasses
behind me. I like swapping risqué stories or winning a game of
Chinese patience – a narrow victory, but a worthy one – and
when I've won I like to order everyone a jug of beer. However,
enough of all that.

Japheth served us and we started to talk about war. One-
legged Polythemes declared that if this were a war then mobili-
zation would have begun already, but Paral objected to that,
saying that if it were war, we would know nothing about it. I
don't like talking about war and would have been glad to move
the conversation on to the question of pensions, but then who
am I to ... Polythemes laid his crutch on the table and asked
how much Paral personally knew about war. Paral just
shrugged his shoulders and Polythemes finally lost his temper.
Then, when he had vented his spleen, he fell to reminiscing over
the tank attack we had all beaten back in the snow.

We sat ourselves down and I decided to have lunch at the
same time. Normally the food at Japheth's is very good, but
today his dumpling soup à la maison had a foul smell of cheap
oil about it – and I told Japheth as much. It turned out that
Japheth had been suffering from toothache for the past three
days, and it was so bad that he couldn't taste what he was preparing. 'And do you remember how I knocked out one of your
teeth, Feb?' he asked mournfully.

How could I forget! It was way back in the seventh class
when we were both running after Iphigenia and fought over
her daily. Good God, the days when I could fight are far away
now! And apparently Iphigenia has married some engineer in
the south and already has grandchildren and heart trouble.

When I passed Mr Laomedontes' house on my way to see
Achilles, that horrible red car with the bullet-proof windows

was standing there, and that vile thug who always pokes fun at me was sitting smoking behind the wheel. He started off with his usual abuse, so that I was obliged to cross in a dignified manner to the other side of the street, without paying any attention to him. Achilles was seated in state behind the cash register, thumbing through his *Cosmos*. Ever since the day he got hold of that blue triangular stamp with the silver seal, he's made it a rule to reach out for the album, as if quite by chance, as soon as I walk in. I can see right through him and so I'm careful not to show any reaction. Though, to tell the truth, it always makes the blood rush to my heart. My one consolation is that the triangular stamp is franked. I told him so. 'Yes, Achilles,' I said, 'there's no doubt about it – it's a beautiful thing. Just a pity that it's franked.' He looked angry and muttered something about sour grapes.

But in general we passed the time quite happily together. He tried to persuade me that yesterday's fireworks were in fact a polar radiance of a very rare kind, which happened purely by chance to have the same appearance as an earthquake, and I tried to make him understand about the manoeuvres and the explosion in the marmalade factory. It's no good arguing with Achilles. And it's plain that the man doesn't believe what he's saying himself, and only argues from sheer cussedness. He sits there like a Mongolian statue, looks through the window and repeats the same thing over and over again, the general drift of it being that I'm not the only man in this town to understand natural phenomena. From the way he talks you might suppose that in his pharmaceutical college they had been trained in the serious sciences. No, not with a single member of our group can you carry an argument to a rational conclusion.

Our argument ended when Achilles brought out his precious bottle, and we both had a glass of gin. Achilles doesn't have a great deal of trade. I get the impression that if it weren't for Madame Persephone he wouldn't even have enough money for gin.

Even today she had sent somebody in. 'May I suggest a stomach settler?' asked Achilles in a delicate whisper.

'No,' replied the girl. 'Madame would like something more reliable, please.' *She* dares to ask for something more reliable ... Japheth's young cook came running in to get him some tooth drops, and apart from that there was nobody, so we could chat to our heart's content.

June 3rd. Sometimes I'm seized by terror at the thought that the problem of my pension is making no headway. I tense up inside and can't settle to anything.

If only I had some contacts! But, well, there *is* one of my former pupils, a general what's more, Alcimes, who is now in the Lower Congress. Maybe it would be worth writing to him? He's bound to remember me: we had lots of those stupid conflicts which pupils love to remember once they have become adults. Christ, I'll write to him. And I'll start the letter quite simply: 'Hello, young man. Here I am, an old man already . . .' I'll wait a little and then I'll write.

Today I spent the whole day at home: yesterday Hermione went to visit her aunt and she came back with a large packet full of old stamps. Sorting them out gave me great satisfaction. It's an incomparable occupation – something like an unending honeymoon. There turned out to be several really fine specimens – all franked, though, and they'll need touching up. Myrtil has pitched tent in the courtyard of his house and is living there with his entire family. He was boasting that he could gather his belongings and leave in ten minutes. He said that there was still no communication with Marathon. No doubt he's lying. Minotaur, blind drunk, had driven his dirty cart into Mr Laomedontes' red car and had had a fight with the chauffeur. Both of them had been taken to the police station. Then Minotaur had been locked up until he sobered and apparently the driver had been taken to hospital. There's some justice in the world after all. Artemida is sitting at home, quiet as a mouse; Charon should be back any day now. And I'm not going to say anything to Hermione. Maybe it will all sort itself out somehow. If I could just get the first instalment of my pension!

June 4th. I've just finished reading the evening paper, but I still can't understand anything. No doubt about it, there's been some kind of change. But what exactly? And as the result of what events? Our papers like to tell lies, that's all.

This morning I had a cup of coffee then made my way to The Five Clinks. It was a fine, mild morning. (Temperature –

+18°C; cloud density – 0 degrees; wind – southerly, 1 metre per second, according to my wind-gauge.) As I came out of the garden gate I saw that Myrtil was busy with his tent which he had spread out on the ground. I asked him what he was doing.

'All right, all right,' he replied in a tone of intense irritation. 'You lot have got all the answers. You sit and wait for them to come and finish you all off if you want to.'

I've no faith in what Myrtil says, but such talk always upsets me. 'Well, what has happened now?' I asked. 'The Mars-men,' he answered briefly and started folding the tent between his knees. I didn't understand what he meant straight away, and maybe that's why this strange word struck a chill in my heart, as if something terrible and insuperable were at hand. My legs felt weak and I sat down on the bumper of the lorry. Myrtil said nothing more, just puffed and panted. 'What was it you said?' I asked. He wrapped up the tent, threw it into a basket and lit a cigarette.

'The Mars-men have attacked,' he said in a whisper. 'It's the end for all of us. They say that Marathon has been razed to the ground, and that ten million have been killed in one night – can you imagine it? And now they're in our town hall. They're in power now and that's all there is to it. They've already forbidden us to sow our crops, and now people say that they're going to cut out our stomachs. Can you imagine it, they need our stomachs for something or other? Well, I'm not waiting for that – I need my stomach myself. When I heard all that, I decided straight away – these new régimes aren't for me. The rest of you can go to the devil, for all I care, but I'm off to my brother's farm. I've sent the old woman and the children off by bus already. We'll sit it out there, see what's happening, and then we'll decide what to do.'

'Wait a minute,' I said, realizing that it was all plainly a pack of lies, but none the less feeling weaker with every moment. 'Wait a minute, Myrtil. What on earth are you saying? Who's attacked us? Who's razed Marathon? – I've got a son-in-law there at the moment.'

'Your son-in-law is lost,' said Myrtil sympathetically, and threw away his cigarette butt. 'You may as well count your daughter a widow. She can make free with the secretary now. Well, I'm off. Farewell, Apollo. We always got on well together. I've got no grudge against you, and you – well, think kindly of me.'

'Good Lord!' I cried out in desperation, all my strength gone. 'But *who* has attacked?'

'The Mars-men, the Mars-men!' he said, dropping to a whisper again. 'From up there!' He pointed his finger at the sky. 'They came from a comet.'

'Maybe you mean the Martians?' I asked hopefully.

'All right, all right,' he said, getting into his cabin. 'You're the teacher, you know best. But, as far as I'm concerned, it doesn't make any difference who it is that's letting my guts out ...'

'Good heavens, Myrtil,' I said, having finally grasped what all this nonsense was about. 'How can you carry on like this? You're an old man with grandsons of your own. What Martians can there be when Mars is a lifeless planet? There's no life on Mars, and that's a scientific fact.'

'All right, all right,' muttered Myrtil, but it was clear that he was beginning to have doubts. 'What more facts have you got up your sleeve?'

'Enough of your "all rights". That's the plain truth. Ask any scholar. Or you don't even need to ask a scholar – every schoolboy knows that!'

Myrtil grunted and climbed out of his cab. 'The devil take them all,' he said, scratching the back of his head. 'Who on earth is one to listen to? Should I listen to you? Or should I listen to Panderei? I can't make head nor tail of anything.' He spat and went off into his house.

I decided to go back in and telephone the police. Panderei turned out to be very busy – Minotaur had broken the grille of his cell and escaped, so that now he, Panderei, had to organize a round-up. He said that some people had quite definitely driven up to the town hall about an hour and a half ago, authorities from somewhere, and maybe they were Martians even. There were certainly rumours around that it was the Martians, but no orders had been received regarding cutting out stomachs, and, anyway, he wasn't very interested in the Martians, since in his opinion one Minotaur by himself was more trouble than all the Martians put together.

I hurried along to The Five Clinks. Almost all our group were crowded around the entrance to the town hall and were arguing violently about some strange marks in the dust. These marks had been made by one of the Martians who had just arrived – that much they knew for a fact. Morpheus repeated over and over again that even he, a veteran hairdresser and masseur, had never seen such monsters.

'Spiders,' he said. 'Great hairy spiders. The males are hairy and the females hairless. They walk on their hind legs and grab hold of things with their front legs. Have you seen their marks? It's terrible! Just like holes. Here's where he's walked past.'

'He didn't walk past,' said Silen soberly. 'The force of gravity is greater on earth, as Apollo will confirm, which means that they simply cannot use their legs for walking. They have specially-sprung stilts to walk with and it's the stilts that leave the marks in the dust.'

'Quite right, stilts,' Japheth corroborated him. His cheeks were covered by a bandage and he spoke indistinctly. 'Only they're not stilts. It's a special vehicle that they have – I've seen it at the cinema. Their vehicles don't move on wheels but on levers – something like stilts.'

'Our treasurer's gone out of his mind again,' said Paral. 'Last time it was hail of an unusual force, the time before that it was locusts and this time he's hit on the idea of the Martians – more on a level with the age; in tune with assimilation of cosmic expanses.'

'I can't look at those marks and stay calm,' repeated Morpheus. 'It's terrible. Well lads, let's go for a drink, eh?'

Kalaid, who had been struggling with himself for some time already, finally spluttered: 'It-t-t's f-f-fine w-weather to-to-to-d-d-ay, f-f-f-riends. Did y-y-ou s-s-sl-leep w-w-w-well?' Because of his speech defect he is always out of touch with events. All the same he's a veteran and might have had something interesting to say about the marks.

'And Myrtil has taken his leave already,' said Dimant, giggling stupidly. ' "Farewell, Dimant," he said, "we were always good friends. Look after my petrol pump, and if anything happens, burn it rather than leave it to the enemy." '

At this point I asked cautiously what news there was of Marathon.

'They say that Marathon has been burnt to the ground,' said Dimant readily. 'It seems that they've phoned from there offering peace.'

I was quite convinced that all this was stupid rumour, and I was ready to disprove them, but at that moment a police siren wailed and we all turned round.

Zigzagging like a hare, reeling, bruised and swollen-faced, Minotaur came running across the square; and behind him in hot pursuit came Panderei in a police jeep. Panderei was standing up, holding on to the windscreen, shouting something and brandishing a pair of handcuffs.

'That's it – he'll get him now,' said Morpheus.

'How can you say that?' objected Dimant. 'Just look at what he's doing!'

Minotaur had run up to a telegraph pole, clasped his arms and legs round it and begun to clamber up. However, Panderei had already jumped down from the jeep and grabbed a firm hold of his trousers. With the help of the junior policeman he dragged him away from the post, thrust him into the jeep and put on the handcuffs. After this the junior policeman drove off and Panderei, mopping himself with a handkerchief and unbuttoning his tunic, walked over towards us.

'There, he's caught him,' said Morpheus, turning to Dimant.

Panderei drew near and asked what news there was. He was told about the marks left by the Martians. He quickly got down on his haunches and buried himself in an examination of the circumstantial evidence. I even felt an unwilling respect for him, because straight away a really professional understanding showed itself in his eyes: he looked at the marks from the side, and didn't touch anything with his hands. I had a presentiment that everything would be explained now. Panderei moved along the length of the marks like a duck wagging its fat behind, and kept repeating: 'Uh, huh. Quite clear. Uh, huh, quite clear . . .'

We waited in impatient silence – only Kalaid tried to say something and brought out a hiss. At last Panderei righted himself with a groan and, surveying the square for all the world as if he expected to discover something, pronounced abruptly: 'Two of them. Carried off money in a sack. One of them has a walking stick with a blade, the other smokes "Astra".'

'I smoke "Astra" too,' said Paral.

Panderei immediately fixed his eyes on him.

'Two what?' asked Dimant. 'Martians?'

'I didn't think locals had done it at first,' said Panderei slowly, never taking his eyes off Paral. 'At first I thought it was the lads from Milese. I know what they're like.'

At this point Kalaid burst out: 'N-n-no. Y-y-you c-c-can't c-c-catch him in a car.'

'And how can they be Martians?' said Dimant. 'I don't understand . . .'

Panderei, ignoring direct questions as before, looked Paral up and down. 'Give me your cigarette, old man,' he said.

'What do you want it for?' asked Paral.

'I want to see how you bite it,' announced Panderei, 'and as well I want to know where you were between six and seven AM this morning.'

We all looked at Paral, and Paral said that in his opinion Panderei was the biggest fool in the world, with the exception of the cretin who took Panderei into the police force. We were forced to agree with him and started to clap Panderei on the back saying: 'Yes, Panderei, you've made a blunder, old fellow. Can't you understand, old man? These are Martian marks. This isn't one of your lavatory attendants!' Panderei began to swell with indignation.

But at that moment one-legged Polythemes came out of the town hall and burst into the middle of our merriment. 'It's a rotten business, lads,' he said in a worried tone. 'The Martians are advancing. They've taken Milese. Our men are retreating, they're burning the crops and tearing down the bridges after them!' My legs went quite weak again and I didn't even have the strength to push my way to a bench and sit down. 'They've made a landing in the south, two divisions,' croaked Polythemes. 'They'll be here soon!'

'They've been here already,' said Silen, 'on special lever-stilts. Look, here are their tracks . . .'

Polythemes gave them no more than a glance, then said, indignantly, that those were his tracks, and at once everybody realized that, in fact, they were his. I felt very relieved. But as soon as he had understood Panderei buttoned up his tunic from top to bottom and, looking over our heads barked out: 'That's enough, all of you! Move on! In the name of the law.'

I went into the town hall. The place was crowded out with flat sacks of some kind, which were stacked along the corridor walls, on the landings and even in the reception room. An unfamiliar smell came from these sacks, and the windows were wide open everywhere, but apart from that everything was as usual. Mr Nikostratos was sitting at his table, polishing his fingernails. Smirking strangely and pronouncing his words very indistinctly, he gave me to understand that, in the course of his official duty, he was not entitled to spread information concerning the Martians, but that he could positively affirm that all this could hardly have any bearing on the question of my pension. One thing was certain: from now on it would be unprofitable to sow wheat in our region, but it would be very profitable to sow some new cereal, which had what he described as 'universal properties'. The seed was being kept in those sacks, and from today onwards they would begin to divide it among the farms round about.

'And where have these sacks come from?' I asked.

'They were supplied,' he replied impressively.

I overcame my timidity and inquired who had supplied them.

'Official personages,' he said, got up from behind his table, excused himself, and with his straggling gait went off to the mayor's room.

I went out to the general office and chatted with the typists and the watchmen for a bit. Strange though it may seem, they confirmed almost all the rumours about the Martians, but they did not give me the impression of having genuine information. Oh! I've had enough of these rumours already! Nobody believes in them, yet everybody repeats them. It means that even the most simple facts are distorted. For example, Polythemes was declaring that the bridges had been torn down. And what had happened in actual fact? Somebody saw him through a window and asked him to come into the mayor's office and repair a typewriter. While he was at work, and amusing the girls with the story of how he lost his leg, the mayor came into the office, stood there for a moment, listened with a thoughtful expression on his face and said ambiguously: 'Yes, sirs, our bridges seem to have been burned' – and then returned to his room, from where he shortly ordered sardine sandwiches and a bottle of Fargosskii beer. But Polythemes explained to the girls that retreating troops generally tear down bridges behind them so as to obstruct the enemy's advance. The rest is plain. What stupidity! I decided it was my duty to explain to the town-hall employees that the secret phrase uttered by the lord mayor only meant that some irrevocable decision had been taken. Naturally relief immediately showed itself on the faces of all around, mixed, however, with some disappointment.

Nobody could be seen at The Five Clinks – Panderei had chased them all away. Feeling almost completely reassured already, I set off to see Achilles. I wanted to tell him about my latest discoveries and also to sound out the ground regarding the architectural series: maybe he would take the soiled one since it was impossible to get an unmarked one anyway – after all, he'll take franked stamps! But Achilles too was oppressed by the steadily-growing rumours. To my proposal he replied absent-mindedly that he would think it over. Then, not even noticing the importance of it himself, he gave me an excellent idea.

'The Martians are a new power,' he said. 'And you know, Feb, a new power means new stamps.'

I was astonished that this simple idea had not occurred to me. Certainly, even if the rumours were only partly true, the first rational action of these mythical Martians would have been to issue their own stamps, or at least to overprint our old ones. I hurriedly said goodbye to Achilles and headed straight for the post office. But of course no letters with new stamps had appeared, and in general there was nothing new in the post office. When, finally, will we teach ourselves not to believe rumours? After all, it's well known that Mars has an extremely rarefied atmosphere, that its climate is excessively harsh and that water – the basis of life – hardly exists there. The myths about the Martian canals were decisively debunked long ago, and they turned out to be nothing more than an optical illusion. In short, all this reminds me of the panic the year before last, when one-legged Polythemes ran about the town with a shotgun, shrieking that a gigantic man-eating triton had escaped from the zoo in the capital. That time Myrtil was clever enough to carry off his whole house, and it took two weeks before he made up his mind to return to the town.

The dim intelligence of my fellow citizens, blunted by a monotonous life, gives birth to the most fantastic images, whenever something happens that is even slightly outside the usual. The world of our town is like a hen-house buried in sleep – you need only accidentally brush against the plume of some cockerel, as it drowses on the perch, and at once indescribable pandemonium is let loose. The whole brood flaps around, cackling and making a complete mess of the hen-house. But, in my opinion, life is troubled enough as it is. We should all be more careful of our nerves. I reckon that these rumours are a lot more harmful to the health than even smoking. A writer who had the necessary figures to hand proved this. As well, he wrote that the reciprocal strength of the panic rumour was directly proportionate to the ignorance of the masses. And that's true, although I must admit that even the most highly educated among us succumb surprisingly easily to the general mood, and are ready to go anywhere along with the panic-stricken crowd.

I had decided to explain all this to our group but on my way to the bar I noticed that a crowd had gathered again at The Five Clinks. I turned round and went there instead, and was soon convinced that the rumours had already shown their destructive nature. Nobody would listen to my arguments. They were all impossibly worked up, and the veterans were brandishing their guns. Somebody explained to me that the soldiers from the barracks of the 88th infantry regiment had been discharged and had an extraordinary tale to tell.

The night before last the regiment was woken by an alarm call, and had spent some time – to be precise, until the morning – camped in armoured carriers and lorries in the square, in full military readiness. In the morning they had called off the alarm and yesterday everything had been normal. But last night exactly the same had happened, with the one exception, however: in the morning the general staff colonel had arrived in the barracks by helicopter, had ordered them to reconstruct the regiment as a punishment, and, not even getting out of his helicopter, had delivered a long, completely unintelligible speech, after which he flew off, and then almost the entire regiment were discharged. I must add, however, that the soldiers, who had already got themselves pretty well oiled at Japheth's, spoke extremely distinctly, and now and then started singing that coarse song: 'Niobe, Niobe, Come and lie nigh o' me'. However, it was quite plain that not a single word had been said about the Martians in the general staff colonel's speech. As a matter of fact, the colonel spoke only of two things: the patriotic duty of the soldier, and his gastric juices; and then in some elusive manner he managed to link these two concepts together. The soldiers themselves hadn't understood all these subtleties, but they had understood something else: from that day onward anyone whom a sergeant caught with the chewing gum 'Narko' or with an 'Opi' cigarette would find himself bump in the punishment cell and would be left there to rot for ten days and nights. As soon as the colonel had flown off, the regimental commander, far from forgetting the punishment, had ordered the junior officers and sergeants to conduct a thorough search of the barracks, with the object of removing all cigarettes and chewing gum that contained toxic elements. Apart from that the soldiers didn't know anything and didn't want to know any more. Hugging each other by the shoulders they burst forth with such a threatening air into: 'Niobe, Niobe, Come give yourself to me', that we gave way to them in a hurry and left them alone.

By now Polythemes had climbed up on to a bench with his crutch and shotgun and was shouting that the generals had betrayed us, that there were spies all round, that the real patriots must rally round the banner, that patriotism was the thing needed, and so on. That Polythemes cannot live without patriotism. He can live without a leg but he can't do anything without patriotism. At length he became hoarse and stopped talking so as to finish his cigarette. I had a shot at making our group see some sense. I started to tell them that there was not, and could not be, life on Mars, that it was sheer invention. Once again, however, they wouldn't let me have my say. First Morpheus stuck the morning paper with a long article entitled 'Is there life on Mars?' under my nose. In this article all former scientific facts were subjected to ironical doubt: and when, by no means subdued, I tried to discuss the article, Polythemes pushed his way up to me, grabbed me by the collar and wheezed threateningly: 'You're forgetting your vigilance, aren't you, you Martian spy? Balding shit! To the wall with you!'

I can't bear it when people treat me like that. My heart started to pound and I yelled for the police. Sheer hooliganism! I'll never forgive Polythemes for that. Who does he think he is? I pulled myself free, called him a one-legged swine and went off to the bar.

It was pleasant to be persuaded that Polythemes' patriotic

howls were distasteful to others besides myself. Some of the group had already gathered in the bar. They had all planted themselves round Kronid the archivist and were taking it in turns to ply him with beer, while they tried to extract information from him regarding the morning's visitation by the Martians.

'Nothing special about them,' said Kronid, rolling the whites of his eyes with difficulty. 'Well, they're just – Martians. One of them was called Calchand, the other Elias, both of them southerners, with great long noses like this ...'

'Yes, yes, but what about their vehicle?' he was asked.

'Just an ordinary machine, black, flies ... No, not a helicopter. Flies, that's all. What do you think I am, a pilot or something? How would I know how it flies? ...'

I had lunch and waited for them to leave him alone, then got two portions of gin and sat down beside him. 'No further news about the pensions?' I asked him. But Kronid was already past understanding.

His eyes had filled with tears, he downed glass after glass like a machine, and muttered: 'Martians – well, just Martians, one of them called Calchand, the other Elias ... Black machines ... they fly ... No, not airships, Elias I said ... Not me, the pilot ...' and then he fell asleep.

When Polythemes and his gang flocked into the bar I pointedly left for home. Myrtil hadn't left after all. Once again he had pitched his tent and was sitting cooking supper on a gas ring. Artemida wasn't at home; she'd gone off somewhere without saying anything, and Hermione was beating the carpets. I started touching up my stamps to calm myself. It's pleasant, for all that, to reflect on the art I've managed to perfect. I don't know if anyone else could distinguish my special glue from real glue, but, in any case, Achilles can't.

And now to today's papers. Nowadays, the papers are quite amazing. Almost every page is taken up with the opinions of different medical men regarding rational modes of nutrition. Medicinal preparations containing opium, morphine and caffeine are discussed with a certain unnatural indignation. So what, if I have liver pains now, then I'm just supposed to put up with it? Not a single paper has a philatelists' section, there's not a word about football, and, what's more, all the papers have printed the same huge, and entirely meaningless, article about the importance of gastric juice. Anyone would think that I couldn't possibly know what was the importance of the gastric juices without them to tell me. Not a single telegram from abroad, not a word about the results of the embargo – instead a long discussion about wheat. They say there aren't enough vitamins in wheat, and wheat, apparently, is too easily infected by pests. And a certain Martius, an MA in agriculture, has managed to persuade himself that the one thousand years' history of the cultivation of wheat and other useful cereals (oats, Indian corn, maize) represents a universal error on the part of mankind, although it is still not too late to correct this error. I don't know much about wheat, and a specialist would say more than I can, but the article was written in an intolerably fault-finding, not to say perversive manner. You can see at once that this Martius is a typical southerner – a nihilist and a shouter.

Twelve o'clock already and still no sign of Artemida. She's not in the house and there's no sign of her in the garden, and apart from anything else the streets are full of drunken soldiers. She could at least have telephoned to say where she was. I'll get the lot – Hermione will come in and ask what's going on with Artemida. And I've no idea how to reply. I just can't do with that kind of conversation. The question is: how did I come to have such a daughter? The other one, dead now, was a modest girl. She amused herself a little just the once, with the town architect, and amusement was all it was – two or three notes, one letter. And I'd never been a great dog, as Polythemes would put it. I still remember my visit to Madame Persephone with horror. No, such pastimes are not for a civilized man. For all that, love, even the most sensual, is a sacrament, and it is by no means so entertaining to have an affair, even with familiar and well-meaning people, as some books would have it. Good heavens, I certainly don't think that Artemida is indulging in an orgy of drink and bacchanalian dances right now, but she might at least have telephoned. The stupidity of my son-in-law amazes me. In his place I'd have been back long ago.

I was already on the point of closing my diary and going off to bed when the following thought occurred to me. Obviously Charon had had a good reason for staying in Marathon. It's a frightening thought, but I think I can guess what has happened. Can it really be that they've decided on it? Now I can remember all those gatherings under my roof, those strange friends of his with their vulgar habits and appalling manners – some kind of mechanics with coarse voices who drank whisky without soda and smoked revolting cheap cigarettes. As well there were some short-haired shouters with unhealthy complexions who strutted about in jeans and gaudy shirts and never wiped their feet before coming into the house. I can remember all their talk about a world government, about some kind of technocracy and about these unthinkable 'isms' – the organic rejection of everything that guarantees peace and security to the ordinary man. I can remember it all now, and now I understand what has happened. Yes, my son-in-law and his associates were extremists and this is what they've done. All this talk about Martians is obviously the distorted version of something that has really happened. Conspirators have always worshipped fine, mysterious-sounding words, and you can't rule out the possibility that they are calling themselves 'Martians' or some 'society for the improvement of Mars' or even, say, 'The Martian renaissance'. Even the fact that the MA in agriculture bears the name Martius seems to me to be very significant: it's more than likely that he's the leader of the coup. What I cannot understand is the hostility of the putschists to wheat and their unintelligent interest in the gastric juices. Quite likely, it's just a manoeuvre to distract people and bewilder the public.

If Charon has the sense not to remain in the back ranks, then at least I'm assured the first category pension.

June 5th. Last night I slept badly. First I was woken by Artemida, who didn't come home till nearly 1 AM. I had quite decided to speak frankly to her, but nothing came of it: she kissed me goodnight and shut herself up in her bedroom. I had to take a sleeping pill to calm myself. I dozed off and dreamt some kind of nonsense. Then at 4 AM I was woken again, this time by Charon. Everyone is asleep, yet he holds forth to the whole house in a loud voice, as if there were no one there but himself. I threw on my dressing-gown and went into the sitting-room. My God, but it frightened me just to look at him! I realized at once that the coup had not been successful.

He was sitting at the table greedily devouring everything that the sleepy Artemida brought to him: and the oily parts of some kind of gun were scattered on the table too, right on the tablecloth. He was unshaven, his eyes were red and inflamed, his hair dishevelled and sticking up in matted locks, and he gobbled his food like a lavatory attendant. He didn't have a jacket, and I dare say he had arrived at the house in just this state. There was nothing of the chief editor of a small but respectable paper left in him now. His shirt was torn and soiled, his hands were filthy, his fingernails broken, and on his chest you could see some horrible swollen-looking scratches. He didn't even think of greeting me, merely glanced at me with the eyes of a madman and muttered, choking down his food: 'At last, you scum!'

I let this fierce greeting pass, since I could see that the man was not himself, but my heart sank and my legs felt so weak that I was obliged to sit down on the divan without further ado. And Artemida was very frightened – although she tried to hide it in every way. We had no conversation in the normal sense of the word. Trying in vain to control the pounding of my heart I asked Charon if he had had a good trip. In reply he snarled completely unintelligibly that he'd had a bloody awful trip.

I tried to change the topic and direct the conversation into a more peaceful channel, and inquired about the weather at Marathon. He looked at me as if I had insulted him mortally, but in return only snarled into his plate, 'Stupid idiots'. Obviously it was no good talking to him. He swore horribly the whole time – during the course of his meal and when, after he had finished eating, he pushed away the plates with his elbow and started with renewed vigour to sort out the gun parts. In general it went something like this: 'The whole bloody business is in such a bloody state that any bloody wretch can do what he wants with the whole bleeding business and not a single bleeding man will stir a hand to stop all the bleeders carrying on with their filth'.

Poor Artemida stood at his shoulder, wringing her hands, the tears running down her cheeks. From time to time she glanced at me imploringly, but what could I do? I needed help myself – everything had gone black in front of my eyes, like a shroud, from nervous exhaustion. Still keeping up the oaths he fitted his gun together (it turned out to be a modern military automatic), he inserted a cartridge clip and got heavily to his feet, throwing two plates to the floor. My poor little Artemida, her face drained of blood, strained towards him and then he seemed to soften a little.

'Now, now, little girl,' he said, stopping his oaths for a moment and taking her clumsily by the shoulders. 'I could take you with me, but it would hardly make you very happy. I know very well what you're like.'

Even I was tormented by the need for Artemida to find the right words now. And just as if she had caught my telepathy she asked what seemed to me to be a very important question: 'What will happen to us now?' At once I understood that from Charon's point of view these words were quite superfluous.

He thrust his automatic under his arm, slapped Artemida on the bottom and grinning pleasantly said: 'Don't worry, little girl, there'll be nothing new here', after which he headed straight for the door. But I couldn't let him go like that without giving any explanation.

'Just a minute, Charon,' I said, overcoming my weakness, 'just what will happen now? What will they do to us?'

This single question of mine drove him into an indescribable frenzy. He stopped in the doorway, turned halfway round, his knee twitching painfully, hissed the following strange words through his teeth: 'If just one bloody wretch would ask what he should do. But no, every single bloody beast just wants to know what will happen to him. Don't worry, you'll get your heaven on earth.' And with that he went out slamming the door loudly behind him, and a moment later his car engine could be heard muttering as he drove away down the street.

For the next hour I might have been in hell itself. Artemida started something like hysterics, although it looked more like a fit of uncontrollable anger. She broke all the china that was left on the table, snatched hold of the tablecloth and flung it at the television, banged on the door with her fists, and in a stifled voice screamed something that sounded like this: 'So I'm just your fool, am I? Your fool, that's it, isn't it? ... And you? ... And you ... I couldn't care a damn about you! You can do what you want and I'll do what I want! ... Get it? ... Get it? ... Get it? ... You'll come running to me on your knees yet! ...'

I should probably have given her some water, slapped her on the cheeks and all the rest of it, but I myself was lying prostrated on the divan and there was nobody to bring me a validol tablet. Finally Artemida rushed off into her room, without paying any attention to me, and when I had rested a little I dragged myself to my bed and lost consciousness.

The morning turned out overcast and rainy. (Temperature – +17°c; cloud density – 10 degrees; no wind.) Mercifully, I slept through Artemida's explanation to Hermione regarding the chaos in the living-room. I only know that there was a great row and that both of them are now going about sulking. The intention of giving me a dressing-down, too, was written large on Hermione's face, as she poured out the coffee, but she kept her peace. No doubt I'm looking pretty ill – and she's a kind-hearted woman, which is why I respect her. After coffee I was summoning the energy to go out to The Five Clinks when a young messenger-boy appeared on the scene, bringing me a so-called summons, signed by Polythemes. It seems that I am a rank-and-file member of the 'Town Voluntary Anti-Martian Brigade' and I was already directed to 'Present myself on Concord Square by 9 AM having with me a gun, or some other weapon, and food rations for three days'. What does he think I am, some raw youth? Of course, I didn't go anywhere, on principle.

Myrtil, who is still living in his tent, told me that farmers had been arriving at the town hall since dawn, collecting sacks of the new cereal and carrying it off to use on their farms. Supposedly, this year's standing wheat harvest, doomed to destruction, was being bought up by the Government on advantageous terms, and deposits were also being taken on the new cereal harvest. The farmers suspect the usual shady agrarian transactions, but while neither money nor written undertakings are demanded from them they don't know what to think. Myrtil assures me (!) that there are no Martians, because life on Mars is impossible. There is just a new agrarian policy. However, he's ready to leave the town at any moment and he, too, has taken a sack of the new seed, just in case. The same as yesterday, there's nothing but wheat and gastric juices in the papers. If it goes on like this much longer I'll give up my subscription. On the radio – nothing but wheat and gastric juices too. I've stopped listening to it already and just watch the television, where everything is as it was before the coup. Mr Nikostratos turned up in his car, Artemida rushed out to meet him and they rolled off together. I don't want to think about it.

Since the babble about wheat and gastric juices hasn't come to an end it seems that the coup has been successful after all. No doubt Charon, with the quarrelsome nature peculiar to him, hadn't got what he wanted, had fought with the gang there and had found himself in the opposition. I'm afraid that there's still trouble in store for us because of him. When madmen like Charon get hold of an automatic they shoot. Good God, will there ever be a time when I don't have any worries?

June 6th. Temperature – +16°C; cloud density – 9 degrees; wind – south-westerly, 6 metres per second. I've mended the wind-gauge.

June 7th. My eye is still hurting, my eyelid is swollen and I can't see anything through it. It's a good thing it's my left eye. Achilles' eye-lotion doesn't help much. Achilles says that the bruise will be visible for at least a week. At the moment it's reddish-blue, then it will turn green, then yellow and then it will disappear entirely. All the same, what cruel, uncultured behaviour: to strike an elderly man, who had done nothing more than ask an innocent question. If the Martians begin like this, heaven knows how they'll finish. But complaining won't do any good – there's only one thing left to do: wait for the situation to clear up. My eye is so sore that it's an effort even to remember how much the calm morning delighted me. (Temperature – +20°C; cloud density – 0 degrees; wind – southerly, 1 metre per second.)

When I went up to the attic after breakfast to carry out some meteorological observations I noticed, with some surprise, that the fields beyond the town had taken on a distinctly bluish tinge. In the distance the fields had so merged with the azure of the sky that the line of the horizon was completely indistinct, even although the air was beautifully clear and there was absolutely no haze. This new Martian seed has come up remarkably quickly. It looks as if it will wipe out the wheat completely in a matter of days.

Coming into the square I saw that almost the whole of our

group, and besides them a great number of other townsfolk, such as farmers, who should have been at work at this time, and schoolboys, who should have been playing games, were crowding round three large vans, which had been decorated with different-coloured placards and posters. I would have guessed that it was a travelling circus, especially since the posters invited one to admire the incomparable rope-walkers and other unusual heroes of the arena, but Morpheus, who had been there for some time already, explained to me that it was not a circus, but a mobile donor point. Inside them were special pumps and hoses and beside each pump sat a hefty young fellow in a doctor's gown, who invited everyone who came near to have their excesses drawn off, and who paid remarkably highly: five roubles per glass.

'What excesses?' I asked. It turned out to be gastric-juice excesses. The whole world was obsessed with gastric juice. 'Is it really the Martians?' I asked.

'What Martians?' said Morpheus. 'They're just great, hairy fellows. One of them's lost an eye.'

'And what's proved by the fact that he's lost an eye?' I objected quite naturally. 'A member of any race, whether on Earth or on Mars, will lose the use of an eye if it is injured.' I didn't know then that my words were prophetic. Simply, Morpheus's self-importance irritated me.

'Well, I've never heard of one-eyed Martians,' he declared. The people round about were listening to our conversation and, in a fit of vainglory, he decided that it was necessary to boost his doubtful reputation as a debater. And yet he doesn't understand the first thing about the art of debate! 'Those aren't Martians,' he announced. 'They're ordinary fellows from the suburbs of the capital. You can see a dozen like them in every bar.'

'Our information concerning Mars is so meagre,' I said calmly, 'that to suggest that Martians are like fellows from the suburban bars would certainly not contradict any scientific evidence.'

'That's right,' butted in an unknown farmer who was standing beside us. 'You said that most convincingly, Mr I-don't-know-what-your-name-is. That one-eyed character has got his arm tattooed right up to the elbow, nothing but naked women too. He rolled up his sleeves and bore down on me with that hose – and I thought to myself, no, we won't need the likes of him.'

'So what does science have to say regarding Martian tattooing?' Morpheus asked maliciously. He thought he'd catch me with that. A cheap approach, just what you'd expect from a hairdresser. You won't get me with that kind of trick.

'The chief astronomer of the Marathon observatory, Professor Zephyr,' I said, looking him straight in the eyes, 'does not deny the existence of such a habit among the Martians in a single one of his many articles.'

'That's quite right,' the farmer corroborated me. 'And astronomers wear glasses, so they can see better.'

Morpheus had to swallow it all. He developed a sudden coughing fit and with the words 'I need a glass of beer' made his way out of the crowd. I stayed on, however, to see what more would happen.

For some time there was nothing. Everyone just stood around gaping and chatting quietly. Farmers and tradesmen – an indecisive crew. And then someone started to move at the front. Some rural fellow suddenly tore off his straw hat, trod it beneath his feet with all his might, and shouted out loudly: 'Well, so what? Five roubles . . . it's all money, isn't it?'

With these words he walked decisively up the steps and pushed his way through the door of the van, so that all we could see was his back, muddy and covered with feathers. What he said and what he asked – we couldn't make out because of the distance. I could only see that at first his pose was tense, and then he seemed to relax, started shifting about from one foot to the other, thrust his hands in his pockets and, stepping backwards, shook his head. Then he cautiously let himself down to the ground, without looking at anyone, picked up his hat, shook the dust from it carefully and disappeared into the crowd. A man, who was certainly very tall and certainly had only one eye, appeared in the doorway of the van. If it weren't for his white gown, what with the black bandage across his face, his unshaven stubble and hairy tattooed arms, he would have looked just like the criminal inhabitant of some vile den. Looking at us gloomily he slowly rolled down his sleeves, took out a cigarette and, lighting it, said in a coarse voice: 'Well, come along in then. Five roubles a time. Five roubles a time. Five roubles for every glass. Real money! Ready cash. How long do you sweat to earn your-selves five roubles? Here you just swallow a tube and it's done. Well, what about it?'

I looked at him and felt amazed at the short-sightedness of the administration. How could anyone reckon that the man in the street, even a farmer, would be willing to entrust his organism to such a thug? I made my way out of the crowd and went off to The Five Clinks.

Our group were there already, all of them with shotguns and some of them with white bands on their sleeves. Poly-themes had struggled into his old uniform cap, and was de-livering a speech from a bench, with the sweat pouring off his face. According to him, the infamous behaviour of the Martians had become absolutely intolerable; the hearts of all patriots were bleeding in anguish under their yoke; and the time had come, at last, to repulse them once and for all. And it was deserters and traitors such as fat-bottomed, guzzling generals, the chemist Achilles, the coward Myrtil and that recreant Apollo, he maintained, who were responsible for it all.

My eyes saw red when I heard the last words. I quite lost the power of speech and only came to my senses when I noticed that, apart from me, nobody was listening to Poly-themes. They weren't listening to that one-legged fool, but to Silen, who had just returned from the town hall and was saying that from now the payment of taxes would only be accepted in gastric juice, and that an edict had come from Marathon, putting gastric juices on the same footing as or-dinary coinage. Now, apparently, gastric juice will be just as valid as money, and all savings and other banks will be pre-pared to change it for currency.

Paral at once remarked: 'So it's finally come to that. They've squandered the gold reserves and now they're trying to insure the currency with gastric juice.'

'How can that work?' said Dimant. 'I don't understand! Does it mean they'll have to bring in special glass containers shaped like purses? And what if I bring them water instead of gastric juice?'

'Listen, Silen,' said Morpheus, 'I owe you ten roubles. Will you take it in juice?' He was quite transformed – he never had enough money for a drink and was always getting other people to pay for him. 'It's a great age, lads,' he exclaimed. 'For example, if I want to have a drink now, I go off to the bank, divide out my excesses, get some ready cash and – off to the bar.'

At this point Polythemes began to shout with renewed vigour. 'You've been bought!' he yelled. 'You've sold yourselves to the Martians for gastric juice. You've sold yourselves and they're driving round the town as if it were their own Mars!'

And in actual fact a very strange vehicle, black in colour, and apparently quite bare of wheels, doors or windows, was moving slowly and completely silently across the square. Small boys ran after it, shouting and whistling, and some of them tried to clamber on to the back of it, but it was as smooth as a grand piano and there was nothing to cling to. A very strange vehicle.

'It can't really be a Martian vehicle can it?' I asked.

'Well, who else does it belong to?' said Polythemes in an irritated tone. 'Is it yours?'

'Nobody's saying it's mine,' I objected. 'There are enough cars in the world, why should they all belong to the Martians?'

'And I'm not saying they're all Martian, you old fool!' yelled Polythemes. 'I'm saying that the Martians, the skunks, are driving about the town as if it belonged to them! And you lot have all sold yourselves.'

I merely shrugged my shoulders, not wanting to become involved, but Silen rebuked him sharply. 'Excuse me, Polythemes, but your shrieks are beginning to annoy me. And not just me. In my opinion we have all carried out our duty. We've joined the brigade, cleaned our guns; just what more do you want, I'd like to know?'

'Patrols! We need patrols!' said Polythemes tearfully. 'We must close the roads. We mustn't let the Martians into the town!'

'And how will you stop them from getting past?'

'Oh, to the devil with you, Silen. How will I stop them getting past? Very simply! – Stop, who goes there? Stop or I'll shoot!'

I can't take that kind of talk. He's not a man – he's a military barracks.

'Well, we could form patrols,' said Dimant. 'But we'll find it a bit difficult won't we?'

'That's not our job,' I said firmly. 'Silen here will tell you that it's illegal. That's what the Army's for. Let the Army form the patrols and do the shooting.'

I cannot abide these military games, especially when it's Polythemes in charge. It's just like a kind of sadism. I remember when we had some anti-atomic bomb training in the town, and to make it more real Polythemes threw smoke-boxes all round, so that nobody would shirk using their gas masks. And the number of people who were poisoned – a real nightmare. Besides, he's a non-commissioned officer and you can't trust anything to him. And once he burst into a school gym class, swore at the teacher in foul language and started to demonstrate the goose-step to the children. If they put him in a patrol he'd be firing at everybody with his shotgun until people would refuse to bring rations into the town. Let him have a good go at the Martians and in revenge they'll take the town and burn it. But, my God, old men are like children. Tell them to form a patrol and – they'll form a patrol. I spat ostentatiously and went into the town hall.

Mr Nikostratos was polishing his fingernails and answered my confused questions roughly like this: under the new conditions the financial policy of the Government was changing somewhat. From now on the so-called gastric juices would play an important role in monetary affairs. One could expect that gastric juices would soon be used in the same way as money. As yet there were no special instructions concerning pensions, but there was good reason to suppose that once taxes were accepted in the so-called gastric juice, then pensions, too, would be paid in the so-called gastric juice. My heart sank but I plucked up courage and asked Mr Nikostratos straight out whether I would be wrong in taking his words to mean that this so-called gastric juice was not, properly speaking, gastric juice, but represented some symbol of the new financial policy.

Mr Nikostratos shrugged his shoulders vaguely and, continuing to examine his nails, announced: 'Gastric juice, Mr Apollo, is gastric juice'.

'And what do I want with gastric juice?' I asked in complete despair.

He shrugged his shoulders for a second time and observed: 'You know very well that gastric juice is vital to every human being'. It was quite plain to me that Mr Nikostratos was either lying or keeping something back. I was in such despair that I demanded an interview with the mayor. But I was refused. Then I left the town hall and enrolled in the patrol.

If a man who has given thirty years of unblemished service in the field of human enlightenment is offered as a reward a phial of gastric juice, then that man is quite entitled to demonstrate his dissatisfaction as much as he wants. It's not really important whether the Martians are to blame or not. I can't abide anarchistic behaviour, but I'm ready to take up arms for my rights. And although everyone can see that my protest has a purely symbolic character, they can think about this, and know this: they're not dealing with a dumb animal. Certainly, if the donor points were systematized, and if ordinary banks and savings banks did in fact accept gastric juice in exchange for currency, then I would have a different attitude to it all. But the only one to talk about savings banks has been Silen, so for the moment it is nothing more than unsubstantiated rumour. On the subject of donor points, however, Morpheus, who had enrolled in the patrol and decided to celebrate the fact straight away put himself in the hands of the one-eyed thug and returned with red, tear-stained eyes and, showing us a shining new five-rouble piece, told us that the vans were leaving. Which means that there's no question of any system: they've come and they've gone. If you managed to give your excesses – fine; if you didn't – so much the worse for you. In my opinion it's disgraceful.

Polythemes appointed the stutterer Kalaid and myself to patrol Concord Square, and the streets adjacent, from twelve to two AM. Having given us identification cards made out by Silen, he slapped me on the back with great emotion and said: 'The old guard! We won't give these filthy scum any help, will we, Feb? I knew you'd be with us when it came to the crunch.'

We embraced and both shed a few tears. Basically Polythemes is really not a bad sort, it's just that he wants people to obey him unquestioningly. A quite understandable desire. I asked his permission to be dismissed and set off to see Achilles. A patrol is all very well, but one has to take some provision on one's own account. I asked Achilles what gastric juices were, who needed them and what were their uses? Achilles said that one needed this juice to digest one's food properly and for nothing apart from that. I didn't need him to tell me that.

'Soon I'll be able to offer you a large dose of this so-called gastric juice,' I said. 'Will you take it?'

He said he would think it over and proposed swapping my incomplete zoological series for an indentated '28 airmail stamp. There's no doubt about it, an indentated stamp is pretty well unique, but the one Achilles has is double-franked and has a greasy spot on it. I don't know. I really don't.

As I came out of the chemist's I saw the Martian vehicle again. Maybe it was the same one and maybe it was another. Breaking all the rules for street traffic it was bearing along in the middle of the road, moving at walking speed, it's true, so that I could examine it thoroughly – I was on my way to the bar and took the same road. My first impression seemed quite correct – more than anything else the vehicle resembled a dusty grand piano with streamlined contours. From time to time something sparked underneath it and it bobbed up and down slightly, but evidently this was not a fault, since it continued to move implacably forward without halting for a second. Even from a short distance I couldn't make out door or windows. But more than anything else I was struck by the absence of wheels. True, my build did not permit me to stoop low enough to look underneath it. Probably there were wheels there all the same – it's quite impossible for there not to be any wheels at all.

Suddenly the vehicle stopped. And right enough it stopped in front of Mr Laomedontes' villa. I remember that I thought bitterly – well, for some people it really doesn't make any difference who it is, whether it's a new president or an old president, the Martians or anybody else. Any new power always treats them with far more respect and attention than they deserve. Whereas, as far as respect is concerned, they deserve the opposite. However, something quite unexpected now took place. Guessing correctly that somebody would get out of the vehicle, and that at last I would glimpse a live Martian, I stopped in a corner to watch, along with some other passers-by, whose thoughts clearly coincided with my own. To our

amazement and disappointment, however, no Martians got out
of the vehicle but some very fine young men in narrow coats
and identical berets. Three of them went up to the front door
and rang while another two, their hands thrust deep into their
coat pockets, arranged themselves in careless poses beside the
vehicle, leaning on different parts of its body. The front door
opened, the three went inside, and at once strange, not very
loud, sounds could be heard from within. It was just as if one
of them had started carelessly shifting the furniture about and
the others had started to beat the carpet with measured blows.
The two who had remained beside the vehicle didn't pay any
attention to this noise. They remained in their former poses:
one of them looked absent-mindedly along the street, while
the other, yawning, cast his eye over the upper storey of the
house. When a moment later my humiliator, Mr Laomedontes'
chauffeur, like a blind man walked slowly and cautiously out
of the front door they didn't change their poses either. His face
was white, his mouth wide open, his eyes bulging and glassy
and both hands were pressed to his stomach. He got on to the
pavement, took a few steps, sat down with a groan, stayed sitting for a few moments, stooping more and more, then fell
over heavily on to his back, writhed, pawed the ground and lay
deathly still. I must admit that at first I couldn't understand
anything. It all took place so unhurriedly, in such a peaceful,
workmanlike manner and against the background of such normal town noise, that at first the feeling was born in me that
this was something which ought to happen. I felt no dis-
quiet and sought no explanation. I simply trusted these young
men who were so refined-looking and so restrained ... At this
point one of them absent-mindedly glanced at the recumbent
chauffeur, lit a cigarette, and once again continued his
examination of the upper storey. It even seemed to me that he
was smiling. Then the clatter of feet could be heard and out of
the door, one after the other, walked: one young man in a
narrow coat, wiping his lips with a handkerchief; Mr Laomedontes in a luxurious Oriental dressing-gown, without a hat
and in handcuffs; the second young man in a narrow coat, who
was in the middle of taking off his gloves; and, finally, the
third young man in a narrow coat, loaded with guns. With his
right hand he was clutching three or four sub-machine-guns to
his chest, and in his left hand he carried several pistols, his

fingers thrust through the trigger-guards, and, apart from that, light machine guns were hanging from each shoulder. I only looked at Mr Laomedontes once and that was quite enough for me – the impression of something red, wet and sticky has remained in my mind ever since. The whole cavalcade crossed the pavement at a leisurely pace and hid itself in the womb of the vehicle. The two young men who had been leaning against the polished side of the vehicle now straightened themselves casually, walked up to the recumbent chauffeur, took him carefully by the arms and legs, swung him slightly and threw him into the entrance of the house. Then one of them took a piece of paper from his pocket and pinned it neatly to the doorbell, after which the vehicle, without first turning round, moved off at its former speed in the opposite direction. The two remaining young men, with the most unassuming air, passed through the crowd, which parted for them, and disappeared round a corner.

When I recovered from the stupor, into which the suddenness and strangeness of what had just taken place had plunged me, and re-discovered the power of reflection, I experienced something in the nature of a psychological earthquake. It was as if a turning-point in history had been accomplished in front of my eyes. I'm sure that the other witnesses experienced something similar. We all jostled each other in front of the doorway, but nobody could pluck up the courage to go in. I put on my glasses and over the heads of the rest read the proclamation which had been pinned beneath the doorbell. It read: 'Narcotics are the poison and disgrace of the nation! The time has come to put an end to them. We will wipe them out and you will help us. We will punish mercilessly those who spread narcotics.'

If our group had been there it would have made a topic of conversation for a good two hours, but here everybody merely muttered and grunted, unable to overcome their habitual timidity. 'I-yi-yi-yi . . .' 'Well, think of that!' 'Ohhhh . . .' 'Good God! . . .' Someone sent for the police and a doctor. The doctor went into the house and set to work on the chauffeur. Then Panderei turned up in a police jeep. He hung around the doorway, read through the proclamation several times, scratched the back of his head and even glanced through the door, but was too cowardly to go inside – although the doctor shouted to him crossly and called him some very rude names. He stood in the doorway, shuffling from one foot to the other, thrusting his palms into his belt and puffing himself up like a turkey cock. With the appearance of the police, the crowd became slightly more bold and started talking more freely. 'So that's their way, eh?' 'Yes, you can see it all there, it's all plain ...' 'Very interesting, very interesting, gentlemen!' 'I'd never have believed it ...' I felt uneasy that their tongues were becoming loosened and I would have liked to get away, but curiosity was overcoming me.

At this point, however, Silen turned to Panderei with a direct question: 'And so the law has triumphed after all, Pan? You finally made up your minds?'

Panderei pursed his lips significantly and said hesitantly: 'I don't think *we* decided on this'.

'What do you mean, *you* didn't? Well, who did then?'

'I suppose it was the gendarmerie from the capital,' said Panderei in a stage whisper, glancing to either side of him.

'What kind of a gendarmerie is that?' came objections from the crowd. 'A gendarmerie that suddenly appears in a Martian vehicle! No, that's no gendarmerie.'

'Well, who do you think it was then? The Martians themselves, eh?'

Panderei puffed himself up still further and barked out: 'Hey! Who's that talking about Martians? Take care!' But nobody was paying any attention to him now. The tongues had finally become completely unloosened.

'Maybe it was a Martian vehicle, but those weren't Martians, that's for sure. They behave like human beings.'

'Quite right! And why should Martians worry about narcotics either?'

'A new broom sweeps clean, you know, old fellow.'

'And why should the Martians worry about our gastric juices?'

'No, gentlemen, those weren't men. They were too calm, too silent. Do you get my meaning? I think they were, in fact, Martians. They work like machines.'

'That's it, machines! Robots. Why should Martians dirty their hands? They've got robots to do their work for them.'

Panderei, unable to restrain himself, added a suggestion too.

'No, lads,' he announced. 'Those weren't robots. It's a new system we've got. They're only taking deaf-mutes into the gendarmerie now. In the interests of guarding State secrets.'

This hypothesis caused astonishment and then malicious rejoinders, most of them very witty, but I can only remember the observation made by Paral who expressed himself in this vein : that it wouldn't be a bad thing only to take deaf-mutes into the police force, not in the interest of guarding State secrets, but in the interests of protecting entirely innocent people from the utter tripe loosed at them by these officials.

Panderei, who had earlier unbuttoned his tunic, now immediately buttoned it up again and roared: 'You've said your bit – that's all!' So unfortunately we had to disperse although the ambulance was driving up at just that moment. That old donkey got into a rage so that we could only watch from a distance as they carried the mutilated chauffeur from the entrance. Then to our surprise they carried out two more bodies. It's still not known who these two were.

All our chaps went off to the pub, and so did I. Those same two young men in the tight coats had settled themselves down comfortably at the bar. They were as calm and silent as before, just drinking gin and staring into space. I ordered a complete meal and, having satisfied my hunger, watched the more curious of our group gradually edging their way towards the young men. It was amusing to see how clumsily Morpheus tried to start up a conversation with them on the subject of the weather in Marathon, while Paral, in an attempt to take the bull by the horns, offered to buy them a drink. The young men seemed oblivious of everyone around them, they promptly swallowed the drinks thrust in front of them, and direct questions they seemed not to hear at all. I didn't know what to think. At moments I delighted in their extraordinary self-control, their complete indifference to all the absurd attempts to draw them into conversation, at other moments I inclined towards the idea that they really were Martian robots, that the repulsive appearance of the Martians prevented them from being seen in person; and there were moments when I suspected them of being actual Martians – of whom up to now we knew essentially nothing. Our chaps got cheekier, began crowding round the young men and, dropping all restraint, started discussing their characters, while some of the bolder ones even felt the material of their coats. Everyone was now convinced that they were faced with robots.

Japheth even started to get worried. Bringing me a brandy he said: 'How can they be robots? – they've had two gins, two brandies, two packets of cigarettes, and who's going to pay?'

I explained that a robot which had been programmed to take into account a need for drink and cigarettes must surely have had taken into account some device for the payment of the goods required. Japheth calmed down, but at that moment a brawl broke out at the bar.

I learnt afterwards that Paral had had a bet with Dimant the donkey that nothing would happen if Dimant pressed a lighted cigarette against the hand of the robot. What I saw with my own eyes was this: Dimant suddenly shot like a cork out of the crowd of people amusing themselves around the robots; on swiftly gyrating legs he flew backwards across the length of the room knocking over tables and people coming into the bar and collapsed in a corner. Hardly a second passed before Paral emerged in exactly the same way, landing in another corner. Our chaps scattered and I, not understanding anything of what had happened at the time, saw the young men sitting at the bar as calmly as ever and with the self-same gesture thoughtfully raising their glasses of alcohol to their lips.

Paral and Dimant were lifted up and dragged away somewhere behind the scenes. I went to find out what had happened. I arrived just as Dimant was coming round. He was sitting up with the most idiotic expression on his face, feeling his chest. Paral had not yet returned to consciousness, but was already swallowing gin washed down with soda. Next to him, holding a towel ready, stood a waitress, preparing to bandage his jaw when he came to. It was there that I discovered the version of the events which I have recorded above, and I agreed with the others that Paral was a provocateur and Dimant simply an idiot, no better than Panderei. However, having made these sensible observations, our chaps were not content. They took it into their heads that the affair could not be left at that. Polythemes, who had kept to the sidelines till then, announced that this would be the first act of war of our fighting brigade. We would get these young thugs as they left the inn, he said, and began issuing commands, which of us should stand where, and when we should begin to fight. I washed my hands of this venture at once. In the first place I am opposed to force in general, there is definitely nothing of the officer in me, in the second place I could see no particular guilt on the side of the two young men. And, finally, I was planning not to fight them, but to talk to them about my own affairs. I slipped quietly out of the corridor and returned to my table and it was in so doing that I, in fact, set in motion events which were to prove so embittering for me.

Incidentally, even now, when I look back on the experiences of that day through quite different eyes, I must observe that the logic of my actions remains unimpeachable. The young men were not from our parts, I reasoned. The fact that they had arrived in a Martian car indicated that they were most likely from the capital. Moreover, the part they had played in the liquidation of Mr Laomedontes was indisputable evidence that they were connected with the powers that be; they would hardly send some common agent to deal with Mr Laomedontes. Thus, out of the very logic of things, flowed the conclusion that the young men must necessarily be well informed on the new situation and could tell me much on the questions that interested me. In my position as the small man, jeered at by Mr Laomedontes' chauffeur, refused information by the town hall secretary, I could not afford to let slip such an opportunity to get accurate information. On the other hand, the young men did not arouse any apprehension in me. The fact that they had dealt with Mr Laomedontes and his bodyguard somewhat severely, did not put me on my guard. They were doing their duty and that had been Mr Laomedontes, who had long ago had it coming to him. As for the incident with Paral and Dimant, well Dimant is so stupid it's impossible to have dealings with him, and Paral can exasperate anyone with acrid wit. Not to mention that I myself would not allow anyone to call me a robot and, moreover, press a burning cigarette into my hand.

So, when I had finished my brandy, I started to make my way towards the young men. I was quite confident in the success of my undertaking. I had thought out all the details of the projected conversation, taking into account both the nature of their activities and their mood in relation to the incident that had just taken place, and their obvious natural quietness and reserve. I meant to apologize first for the wretched behaviour of my fellow citizens. Then I would introduce myself, expressing the hope that I was not imposing on them with my conversation. I would give them some advice on the quality of the brandy, which Japheth frequently dilutes with cheaper varieties, and would offer them a drink from my personal bottle. And only then, when we had discussed the weather in Marathon and in our town, did I intend, delicately and gently, to pass to the basic question. As I headed towards them I noted that one of them was absorbed in smoking a cigarette. The other one was turned away from the bar and attentively and, it seemed to me, with interest, following my progress towards them. For this reason I decided to address myself directly to him. As I came up I raised my hat and said 'Good evening!' Then that young thug made a lazy movement with his shoulder and immediately a grenade seemed to explode in my head. I don't remember anything. I only remember that I lay for a long time in the corridor beside Paral, swallowing gin, washed down with soda, while someone pressed a cold wet towel to my injured eye.

And now I ask myself: what more could you expect? No one came to my aid, no one raised their voice in protest. The same thing was happening again. Young thugs terrorizing people again, beating up citizens, in the streets. And when Polythemes brought me home in his invalid chair, my daughter, as indifferent as everyone else, was kissing Mister Secretary in the garden. But no, even if I had known how it would all end, I would still have felt obliged to try to start up a conversation with them. I would have been more careful, I wouldn't have gone near them, but who else is going to give me information? I don't want to have to tremble over every penny I spend, I haven't the strength to go on giving lessons any more, I don't want to sell the house in which I have lived so many years. All I want is my peace of mind.

June 8th. Temperature 17°C; cloud density – 8 degrees; wind – southerly, 3 metres per second. I'm at home, I don't go out and I don't see anyone. The swelling has gone down and the injured spot hardly hurts at all, but the general appearance is ugly all the same. All day I have been looking through my stamps and watching television. In town everything is as it was. Yesterday night our golden youth besieged Madame Persephones' establishment which was taken over by soldiers. They say there was a regular battle.

The papers say nothing much. Not a word about the embargo – you'd think it had been completely abolished. There was a strange speech by the minister for war, full of small print, about how our participation in the Military Union was a burden for the country and not so justifiable as it might seem at first glance. Thank God they've realized that, after eleven years! But the main news is about a farmer called Periphant, remarkable in that he is able to give up to four litres of gastric juices in one day without any ill-effects to his own organism. His difficult life story is told with many intimate details, there is a report of an interview with him and scenes from his life have been shown several times on television. A sturdy rough-looking man of about forty-five, completely unintelligent – to see him you would never think that you were confronted by such a surprising phenomenon. He continually stressed his habit of sucking a piece of sugar in the mornings. I must try it.

Yes, of course! In the paper there's an article by the veterinary surgeon Kalaid about the harmfulness of narcotics. Kalaid says straight out that the regular use of narcotics by heavy horned cattle is without exception damaging to the production of gastric juices. There's even a diagram. It's an interesting observation: Kalaid's article has it all in black and white, but it's unbearably difficult to read, as if he were writing with the hiccups. But the general impression is that Mr Laomedontes was done away with because he prevented citizens from giving gastric juices freely. It gives the impression that gastric juices represents some sort of corner stone of new Government policy. It's unprecedented, but if you think about it, why not?

I've just come back from a visit with Hermione. Over supper she said that a donor's point for the collection of stomach juices was being set up in the former residence of Mr Laomedontes. If this is true, I approve and support the move. I am generally for all setting up of points and for stability.

My little stamps, dear little stamps! Only you never upset me.

June 9th. Temperature 16°C; cloud density – 5 degrees; slight rain. The swelling has completely disappeared. However, as Achilles predicted, all the area around the eye has turned an ugly green. It's impossible to go out: never mind, apart from stupid jokes, you don't hear anything worthwhile. In the morning I rang the town hall, but Mr Nikostratos chose to be in a humorous mood and told me absolutely nothing on the subject of the pension. Of course, I got worked up, tried to calm myself with the stamps, but even the stamps couldn't soothe me. I sent Hermione to get me some sedatives, but she came back empty-handed. It seems Achilles had received a special circular telling him to issue sedatives only on the prescription of a city doctor. I lost my temper and rang him, started an argument, but to be honest, how is he to blame? A strict check is being kept on all medicines containing narcotics by the police and others specially empowered by the town hall. But what can you do? If you cut down a forest, chips will fly. I had a glass of whisky, right in front of Hermione. It helped. I even felt better, and not a squeak out of Hermione.

In the morning Myrtil's family – he's still living in the tent – came back. To tell the truth, I was pleased. It was a real sign that the situation in the country was becoming stabilized. But suddenly after lunch I saw that Myrtil was once again seeing them all on to the bus. What was happening? 'All right, all right,' Myrtil replied in his usual manner. 'You're all the clever ones around here, and I'm a fool ...'

It appeared he had been to The Five Clinks and had found out there that both the treasurer and the architect were to be called by the Martians to answer for embezzlement of funds and intrigue; they had already been summoned somewhere. I tried to explain to Myrtil that this was a good thing and that it was just, but it was hopeless. 'OK,' he said. 'Just, is it? Today the treasurer and the architect, tomorrow the mayor, the day after, I don't know who, me perhaps. It's no good. They gave you one in the eye – is that just too?' I just can't talk to him. Let him be.

Mr Coribanth rang me. He, it seems, is replacing Charon on the paper. His voice trembled pitifully. The paper was having some kind of unpleasantness with the authorities. He begged me to tell him whether Charon would be back soon. I, of course, spoke to him very sympathetically but didn't say a word about the fact that Charon had already been back once. I felt intuitively that it wasn't worth spreading that about. God knew where Charon was now and what he was doing. All I needed was unpleasantness over politics. I don't talk about him to anyone myself and I have forbidden Artemida and Hermione to do so. Hermione understood at once, but Artemida made a scene.

June 11th. Only now am I more or less myself again, although I am still just as sick and exhausted. And I am constantly dogged by sinister phantoms which I would like to shake off, but can't. I can understand going off with a gun to kill when it's kill or be killed. That, too, is distasteful and nasty, but at least it's normal. But no one is forcing them. Partisans! I know very well what that means, but how could I have expected that in my declining years I would see it once again with my own eyes?

It all began when yesterday morning, against all expectations, I received a very friendly reply from General Alcimes. He wrote that he remembered me well, had liked me very much and wished me all the best. His letter excited me so much, I just didn't know what to do with myself. I consulted Hermione and she was obliged to agree that such an opportunity wasn't to be missed. There was just one thing that worried both of us – the troubled times. But at that moment we saw Myrtil roll up his temporary shelter and begin carrying his things back into the house. This was the deciding stroke. Hermione made me a very elegant black bandage for my injured eye, I took the bundle of documents, got into my car and set off for Marathon.

The weather favoured me. I drove peacefully down the empty highway between the blue fields and thought over various possible courses of action, depending on different circumstances. However, as usual the unforeseen soon happened. About forty miles from town, the motor began to cough, the car began to lurch and to pull badly and then stopped altogether. This happened at the top of a hill and when I got out on to the highway a peaceful country scene opened up before me. It's true it looked a little unusual because of the blueness of the ripening ears of grain. I remember that, in spite of the delay, I was completely calm and didn't restrain myself from admiring the neat, white farms scattered in the distance. The blue wheat stood very tall, reaching a man's height in places. Never before had such an abundant harvest flourished in our district. The highway, straight as an arrow, could be seen right to the horizon.

I opened the bonnet and examined the motor for a while hoping to locate the fault, but I'm too hopeless a mechanic and I despaired very soon, straightened my tired back and looked around, trying to decide where to turn for help. However, the nearest farm was too far away and on the highway I could see only one car, approaching from the direction of Marathon at quite a speed. At first I was cheered but soon to my great disappointment I saw that it was one of the black Martian cars. I didn't give up hope altogether though, since I remembered that ordinary people also drove about in Martian cars. The prospect of deciding which didn't attract me very much, I feared that the occupants might nevertheless turn out to be Martians, whom I instinctively feared. But what else was there for me to do? I stretched out my hand across the road and took a few steps towards the car which had already reached the foot of the hill. And then a terrible thing happened.

The car was about fifty yards from me when suddenly something exploded with a yellow flash. The car appeared to stand on end. A thunderous bang rang out, the highway was lost in a cloud of smoke. Then I saw the car apparently trying to take to the air; it had already risen above the cloud lurching sharply on its side, but then two more flashes burst one after another alongside it. The double blow overturned it, and it crashed with all its weight to the asphalt so that I felt the earth shudder under my legs, which were in any case giving way under the impact of the unexpectedness of it all. 'What a terrible smash,' I thought in the first moment. The car was beginning to burn and some black, flaming figures were climbing out of it. At that moment shots broke out. I couldn't see who was shooting, where the shots were coming from, but I clearly saw who they were shooting at. The black figures stumbled about in the smoke and flames and fell, one after another. Through the crackle of gunfire I heard their heartrending inhuman screams and then they all lay spread out beside the overturned car which continued to burn; but the shooting still didn't stop. Then the car exploded with a terrible crash, an unearthly white light hit me in the eyes and thick burning air slapped me in the face. I involuntarily shut my eyes and when I opened them again I was horrified to see, coming towards me along the highway, and leaping like an enormous monkey, a black creature enveloped in flames and trailing a tail of black soot. At that moment a man sprang out of the blue wheat fields on my left, wearing a military uniform and holding a gun at the ready. He stopped in the middle of the road with his back to me, squatted down quickly and started shooting at the flaming black figure, almost point-blank. My horror was so great that the initial numbness left me and I found in myself the strength to turn around and run towards my car as fast as my legs would take me. Like a madman I pressed the starter, blind to everything in front of me, and forgetting that the motor wasn't working; then my strength ebbed again and I remained sitting in my car, staring stupidly in front of me, the passive and deafened witness of a terrible tragedy.

Indifference overwhelmed me. As if in a dream I saw armed men coming into the road one after another, I saw them surround the site of the disaster and bend over the burning bodies, turning them over and exchanging brief shouts hardly audible over the noise of the blood beating in my temples.

Four of them had gathered at the foot of the hill, but the man in the military uniform – an officer judging by the epaulettes – stood in his former place a few paces from the last man killed and was reloading his automatic. Then I saw him unhurriedly approach the man on the ground, lower the barrel of the automatic and give a short burst of fire. Then the most frightful part of all began.

The officer glanced swiftly over the sky, then turned and looked at me – I will never forget his cold, merciless glance – and, holding his automatic at the ready, he headed towards my car. I heard those standing below shout something to him, but he didn't turn around. He was walking towards me. I probably even lost consciousness for a few seconds because I don't remember any more until the moment when I came to, standing alongside my car in front of that officer and two more of the rebels. God, what people! All three were long unshaven and dirty and their clothes were grubby and ragged; the officer's uniform, too, was in a terrible state. The officer wore a cap, one of the civilians had a black beret, the other was wearing glasses and had no headgear at all.

'Are you deaf or something?' the officer was saying sharply, shaking me by the shoulder.

The man in the beret grimaced and said through set teeth: 'Leave him alone. What do you want with him?'

I gathered together what remained of my feeble strength and forced myself to speak calmly, I realized my life was at stake. 'What is it you want?' I asked.

'He's just an ordinary person,' said the man in the beret. 'He doesn't know anything and doesn't want to know anything.'

'Just a minute, engineer,' said the officer irritably. 'Who are you?' he asked me. 'What are you doing here?'

I hid nothing, explained everything to him, and while I talked he kept looking around, examining the sky, for all the world as if he were afraid of rain.

The man in the beret interrupted me once to shout: 'I don't want to risk it. I'm going, you do what you want!' After which he turned and ran down the hill. But the other two remained and heard me out to the end, while I tried to guess from their faces what my fate was to be − I didn't see anything that augured well for me there.

A saving thought came into my head and forgetting everything else I blurted out: 'Bear in mind, sirs, that I'm the father-in-law of Mr Charon'.

'Who's Charon?' asked the rebel in glasses.

'The chief editor of the local paper.'

'So what?' asked the rebel in glasses, and the officer went on looking at the sky.

I got confused: they obviously didn't know Charon. But I said nevertheless: 'My son-in-law took a gun on the very first day and left home'.

'I see,' said the rebel in glasses. 'That does him credit.'

'That's all rubbish,' said the officer. 'What's going on in town? What's happening with the Army?'

'I don't know,' I said. 'Everything's peaceful in town.'

'Is the entry into town free?' asked the officer.

'As far as I know, it is,' I said, and thought it my duty to add, 'but you might be held up by the patrols of the Anti-Martian Brigade.'

'What?' said the officer, and on his stern face for the first time there appeared something like surprise. He even stopped looking at the sky and began looking at me. 'What sort of brigade?'

'Anti-Martian,' I said. 'Under the leadership of Officer Polythemes. Perhaps you know him? He's an invalid.'

'How very curious,' said the officer. 'Can you take us to town?'

My heart sank. 'I would, of course,' I said, 'but my car . . .'

'Yes,' said the officer. 'What's wrong with it?'

I gathered up my determination and lied, 'It seems the motor's jammed'.

The officer whistled and without saying another word turned and disappeared in the wheat. The rebel in the glasses went on staring at me fixedly and then suddenly asked:

'Do you have any grandchildren?'

'Yes,' I lied in utter despair. 'Two! One's an infant in arms . . .'

He nodded sympathetically. 'It's terrible,' he said. 'That's what torments me more than anything. They don't know anything and they won't ever know . . .'

I didn't understand a word he said and I didn't want to understand. I just prayed that he would go away as quickly as possible and do nothing to me. For some reason it suddenly seemed to me that this quiet man in the glasses was the most terrible of all of them.

He waited for me to reply for a few seconds and then he slung his automatic across his shoulder and said: 'I advise you to get out of here as quickly as you can. Goodbye.'

I didn't even wait for him to disappear, I turned and ran as fast as I could away from the hill in the direction of town, as if a whirlwind were carrying me on its wings. I didn't feel my legs, I didn't feel my breathing. I thought I heard some kind of mechanical rumble behind me, but I didn't even turn around, I just tried to run.

I hadn't gone far when a small lorry filled to overflowing with farmers turned out of the village road and came towards me. I was half senseless, but I found enough strength in me to bar their way. I waved my hands and shouted: 'Stop! Don't go on. There are partisans over there!'

The lorry stopped and I was surrounded by rough, common people who for some reason were armed with machine guns. They grasped me by my shirt front, shook me, shouted and swore at me and I didn't understand anything that was happening, I was terrified and only after a while realized that they were taking me for an accomplice of the rebels. My legs gave under me, but then the driver climbed out of the cabin and proved to be a former student of mine.

'What are you doing, mates?' he shouted, grabbing their hands. 'That's Mr Apollo, the town teacher, I know him.'

Eventually they all calmed down and I told them what I had seen.

'Aha,' said the driver, 'that's what we thought. We'll hunt them out now. Let's go, mates.'

I wanted to carry on into town, but he convinced me that it was safer for me to be with them and that he would repair my car in peace while the rest hunted the bandits. They sat me in the cabin of the lorry and moved off towards the site of the tragedy. We came to the crest of the hill and saw my car, but farther on the road was completely empty. There were no bodies, no pieces of broken metal, only the burnt patches on the asphalt remained and the shallow pit in the place where the explosion had happened. 'It's obvious,' said the driver, as he stopped the lorry, 'they've collected everything up already. There they are in the air ...' Everyone started talking and also pointed to the horizon in the direction of Marathon but much as I stared far into the calm sky with my one eye, I couldn't see anything.

Then the farmers, with a skill that indicated a certain experience, without any unnecessary fuss or argument, broke into two groups of ten men. The two groups spread into a chain and began combing the wheatfields, one to the right, the other to the left.

'They've got automatics,' I warned them, 'and grenades, too, I think.' 'We know that very well,' they replied, and after a while I heard shouts that indicated they had come across a trail. The driver busied himself for a while with the repair of my car while I flung myself down on the back seat and fell into a blessed half-consciousness as I finally got a chance to rest my nerves. The driver located the fault (it proved to be an air-lock in the petrol pipe). Tears of gratitude came to my eyes. I squeezed his hand and paid him as much as I could. He was content. This simple, good man (I never did manage to remember his name) proved to be very talkative as well, as distinct from the majority of farmers who are also simple and kind people, but morose and reserved. He explained a lot to me about what had happened. It seems that the rebels, whom the people had simply termed bandits, had appeared in the district as early as the second day after the arrival of the Martians. At first they fraternized in a friendly way with the farmers and it was obvious then that the majority of them were residents of Marathon, mostly educated and at first glance harmless people, if you didn't count the soldiers. What they were after was incomprehensible to the farmers. At first they called on the villagers to rise against the new authorities, but they explained the need for this in a very muddled way, kept on about the death of culture, renaissance and other literary things which didn't interest the villagers. Nevertheless, the farmers fed and lodged them because the situation remained unclear and it was still not known what was to be expected from the new order. However, it became clear that the new authorities represented nothing bad – only good, in fact. They bought up the growing wheat at a good price (not even the harvest, but the shoots). They gave them a generous advance on the harvest of blue corn and money started pouring in as if from the sky for hitherto useless gastric juices. On the other hand, it became clear that the bandits were setting up ambushes against the representatives of the administration which was bringing money into the countryside. The representatives from Marathon made it clear that this disgrace must be stopped as soon as possible for the general good, and relations with the rebels changed completely.

Several times we interrupted our conversation and listened. From the fields came the occasional shot and each time we nodded with satisfaction and exchanged glances. I had already recovered and was sitting at the wheel ready to turn the car homewards. I had no intention, of course, of continuing on to Marathon. With things like this happening on the road, Alcimes could remain undisturbed when the hunt returned to the road. First came two farmers with two motionless bodies. One of the dead I recognized. It was the man in the beret whom the officer had called engineer. The other, a young man, hardly more than a boy, was unknown to me. With some relief I saw that he was, fortunately, not dead but just badly wounded. Then the rest of the members of the hunt returned in a crowd, chattering cheerfully to each other. They brought a prisoner with his hands tied whom I also recognized, although he no longer had his glasses. The victory was complete, none of the farmers had suffered. I felt an enormous moral satisfaction seeing how these simple people, with the heat of battle still on them, none the less showed unmistakable spiritual dignity, treating the defeated enemy in an almost knightly way. They bound the wounds of the injured man and laid him in the lorry carefully enough. Although his hands were still tied, the prisoner was given a drink and a cigarette was thrust in his mouth.

'Well, that's that,' said my driver friend. 'Now the place will be more peaceful.'

I thought it my duty to tell him that there had been at least five rebels.

'Never mind,' he said. 'So two got away. They won't get anywhere. The set-up in the next district is the same as in ours. They're killed or they're caught.'

'Where will you send these?' I asked.

'We'll take them to the Martian garrison about forty miles away. They take them there alive or dead, as you bring them.' I thanked him again, shook his hand, and he went to his lorry saying to the rest, 'Let's go, eh?'

Then the prisoner was led past me. He stopped for a second and looked me straight in the face with his short-sighted eyes. Perhaps I imagined it, but in his eyes was something that made my heart sink. Now I hope that I imagined it. Wretched world! No, I'm not justifying that man. He's an extremist, a partisan. He has killed and must be punished, but I'm not blind. I saw clearly that this was a fine man, not a black shirt, not a fool, but a man with convictions. Now I hope that I was wrong. All my life I have suffered for thinking well of people.

The lorry moved off in one direction and I in the other and in an hour I was already home, absolutely broken, exhausted and ill. I noted incidentally that Mr Nikostratos was sitting in the drawing-room and Artemida was serving him tea. However, I wasn't worried about them. It had been a terrible, torturing day.

Temperature – 17°C; cloud density – 10 degrees; heavy rain.

Yes, these rebels are dangerous people for the general peace. And yet I cannot but pity them, drenched through, muddy, hunted like animals, in the name of what? What is anarchy?

Protest against injustice? But against whom? I definitely don't understand them. It's odd, I now recall that during the hunt there had been no burst of automatic fire, nor the sound of grenades. They must have run out of ammunition.

June 11th. Midnight. Hermione wanted me to spend the whole day in bed, but I didn't take any notice and I did right not to. At midday I felt well enough and straight after lunch I decided to go into town. Man is weak. I won't conceal the fact that I couldn't wait to tell our group about the terrible and tragic events which I had witnessed the previous day. It's true that by lunchtime these events featured in my imagination in not so much a tragic as a romantic light. At The Five Clinks my tale was a great success. I was showered with questions and my little bit of vanity was fully satisfied. It was amusing to watch Polythemes (he was, by the way, now the only member of the Anti-Martian Brigade who still went round with a shotgun). When I related to our chaps my conversation with the rebel officer he spoke up immediately, boasting and claiming a part in the desperate and dangerous activities of the rebels. He even got to the point of admitting that they were brave fellows, although they were acting illegally. I didn't understand what he meant by that, and neither did anyone else. He announced that he would show those peasants the price of a pound of smoke and then a brawl almost broke out because Myrtil's brother is a farmer and Myrtil himself comes from farming stock. I don't like arguments, I can't bear them, in fact, and while they were being separated I went off to the town hall.

Mr Nikostratos showed me marked kindness, inquired, inquired concernedly about my health and with great sympathy heard out my account of yesterday's adventures. Not just he, but all the employees put aside what they were doing and gathered around me, so I had a complete success here too. All agreed that I had acted bravely and that my conduct did me credit. I had to shake a lot of hands and the beautiful Tiona even asked permission to kiss me, which permission I, of course, willingly granted. (Dash it all, it's a long time since I'd been kissed by young girls, I confess I'd even forgotten how pleasant it was.) On the question of the pension Mr Nikostratos assured me that everything would probably be all right and told me in great secrecy that the question of taxes had now been finally settled it seemed, and as from June taxes would be collected in the form of gastric juice.

This entertaining conversation, of course, was unfortunately interrupted by a regular scandal. The door of the mayor's office was flung open and Mr Coribanth appeared on the threshold and, standing with his back to us, he began to shout at the lord mayor that he would not leave things at that, that this was an infringement of freedom and speech, that this was a corporation, that the lord mayor ought to remember the unfortunate fate of Mr Laomedontes and so on. The lord mayor also spoke in a raised voice but rather more quietly than Mr Coribanth and I didn't understand exactly what they were talking about. Mr Coribanth finally left, slamming the door hard behind him, and then Mr Nikostratos explained the matter to me. It seems that the lord mayor had fined the newspaper and closed it down for a week because Mr Coribanth had published a poem in the issue of the day before yesterday signed by a certain 'XYZ' in which had appeared the line: 'And on the distant horizon, fierce Mars is flaming'. Mr Coribanth refused to accept the lord mayor's decision and this was already the second day that they'd been quarrelling, both by telephone and in person. In passing judgement on this event, Mr Nikostratos and I came to the same conclusion, that both sides in this affair were, in their own way, both right and wrong. On the one hand, the penalty inflicted on the newspaper by the lord mayor was excessively severe, especially since the poem was as a whole completely harmless, inasmuch as it was only talking of the author's unrequited love for a night fairy. But, on the other hand, the situation is such that one can't afford to tease the geese – the lord mayor has enough unpleasantness as it is to deal with, what with Minotaur, who the day before yesterday again got blind drunk and damaged a Martian car with his stinking tank cart. I returned to The Five Clinks and rejoined the fellows. The quarrel between Polythemes and Myrtil had already been smoothed over and the usual friendly discussion was in progress. Not without satisfaction I noted that my tale had, it seemed, turned the minds of those gathered there along a particular line. They were talking about the rebels, about the armaments which the Martians had at their disposal and other similar subjects. Morpheus was saying that not far from Milese a Martian flying machine, which was making a forced landing because the pilot was unused to the increased force of gravity, had been attacked by a group of malefactors and had shot everyone of them, down to the last man, with some special electronic missile, after which it exploded itself, leaving behind an enormous hole with glass walls. All of Milese was now going over to look at the hole.

Myrtil, repeating what he had heard from his farmer brother, told us about a terrible band of Amazons who attacked and kidnapped Martians with the intention of having offspring by them. The one-legged Polythemes for his part told us the following: yesterday night, when he was on patrol duty on Park Street, four Martian cars stole up on him silently. An unfamiliar voice in some massacred version of the language and with an unpleasant hiss in it asked him how to get to the pub, and, although the pub is not an object of national importance, Polythemes, simply out of pride and scorn for the conquerors refused to reply, so that the Martians got nothing for their pains. Polythemes assured us that at the time his life hung by a thread, he had even noticed long, black poles directed straight at him, but he didn't waver for a second in his determination.

'What! Were you too miserable to tell them?' asked Myrtil. 'I know that kind of mean wretch. You come to some strange place, you want a drink and they won't for anything tell you where the pub is.'

The affair nearly came to a fight once again, but then Panderei arrived and, with a happy smile, announced that Minotaur had at last been taken out of town – by the Martians. They suspected Minotaur in connexion with the terrorists and sabotage. We were all up in arms about it – leaving us without a cesspit emptier at the hottest time of the year – why, that was a crime!

'Enough!' shouted the one-legged Polythemes. 'We've borne the cursed yoke long enough. Fellow countrymen, hear my command. Arise!'

We had already started to fall into line when Panderei calmed everyone down by saying that the Martians intended to begin work on the sewerage canals in the coming week, and meanwhile Minotaur's place would be taken by a junior policeman. Everyone agreed that that was a different matter and resumed their conversation about the terrorists, about how it was swinish all the same, setting up ambushes.

Rolling his eyes, Dimant told us a terrible story about how for the third day now, some people had been roaming around town and offering sweets to people they met. 'You eat one of those sweets and – piff! – you're gone.' They hoped to poison all the Martians this way. We of course didn't believe the story, but somehow we began to feel bad.

Then Kalaid who had been twitching and spluttering for a long time suddenly blurted out: 'But A-A-Apollo himself has a son-in-law who's a terrorist'. Everyone at once recoiled from me somehow, and Panderei thrusting out his jaw, announced: 'That's true, I have information to that effect'.

I was extremely put out and announced to all of them that: in the first place, a father-in-law was not answerable for his son-in-law; in the second place, Panderei himself had a relation who was last year put away for five years for some sort of debauched activities; in the third place, I had always been at daggers drawn with Charon and anyone could support that, and, in the fourth place, I knew nothing of the sort about Charon – he had gone on a study trip and we had not heard a word from him since. These were unpleasant moments but the stupidity of the accusation was so obvious that everything ended happily and the conversation moved on to gastric juice. It appeared that all our group had been giving gastric juice for the second day running and had got cash for it. Only I was left out. Always, in some incomprehensible way, I proved the exception when there was a profit to be made from something – there are such disorganized people in the world. In Army barracks it is they who are always doing jankers, at the front, it's they who fall into the shit. All the nasty things come to them first, and all the good things last. I'm one of those. Well, that's how it is. All the chaps then started boasting about how satisfied they were. I should think so! All that and then to be dissatisfied!

At this point a Martian car drove across the square and the one-legged Polythemes said: 'What do you reckon, lads, if you took a pot at it with a shotgun, would you punch a hole in it or not?'

'With a bullet, presumably you would,' said Silen.

'Depends where you hit it,' said Myrtil, 'if you got the prow or the stern, not a chance.'

'What about the side?' asked Polythemes.

'If you hit the side, then presumably you would,' replied Myrtil.

I was just going to say that even a grenade wouldn't puncture it when I was forestalled by Panderei who said ponderously: 'No, old chaps, you're wasting your time arguing, they're impregnable'.

'The sides too?' asked Morpheus maliciously.

'Absolutely,' said Panderei.

'What, even with a bullet?' asked Myrtil.

'Yes, even if you shoot at it,' said Panderei very importantly.

At that everyone began shaking their heads and slapping him on the back. 'Oh, Pan! Old boy,' they said, 'you've slipped up there. Yes, Pandy, old fellow, you didn't think, just opened your mouth and babbled.' And Paral the quarrelsome wasted no time in showing his sting – he said: 'If you shot Panderei in the stern you might perhaps make a dent, but if you got him in the head, it would just bounce off'.

Well, Panderei swelled up, buttoned up his tunic and barked: 'You've all said your bit! That's all! Disperse! In the name of the law.'

Without wasting any time, I set off for the donor's point. I was, of course, met by failure again. They took no juice from me and I got no money. It seems there's a regulation that you have to have fasted before you can give juice, and I had had lunch only two hours before. I was given a donor's card and told to come back in the morning. I must say, by the way, that the donor's point made the most pleasant impression on me. The newest equipment. The probe was wiped with the finest-quality vaseline. The juice is taken automatically, but under the supervision of an experienced doctor, not some ruffian. The staff is without exception polite and helpful – it's obvious at once that they're well paid. Everything shines with cleanliness, the furniture is new. In the waiting-room you can read the latest papers or watch television, and the waiting is nothing – fewer people and quicker service than in the pub. And you get your money at once, from an automat. Throughout, you are conscious of a high level of culture, humanity and solicitousness towards the donor. To think that three days ago this house was the den of a man like Mr Laomedontes!

However, I couldn't shake off the thought of my son-in-law and I felt I had to discuss this irritating problem with Achilles.

I found him as usual behind the cash desk looking at his copy of *Cosmos*. The story of my adventures had a tremendous effect on him and I felt that he looked at me in quite a different light as a result. But, when I spoke of Charon, he just shrugged his shoulders and said that the impression made by my actions and the dangers which I had experienced would completely rehabilitate not just me, but perhaps Charon himself. Besides, he actually doubted that Charon would take part in anything illegal. Charon, he said, was most likely now in Marathon doing his bit to restore order and trying to do something useful for his home town as befitted every civilized resident. The local envies, all your Pandereis and Kalaids were only capable of irresponsible gossip and were simply slandering him.

I had my own suspicions on this score, but naturally I was silent and I just felt surprised how badly we citizens of such an essentially small town knew each other. I realized that I had talked about this with Achilles to no purpose and, pretending that his judgement had completely set my mind at rest, I turned the conversation to stamps. And then an extraordinary thing happened.

I remember that at first my conversation was rather forced since it was basically intended to draw Achilles away from the subject of Charon. But it turned out that the conversation turned to that blessed inverted lithographic overprint. In my own time, I put before Achilles absolutely indisputable facts to show that it was a forgery, and the question seemed to be closed. However, the evening before Achilles had read some sort of book and considered himself capable of drawing his own conclusions. This was unheard of in our relationship. Naturally, I was beside myself. I lost my temper and said straight out that Achilles knew nothing about philately, that only a year before he couldn't tell the difference between 'mint' and 'used', and it was no accident that his collection overflowed with defective examples. Achilles also exploded and we completely forgot ourselves in the wrangle that ensued, the kind of wrangle I am only capable of with Achilles, and then only on the subject of stamps.

Through a kind of fog I was aware then that during our argument someone seemed to come into the chemist shop, hold out some kind of paper to Achilles over my shoulder, that Achilles quietened down for a moment, and that I immediately took advantage of this to drive a wedge into his incompetent judgements. Then I remember an irritating sense of being disturbed, something irrelevant was thrusting itself into my consciousness and preventing me from thinking coherently or logically. However, this passed and the next stage in this psychologically curious event was the point when our argument ended and we fell silent, tired and a little offended with each other.

I remember that precisely at that moment I experienced an uncontrollable urge to look around the place and felt a vague surprise at not seeing anything particularly changed. Meanwhile, I was clearly aware that some kind of change must have taken place during our quarrel. Then I noticed that Achilles, too, was in a state of mental unease. He, too, was looking round him and then he went down along the counter and looked under it. Finally he asked: 'I say, Feb, did anyone come in?' He was definitely worried by the same thing that was bothering me. His question dotted all the 'i's: I realized what the sense of my perplexity was.

'The blue hand!' I cried, as an unexpectedly clear recollection came to me. I almost seemed to see in front of me the blue fingers, crumpling a piece of paper.

'No, not a hand!' said Achilles excitedly. 'A tentacle! Like an octopus!'

'But I clearly remember fingers . . .'

'A tentacle, like an octopus!' Achilles repeated, looking round him feverishly. Then he grabbed the prescription book from the counter and hurriedly thumbed through it. Everything in me tensed under the weight of a presentiment. Holding a slip of paper in his hand he slowly raised bulging eyes to me and I already knew what he was going to say.

'Feb,' he said in a choking voice, 'it was a Martian.' We were both shaken and Achilles, as a man versed in medicine, considered it essential to revive our strength with brandy, a bottle of which he took from a carton marked 'Norsulphazolum'. Yes, while we were arguing here about that overprint a Martian had entered the chemist's shop, had given Achilles a written order asking for all medicaments containing narcotics to be given over to the bearer, and Achilles had without remembering or realizing anything wrapped up a package containing these medicaments and handed it over, after which the

Martian had left, leaving nothing in our memories but flashes of recollection and a blurred picture registered out of the corners of our eyes.

I remembered clearly the blue hand covered with thin, short whitish hair, and the fleshy fingers without nails and I was struck by the fact that such a vision had not immediately driven out of my mind any capacity for abstract argument.

Achilles didn't remember any hand, but instead he remembered a long, throbbing tentacle stretched out to him apparently out of nowhere. He remembered, too, how he had angrily thrown the packet of medicine on to the counter without looking, but he had absolutely no recollection of reading or entering the prescription in the book, yet he obviously must have read it (since he had passed over the medicine) and recorded it (since there it was).

We drank another glass of brandy and Achilles remembered that the Martian had stood to my left and had worn a fashionable sweater with a low neck and I remembered that on one of the blue fingers there had been a glittering ring of some white metal set with a precious stone. Besides that, I remembered the sound of a car. Achilles mopped his forehead and announced that the sight of the prescription book reminded him of the uncomfortable feeling he had had, apparently induced by someone's attempts – importunate to the point of rudeness – to force himself into our argument with some completely absurd viewpoint on philately in general and on inverted overprints in particular.

Then I remembered that it was true, the Martian had spoken, and his voice had been piercing and unpleasant. 'Low and patronizing, rather,' said Achilles. However, I stuck to my version and Achilles got heated again and called his junior pharmacist from the laboratory to ask him what sounds he had heard during the last hour. The junior pharmacist, a particularly unintelligent youth, blinked his stupid eyes and mumbled that he had only heard our voices during all that time and at one point it seemed someone had turned on the radio, but he hadn't paid any attention to that. We sent the junior pharmacist back and had another drop of brandy. Our memories finally cleared and, although our opinions still differed as to the external appearance of the Martian, we were nevertheless in full agreement as to the facts of what had taken place. The

Martian had undoubtedly come to the chemist shop in a car and had not switched off the engine while he came into the building, he had stopped to the left of and just a little behind me, had stood there motionless for some time, looking at us and listening to our conversation. (A chill ran over my skin as I realized how vulnerable I had been in that moment.) Then he had made several remarks to us, apparently on the subject of philately and apparently completely incompetent, and then he had held out the prescription to Achilles who had fleetingly looked at it and thrust it into the prescription book. And then Achilles, still furious at the interruption, had passed over the parcel of medicine and the Martian had left, realizing that we didn't want to include him in our conversation. In this way we separated out the detail and established a picture of a being who, although not very competent in the field of philately, was in general not without breeding and a certain humanity, if you considered that in that time he could have done what he liked to us. We had another drink and felt that it was more than we could do to stay here and keep the group uninformed about what had happened. Achilles hid the bottle, put the junior pharmacist in charge and we walked quickly towards the pub.

Our account of the Martian's visit was received in various ways by the group. The one-legged Polythemes frankly considered it a lie. 'Just a whiff of them,' he said, 'they're tanked to the eyeballs.'

The sensible Silen suggested that it had nevertheless been just some Negro: Negroes sometimes have a bluish tint to their skin. And Paral was Paral.

'A fine chemist we've got,' he said acidly. 'Someone, he doesn't know who, comes from somewhere, he doesn't know where, shows him some piece of paper, he doesn't know what, and, without a murmur, he gives him what he wants. Really, with chemists like this, how can we hope to establish a rational society? What kind of a chemist is it who, because of his rubbishy stamps, doesn't know what he's about?'

On the other hand the others were on our side, the whole pub gathered around us and even the golden youth headed by Mr Nikostratos dragged themselves away from the bar to listen. We had to repeat the story again and again, where the Martian stood, how he had stretched out his extremity and so on. Very soon I noticed that Achilles was embroidering the tale with new details which were as a rule of a shattering nature. (Such as that when the Martian was silent he blinked only two eyes, but when he opened his mouth additional eyes opened, one red and one white.) I reproved him at once but he said that cognac and brandy had a remarkable effect on the human memory and that this was a medically established fact. I decided not to argue and, laughing to myself, watched him confidently compromising himself. In some ten minutes everyone realized that Achilles had definitely lied himself to a full stop, and ceased to pay any attention to him.

The golden youth went back to the bar and soon we could hear from their direction remarks such as: '... had enough ... What bores! ... Martians? Rubbish, drivel ... We ought to beat them up.'

At our table the old argument about gastric juice was revived: what it was, what use it was, what the Martians wanted it for, and what use it was to ourselves. Achilles explained that man needed stomach juices for the digestion of food, it was impossible to digest food without it. But his authority had already been undermined and no one believed him.

'You'd better be quiet, you old bag of wind ...' said Polythemes. 'What do you mean, impossible? I've given juice for the third day running and what of it? I'm still digesting I ought to digest you.'

Woefully they turned to consult Kalaid, but naturally that came to nothing. Kalaid after long digressions which the whole pub followed expectantly, blurted out: 'If you want to know, a policeman's finished at thirty'.

These words bore on some half-forgotten conversation which had taken place back at The Five Clinks before lunch and were generally not intended for us but for Panderei who had long since gone on duty. We left Kalaid still giving birth to an answer to our question and started speculating amongst ourselves. Silen suggested that the civilization of Mars had come to a blind alley in the physiological field and were unable to manufacture their own gastric juices, so they had to take over other sources of supply. Japheth put in from behind the bar that the Martians used gastric juices as a kind of ferment for the production of a special kind of energy, 'like atomic energy,' he added as an afterthought. And then Dimant, who had never distinguished himself with bold flights of fancy, announced that human gastric juice was for the Martians what brandy or beer was for us, or say vodka, and with this announcement spoilt the appetite of everyone who was eating at the time.

Someone suggested that the Martians got gold or precious metal from gastric juice and this obviously uneducated suggestion led Morpheus to a very true thought: 'Fellows,' he said, 'whether in fact they get gold or energy from it, it's clear that our gastric juice is very important to the Martians. Are they making fools of us?' At first no one understood what he was getting at, but then it dawned – no one knew the real price of gastric juice and what kind of price it was that the Martians had fixed, we couldn't tell. It was quite possible that the Martians – a very practical people we had to agree – were taking advantage of our ignorance.

'They're buying from us on the cheap,' one-legged Polythemes said, white with anger. 'They take it to some comet and get the proper price.' I risked correcting him on the point that it wouldn't be a comet but a planet, to which with his characteristic rudeness he suggested that I had my eyes seen to before I ventured into arguments. But that wasn't the point.

We were all disturbed by Morpheus' suggestion and a very serious and useful discussion could have resulted, but at that point Myrtil rolled into the pub with his farmer brother, both of them dead drunk. It appeared that Myrtil's brother had for several days been experimenting with the distillation of the grain of the blue wheat and that today his experiments had finally been crowned with success. On to the table were hoisted two respectable flagons of blue first brew. Everyone was at once distracted, and started trying it, and I must say that blue brandy made a big impression on us. Myrtil, to his misfortune, invited Japheth to the table to try it as well. Japheth drank two glasses, stood for a while with his left eye closed as if he were thinking it over and then suddenly said: 'Get out of my sight'.

It was said in such a voice that Myrtil without a word gathered up the empty flagons and his brother who had dozed off, and hurriedly left. Japheth looked us over solemnly and said: 'They've got a nerve – bringing their rot-gut into my establishment', and returned to the bar.

To smooth over the unpleasantness we all ordered a drink but the easy atmosphere had now been shattered. I sat for another half-hour and then I went home.

In the sitting-room, Mr Nikostratos had taken over Charon's chair and was sitting opposite Artemida having tea. I didn't get involved in that affair. First of all, Charon had in any case cut himself off, and it wasn't clear whether he was going to come back at all, and, in the second place, Hermione was somewhere not too far away and I reeked of alcohol so strongly that I could smell it myself. Therefore I preferred to creep past silently to my own room, without drawing attention to myself. I changed and looked through the paper. It's simply amazing. Sixteen sides and nothing of substance, it's like chewing cotton-wool. There was a report of a Press conference given by the president. I read it twice and understood nothing – sheer gastric juice. I'll go and see how Hermione is.

June 12th. Temperature – 20°c; cloud density – 0 degrees; no wind. I'm having revolting belches from that blue brandy; a splitting migraine, and I've been home all day. A gastronomic novelty made its appearance – blue bread. Hermione praised it, Artemida liked it too, but I ate it without any appetite, bread's bread, even when it's blue.

June 13th. Summer weather has finally arrived it seems. Temperature – 20°c and some cloud.

What a business! I don't know where to begin. On the question of the pension, there's nothing new, but that's not what I'm concerned with now. I had just started writing today's entry when I heard a car drive up. I thought Myrtil might have brought the promised quart of blue brandy from the farm and glanced out just in time. First I caught sight of an unfamiliar car, a luxury model too, which was standing under the street-lamp, and then I noticed Charon making his way through the garden straight towards the bench where Artemida and Mr Nikostratos had been settled since the evening. I hardly had time to blink before Mr Nikostratos flew head over heels over the garden wall. Charon flung his stick and hat after him, but Mr Nikostratos didn't stop to pick them up, just ran ever faster. Then Charon turned to Artemida. I couldn't see very well what was happening between them but I got the impression that at first Artemida tried to faint. However, when Charon boxed her ears she changed her mind and decided to display some of her famous temper. She let out a long-drawn-out ear-shattering shriek and clawed Charon's face. I repeat that I didn't see everything. But when, a few minutes later, I looked into the drawing-room, Charon was pacing from corner to corner like a tiger in a cage, his hands behind his back, and on his nose was a fresh, red scratch. Artemida was busily laying the table and I noticed that her face looked slightly asymmetrical. I can't bear domestic scenes, they make me all weak inside and I have to go away somewhere so as not to see or hear anything. However, Charon noticed me before I could hide myself, and to my surprise he greeted me so warmly and welcomingly that I felt obliged to go into the drawing-room and speak to him.

First of all, I was pleasantly struck by the fact that Charon looked completely different to what I had expected. This was not the bearded, ragged tramp who had clanked around with a gun and quarrelled with me here a week ago. To be honest, I had expected him to be still dirtier and more ragged. However, before me stood the former Charon of peaceful times, smooth shaven, well combed, tastefully and elegantly dressed. Only the red scratch on his nose spoiled the general impression a little and the colour of his face, which was unaccustomedly swarthy, witnessed to the fact that in the last few days this office worker had spent a lot of time in the open.

Hermione came in in her curling pins, apologized for her appearance and also sat down to the table. It was like in the old days, we sat there, the four of us, one peaceful family. Until the women left to take out the dishes the conversation was on general topics, the weather, health, who looked how. But when we were left alone Charon lit up a cigarette and said, looking at me strangely: 'Well, Father, our game's over then?'

In reply I simply shrugged my shoulders although I wanted very much to say that if someone's game was over, it certainly wasn't 'ours'. Actually Charon, in my opinion, didn't expect a reply. He had restrained himself in front of the women and only now I noticed that he was in a state of almost unhealthy excitement, in the state when a man can change abruptly from nervous laughter to nervous tears, when everything is boiling inside him and he feels an unbearable need to give vent to some of it in words and so to talk, talk, talk and Charon talked.

People no longer had a future, he said. Man had ceased to be the king of nature. From now and for ever man would be an ordinary phenomenon of nature like a tree, or a horse, and nothing more. Civilization and progress in general had lost all meaning. Humanity no longer needed to develop itself, it would be developed from outside, and for that it did not need schools, institutes, laboratories, social consciousness, philosophy, literature, in other words, all that distinguished man from the animals and that had up to now been called civilization was no longer necessary. As a factory of gastric juice, Albert Einstein, he said, was no better than Panderei, he was inferior probably since Panderei was an exceptional glutton. The history of man would end, not in the thunder of a cosmic catastrophe, not in the flames of atomic war, not even in the press of over-population, but in satiated, peaceful quiet.

'Just to think,' he said, dropping his head in his hands, 'it isn't ballistic missiles that finished civilization, it's nothing more than a handful of coppers for a glass of gastric juice ...'

He spoke much more, of course, and much more effectively, but I assimilate abstract discussion badly, and remembered only what I remembered. I admit that at first he managed to depress me. However, I understood soon enough that this was simply the hysterical outpouring of words of an educated man who could not bear the shattering of his personal ideals. And I felt I had to reply to him. Not, of course, because I hoped to convince him, but because his judgements hurt me deeply, seemed bombastic and arrogant, and besides I wanted to shake off that depressing impression which his lamentations had had on me.

'You've had too easy a life, my son,' I said straight out. 'You're too fussy! You don't know anything about life. It's obvious at once that you've never had a knock in the teeth, you've never frozen in the trenches, never carted logs in prison. You've always had enough to eat, and enough to pay for it with. You've got used to looking at the world with the eyes of a godless man, some sort of superman. What a pity! Civilization has been sold for a handful of coppers! Be thankful that they still give you coppers for it! For you they mean nothing. But what about the widow who has to raise three children alone, who has to bring them up, feed them, educate them? And Polythemes, the cripple, who gets a paltry pension? And the farmer? What do you propose for the farmer? Dubious little social ideas? Books and pamphlets? Your aesthetic philosophy? The farmer would spit on it all. He needs clothes, machines, and faith in tomorrow. He needs the permanent possibility of raising his harvest and getting a good price for it! Could you give him that? You with all your civilization? No one could give him that for ten thousand years, but the Martians have done it. Why be surprised now that the farmers hound you like wild beasts? No one needs you or your civilization talk, your snobbery, your abstract preaching, which so easily turns into shots from an automatic. The farmer doesn't need you, the townsman doesn't need you, the Martians don't need you. I even believe that the majority of your rational, educated people don't need you. You think you are the flower of civilization, and in fact you are mould growing out of its sap. You've grown conceited and now argue that your death is the death of civilization.'

My speech seemed to have shattered him. He sat, covering his face with his hands, trembling all over. He looked so pitiful that my heart was touched.

'Charon,' I said as gently as I could, 'my boy, try at least for a moment to come down from the clouds on to the sinful earth. Try to understand that man needs peace and faith in tomorrow more than anything else in the world. Nothing terrible has happened. You say that man has now turned into a factory of gastric juice. These are strong words, Charon. In fact, something like the opposite has happened. Man, having emerged into new conditions of life, has found a superb means of using his physiological resources for the improvement of his situation in this world. You call it slavery, but every reasonable man would call it the usual commercial transaction which can be mutually beneficial. What sort of slavery can it be if rational man is already weighing up whether or not he is being cheated, and if he is being cheated, then I assure you he will know how to get justice? You talk of the end of culture and civilization, that is really not true! I don't even understand what you mean. The papers come out every day, industry is working, Charon, what more do you ask? You have all that you ever had, freedom of speech, self-government, the constitution. As if this weren't enough you are protected from Mr Laomedontes and you have at last been given a permanent and dependable source of income which is completely independent of any crisis.'

I stopped at this point because I saw that Charon was not at all shattered, he wasn't sobbing as I thought, but in fact giggling in the rudest possible way.

I felt extremely insulted, but when Charon said: 'Forgive me, for God's sake. I don't want to offend you. I was just remembering an amusing story.'

It appeared that two days ago Charon, at the head of a group of five rebels, had captured a Martian car. To their surprise out of the car stepped a completely sober Minotaur with a portable device for the pumping of gastric juice.

'Well, fellows, what's up? Feeling thirsty?' he asked. 'Come on, I'll set you up in a minute, who's first?'

The rebels had even been taken aback. When they recovered themselves they knocked him about a bit for his treachery and let him go together with the car. They had intended to take the car, learn to drive it and then to use it to penetrate into the Martian garrison and start a battle there, but the episode had such an effect on them that they felt like spitting on everything. In the evening two of them went home and the next morning the rest were caught by farmers. I didn't understand at all what relation this bore to the subject of our discussion, but I was struck by the thought that Charon must have been a prisoner of the Martians.

'Yes,' he said in response to my question. 'That's why I laughed. The Martians told me exactly what you have, point for point. They especially stressed the point that I am of the élite in society, that they had a deep respect for me, and did not understand why I and those like me involved ourselves in terrorist activities instead of setting up a rational opposition. They suggested that we fight them by legal means, guaranteed us full freedom of Press and freedom to hold meetings. Wonderful chaps the Martians, don't you agree?'

What could I say to him? Especially when it became clear that they had treated him splendidly, washed him, dressed him, given him medical attention, and a car, confiscated from some owner of an opium den, and let him go in peace.

'I'm speechless,' I said, raising my hands.

'I too,' echoed Charon and his face darkened again. 'I, too, am speechless but I have to find words. We're all worth nothing unless we find them.'

After that he, completely unexpectedly, wished me a sudden

goodnight and went to his room. I was left sitting there like a fool seized by an unpleasant presentiment. Oh yes, we would have more trouble yet with Charon, yes indeed! And what an unpleasant way of leaving, without finishing the argument. It was only one o'clock already and I wasn't in the least sleepy.

By the way, I gave gastric juice for the first time today. There's nothing frightening in it, it's just unpleasant to swallow, but they say you soon get used to it. If you give 200 grams a day, that's 150 a month. Not so bad!

June 14th. Temperature – 22°c; cloud density – 0 degrees; no wind. The new stamps have been issued at last. Lord, what joy! I bought the whole issue in quarter-block and then couldn't resist it, and bought the full sheets. I've economized enough! Now I can allow myself a bit of expenditure. Hermione and I went to give gastric juice – in future I'll go alone. There's a rumour that the Ministry of Education has issued a circular confirming the earlier situation on the question of pensions, however I wasn't able to find out the details. Mr Nikostratos didn't come to work. He sent his younger brother to say that he had caught a chill. They say, though, that it's not the flu, but that he was careless enough to fall over somewhere. Of course, Charon! Artemida goes about as quiet as a mouse.

Oh, yes, I had completely forgotten. Today I looked into the drawing-room and saw Charon sitting there and with him a pleasant-looking fellow with large glasses. I recognized him and literally froze. It was the same rebel whom the farmers had caught before my eyes. He recognized me, too, and also froze. We stared at each other for a time, and then I recovered myself, nodded and left the room. I don't know what he told Charon about me. Anyway, he left soon after. I repeat frankly, I don't like it. If he takes up the battle legally, as they officially suggested to him, with all kinds of meetings, pamphlets, papers – by all means. But if I find just once again any automatics and other kind of ironmongery in my house, I'll say goodbye, dear son-in-law. Here our roads must part. I've had enough.

To calm myself I read over again yesterday's entry of my talk with Charon. In my opinion, my logic is unimpeachable. He was unable to bring forward any reply to it. It's only sad that I wrote it much more coherently and convincingly than I said it. I am no good at all at talking, it's my weakest point.

There was an interesting article in the morning paper about the general demobilization and demilitarization of the country. Thank God, they've come to their senses at last. Evidently the Martians have taken the question of defence completely into their own hands, and now defence won't cost us a penny, if you don't take into account gastric juice, that is. The president's speech doesn't say a word about that directly, but you can read between the lines. The former defence expenditure, he says, will be diverted towards the raising of the standard of living, and developing shipbuilding. There are certain difficulties connected with the cutting of war industries, but this is a purely temporary factor. And he stressed several times that no one will suffer from this reorganization. I understand it this way, the war industries and the generals are to be given a nice lump sum – they're rich people these Martians. Demobilization has begun already. Paral is spreading the rumour that the police will also be abolished. Panderei wanted to put him in jail but we wouldn't let him. Rumours are only rumours, but in Panderei's place I would be more careful now.

Today I don't feel like writing anything. I'll make a fair copy of my yesterday's speech to Charon now. It's a good speech.

June 15th. An unusually clear and bright morning (temperature – 15°c; cloud density – nil; and no wind). How pleasant it is to get up early in the morning, when the sun has already dispersed the morning mist, but the air is still fresh and cool and retains the perfumes of the night. The finest drops of dew tremble and shimmer in a myriad of rainbows, like precious stones, on each blade of grass, on each leaf, on each spider web, which the industrious spider has spun overnight from his little home to an overhanging twig – no, I must say, I don't do too well with artistic prose. On the one hand, everything seems to be correct, beautiful in places, but just the same, somehow I don't know, something's not quite right. Well, never mind.

For the second day running we all show an exceptionally good appetite. They say that it's the blue bread. It is, it's true, an amazing product. Before, I didn't ever eat bread except in sandwiches, and actually I ate very little of it altogether. Now I literally gorge myself on it. It melts in the mouth like pastry and doesn't weigh heavily on the stomach. Even Artemida, who always worried more about preserving her figure than about preserving the family, cannot restrain herself and now eats as a healthy young woman of her age ought to eat.

Charon also eats and praises it. At my not-unmalicious digs he only says: 'One doesn't interfere with the other, Father. One doesn't interfere with the other.'

After breakfast I went to the town hall and came just before the beginning of the session. Our group hadn't yet got to The Five Clinks. Mr Nikostratos doesn't look too well. At each movement he grimaces, grabbing his side, and from time to time he groans quietly. He talked in a painful whisper, didn't pay any attention to his nails. During our conversation he didn't look at me once, but spoke politely without the slightest suggestion of his usual irony. The circular had, indeed, been received, confirming the earlier position on the question of payment of pensions. My papers were probably already with the ministry. We must assume that everything would turn out well and I would be in the first category, all the same it wouldn't hurt to ask the mayor to send a special letter to the ministry in which my personal part in the war against the rebels could be confirmed. This idea pleased me very much and I agreed with Mr Nikostratos that I would put together a rough draft of such a letter and he would edit it and give it to the lord mayor for his perusal.

Meanwhile at The Five Clinks our group had already got together. Morpheus came last and we fined him. Enough of liberalism! We had lately completely neglected our club business. Everyone was extremely interested in one question: had the affair between Charon and Mr Nikostratos ended? They made me describe in the most detailed way all that I had seen, and for some time the one-legged Polythemes and Silen argued about what part of Mr Nikostratos it was that had suffered injury. As a former non-commissioned officer, Polythemes insisted that in such a skirmish Mr Nikostratos must have injured his tailbone, because only an accurately aimed blow from the toe of a boot in the appropriate place could have brought about the kind of departure from the field of battle that I had described.

I was also asked whether Artemida continued to feel warmly towards Mr Nikostratos and when I determinedly refused to answer such a tactless question they concluded to a man that of course she did.

'A woman is a woman,' said Paral the quarrelsome. 'One man never satisfies a woman – it's their biological nature.'

I lost my temper in the end and remarked that he shouldn't judge others by his own standards, and everyone found my joke very witty inasmuch as everyone disliked Paral for his irascibility and we remembered that in his time, before the war, his young wife had run off with a travelling salesman. A perfect situation arose for putting Paral, with his eternal, quasi-philosophical pronouncements, in his place.

Morpheus, a new witticism already on his lips, choked with laughter in advance, and grabbing people by the hand shouted, 'Just listen to what I'm going to say'.

Then, at the wrong moment as usual, that old donkey Panderei butted his way in and not understanding the subject of the conversation announced in his thunderous voice that these days we were acquiring the foreign fashion of living three or four with one woman, like cats. 'What can you do – just throw up your hands and give up.'

Paral at once seized on this speech and immediately turned the conversation to Panderei personally. 'Yes, Pandy,' he said, 'you're in form today, I haven't heard anything like that even from my youngest son-in-law, the major.' Paral's second son-in-law was known far beyond the limits of the town. We couldn't restrain ourselves and we all burst into roars of laughter, but Paral went one better, adding with a mournful expression: 'No, old chaps, it's useless our demilitarizing, we'd be better off depolicifying, or at the thin end of the wedge, depanderizing'.

Panderei at once swelled up, like a blow-fish, did up the buttons of his tunic and barked: 'You've all said your bit – and that's all . . .'

It was still too early to go to the donor's point and I set off for Achilles' shop. I read him the fair copy of my speech to Charon. He listened to me open-mouthed. My success was complete.

Here are his exact words, when I had finished my reading: 'That was written by a real tribune, Feb! Where did you get it from?' I put on a few airs for better effect and then explained to him how it had happened. But he didn't believe me! He announced that a retired teacher of astronomy was simply not capable of formulating so accurately the thoughts and longings of the simple people. 'Only a great writer could do this,' he said, 'or a great statesman. And in our country I don't see much sign of any great writers, or any great statesmen. Feb, you pinched that from the Martians. Admit it, old chap, I won't tell anyone.'

I was quite perplexed. His disbelief at once flattered me and annoyed me. And at that point he suddenly showed me a sealed envelope of thick, black paper.

'What's that?' I asked with deliberate casualness, while my heart already felt a sense of misfortune and contracted from a nasty presentiment.

'Stamps,' said that boaster. 'The real thing. From that place!'

I don't remember how I pulled myself together. Through a fog, I heard his exultations, expressed in a falsely sympathetic tone. And he waved the envelope in front of my nose telling me all the time what a rarity this was, how impossible it was to get hold of them, what fabulous prices he had already been offered for them by Kitone himself and how shrewdly he had acted, demanding compensation for the withdrawal of medicines not in money but in stamps. The sums which he casually mentioned put me in a completely bemused state. It seemed that the market price of Martian stamps was so high that no first category pension and no gastric juice would ever change anything in my situation. But in the end I recovered my composure. I had a brainwave and asked Achilles to show me the stamps. And then everything became clear. That slyboots got confused and put out, and began to babble something about how these stamps, being Martian ones, couldn't be exposed to the light, like photographic paper, that you could only examine them under special lighting and that here in the shop he didn't have the proper equipment. I recovered my courage and asked permission to call round that evening when he was at home. He invited me without much enthusiasm saying that to tell the truth he didn't have the special lighting at home either at the moment, but by tomorrow evening he would try to think of something. It will probably turn out that these stamps dissolve in the air or that they can't be examined at all, only be felt with the fingers.

In the heat of our talk I suddenly heard someone's breathing over my left shoulder and caught a glimpse out of the corner of my eye of some sort of movement next to me. I at once remembered the mysterious visitor and turned around sharply, but it turned out to be Madame Persephone's servant, who had come to ask for something a bit more reliable. Achilles went off to the laboratory to find a preparation to satisfy Mrs Persephone, obviously intending not to return until I had gone. I left, making no effort to hide my sarcasm.

At the donor's point a pleasant surprise awaited me: the appropriate analysis had revealed that, as a result of my chronic internal illness, my gastric juice came under the first type, so that for a hundred grams of juice I would now be paid forty per cent more than all the others. As if this were not enough, the surgeon on duty hinted that by using a moderate but sufficient quantity of the blue brandy, I could achieve a transfer into the extra category and would receive seventy to eighty per cent more for a hundred grams. I don't want to tempt fate, but it seems that at last, for the first time in my life, I've had a bit of luck.

I set off for the pub in a most exhilarated mood and sat there till late at night. It was very jolly. In the first place Japheth now deals at full steam in blue brandy, which he gets wholesale from the local farmers. The blue brandy gives one unpleasant belches but it's cheap, easy to drink and gives you a pleasant, merry kind of intoxication. One of the young men in the narrow coats diverted us very much. I still hadn't learnt to tell them apart, and up to this evening felt towards both of them a natural aversion which most of our group shared. These terrible assassins of Mr Laomedontes, together or singly, usually spent the whole time from lunch to closing time in the pub. They sat at the bar and drank in stubborn silence, as if they didn't notice anyone around them. However, today this young man suddenly broke away from the bar, came to our table and in the guarded silence that followed, first of all ordered drinks all round.

Then he sat down between Polythemes and Silen and said not very loudly, 'Urk!'

At first we all thought he had belched and Polythemes, as was his custom, said : 'Best of luck ! '

However the young man looked slightly offended and explained that Urk was his name and that he had been so named in honour of the son of Zeus and Aegina, the father of Telamon and Peles, the grandfather of Aenthe the Great. Polythemes at once begged his pardon and proposed a toast to Urk's health so that the incident was completely smoothed over. We all also introduced ourselves and very soon Urk was absolutely at home amongst us. He proved a splendid storyteller and we simply split our sides listening to him.

We especially liked their custom of soaping the floor of the drawing-room, undressing young ladies and setting up a chase after them. They called this 'playing tag'; and he told us about it in the most killing way. I must admit that we all felt a little ashamed of ourselves as provincials who'd never heard of anything like this, and for this reason the witty escapade of some of the young layabouts from Mr Nikostratos' band proved very much in place.

They appeared on the square leading on a string a big, gingery-red rooster. My goodness, how funny it was. Singing 'Niobe-Niobe' they proceeded across the square right into the pub. There they surrounded the bar and demanded brandy for themselves and a blue brandy for the rooster. At the same time they announced to everyone listening that they were celebrating the rooster's attainment of sexual maturity and invited all those who wanted to, to join in. Urk laughed too, so that our town was somewhat rehabilitated in the eyes of this resident of the capital, as some sort of centre of witty entertainment.

It was also interesting when Achilles came and announced that six semi-padded chairs had been stolen out of the waiting-room of the town hall. Panderei had already examined the scene of the crime and claimed that he had come across a trail. He said that there were two of them, and one had worn a velvet cap while the other had six toes on his right leg, but actually we were all convinced that the city treasurer had taken the chairs.

Paral said so openly: 'Well, he's pulled himself out of a hole again. Now everyone will be talking about those stupid chairs and completely forget about the latest embezzlement.'

When I came home, Charon was still sitting in the editorial office and we had supper together.

I've just looked out the window. A wonderful summer night has opened up an endless sky over the town, a sky studded with a myriad of glittering stars. A warm breeze is drifting in magical perfumes and caressing the branches of the sleeping trees. Hist! You can hear the gentle humming of a glow-worm lost in the grass on his way to a meeting with his emerald mistress. Dreams and bliss have descended on the little town, tired out by daily cares — no, somehow it's not quite right. Never mind. I'm leading up to how beautiful it was when, like a symbol of peace and security, some enormous space-ships shining with a magical light flew by through the heavens; it was obvious at once that they weren't ours.

I'm going to call my speech 'Peace and faith' and I'll give it to Charon for the paper. Just let him try not to print it. How is it that, when the whole town is for, they, can you believe it, are against! Nothing will come of it, dear son-in-law, nothing will come of it.

I'll go and see how Hermione is.

Translated by D. Matias and P. Barrett

SCIENCE FICTION IN PAN

A SELECTION OF POPULAR READING IN PAN

FICTION

ROYAL FLASH	George MacDonald Fraser	30p
THE FAME GAME	Rona Jaffe	40p
SILENCE ON MONTE SOLE	Jack Olsen	35p
A TASTE FOR DEATH	Peter O'Donnell	30p
TRAMP IN ARMOUR	Colin Forbes	30p
SHOTGUN	Ed McBain	25p
EMBASSY	Stephen Coulter	30p
AIRPORT	Arthur Hailey	37½p
HEIR TO FALCONHURST	Lance Horner	40p
REQUIEM FOR A WREN	Nevil Shute	30p
MADAME SERPENT	Jean Plaidy	30p
MURDER MOST ROYAL	Jean Plaidy	35p
CATHERINE	Juliette Benzoni	35p

NON-FICTION

THE SOMERSET & DORSET RAILWAY (illus.)	Robin Atthill	35p
THE WEST HIGHLAND RAILWAY (illus.)	John Thomas	35p
MY BEAVER COLONY (illus.)	Lars Wilsson	25p
THE SMALL GARDEN (illus.)	C. E. Lucas-Phillips	40p
HOW TO WIN CUSTOMERS	Heinz M. Goldmann	45p
THE NINE BAD SHOTS OF GOLF (illus.)	Jim Dante and Leo Diegel	35p

These and other advertised PAN Books are obtainable from all booksellers and newsagents. If you have any difficulty please send purchase price plus 5p postage to P.O. Box 11, Falmouth, Cornwall. While every effort is made to keep prices low it is sometimes necessary to increase prices at short notice. PAN Books reserve the right to show new retail prices on covers which may differ from those advertised in the text or elsewhere.